HORT LIFE

from

Lindsay

## PRAISE FOR *A SHORT LIFE*

'A twisty, thrilling ride, much like those Cape Town roads where it is set. I zoomed right through to the last hairpin bend!'

– KATE WEINBERG, author of *The Truants* and one of *The New York Times*' Top Ten Crime Writers.

'Gripping and relatable! What would you do if this happened in your friend group?'

– VANESSA RAPHAELY, former editor of *Cosmopolitan*, author of *Plus One*, and founder of the social media parenting group The Village.

'Razor-sharp and artfully rendered, *A Short Life* positively crackles with tension.'

– BIANCA MARAIS, author of *Hum If You Don't Know the Words* and host of the podcast The S**t No One Tells You About Writing.

'Clear your day, because once you start this, you won't want to put it down. Beautiful and evocative!'

– GAIL SCHIMMEL, author of *Little Secrets* and host of the podcast The Hidden Lives of Writers.

# A SHORT LIFE

NICKY GREENWALL

Published in 2024 by Penguin Random House South Africa (Pty) Ltd
Company Reg. No. 1953/000441/07
The Estuaries No. 4, Oxbow Crescent, Century Avenue,
Century City, 7441, South Africa
PO Box 1144, Cape Town, 8000, South Africa
www.penguinrandomhouse.co.za



First edition, first printing 2024
1 3 5 7 9 8 6 4 2

ISBN 978-1-77638-031-2 (Print)
ISBN 978-1-77638-073-2 (ePub)

Cover design by PUBLICIDE
Text design by Chérie Collins
Set in 11 on 14.5 pt Adobe Garamond Pro

Printed and bound by Novus Print, a Novus Holdings company

MIX
Paper | Supporting responsible forestry
FSC® C022948

*For my Bird, my Bear and my BFF*

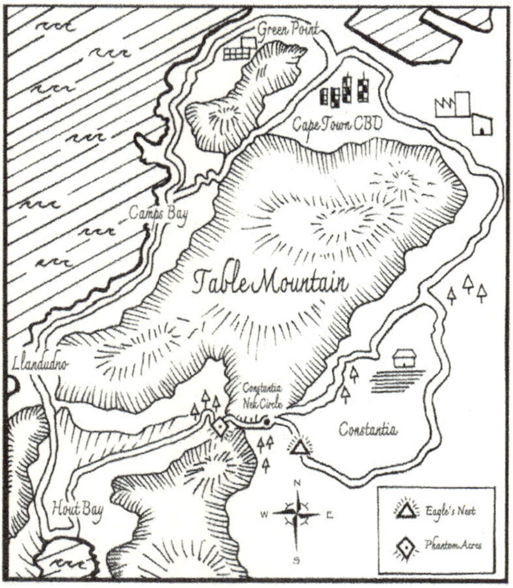
Green Point
Cape Town CBD
Camps Bay
Table Mountain
Llandudno
Constantia Nek Circle
Constantia
Hout Bay
N
W
E
S
Eagle's Nest
Phantom Acres

*The part of life we really live is small.*
*For all the rest of existence is not life, but merely time.*

– *On the Shortness of Life,* Seneca

*But there's solace a bit in submitting*
*To the fitfully, cryptically true*
*What's happened, has happened*
*What's coming is already on its way*
*With a role for me to play*
*And I don't understand, I'll never understand but I'll try to understand*
*There's nothing else I can do*

– 'Red Red Red', Fiona Apple

# FRIDAY

23:55

## Franky

*Constantia Nek Road*

A red-rimmed moon is our searchlight. From my vantage point, the car reminds me of a scarab that has landed on its back. Unlike the creature of my imagination, this car doesn't struggle to right itself. It has resigned to the inevitable. It lies where the foot of the forest meets the bottom of a steep verge – motionless except for a faint plume of smoke curling from beneath the body.

Nocturnal insects throb. The South Easter moves through the poplars and the blue gums above. Clouds shift. Every so often there's a passing car, not slowing down. Twin red lights disappear quickly behind the curve of the mountain. I know it's too dark to see much at that speed, unless you're looking for something at the side of the road – like we were.

'He can't be in there,' says Nick, cutting the engine. My free hand opens the passenger door. Nick's movements mirror mine. The Jeep's doors slam shut with a synchronised thud. I make my way behind the Jeep towards my mother's parked Mercedes. She was here first – called at my request. Her burgundy relic is parked on the shoulder: a painted fingernail marking the spot. As I reach for her passenger door, I turn back to see Nick sliding down the incline towards the wreckage. Moonlight picks out the silver in his hair as he manoeuvres past the roots and rocks. He will be disappointed to get his shoes dirty. I feel certain I hear a siren up ahead, but it could be the wind, or a peacock.

'Jesus,' my mother says, reaching over to release the bygone mechanism of her passenger door. Her windows are the kind that wind down by hand.

'How long have you been here?' I say, sinking into the wrinkled hide of her passenger seat. Her hand is cold and papery.

'About five minutes. I left as soon as you called—'

'Mom, I'm sorry to involve you. I—'

'I can't go and look. I thought I could but … I can't.'

I take in my mother's outfit: cardigan over her pyjamas, gardening shoes still caked in mud.

'I think we should call the police,' I say.

'I've just done that.' Tilt of the chin, flick of grey-gold fringe communicate *I'm not an idiot, you know.* She wraps her cardigan tighter around herself.

'I shouldn't have called you, Mom. I'm sorry, I thought—'

'He called *you*, didn't he? He must be all right.' Her eyes are their deepest hue when she's worried, inexplicably paler when she's angry. Before I'm able to make the distinction, the car's interior lights fade to black, as if marking the end of a scene.

'Where *are* the police?' she says.

I am all but silent, grinding a thumbnail between my teeth. My husband will know what to do. My mother's soliloquy continues: 'Why didn't he call his wife first?' I strain my ears to listen for the sirens I was sure I could hear before. 'Surely she—' She's building up for a lecture, as certain of her opinion as one should be after sixty, but her words dissolve in the air as our eardrums accept the sound of a car starting, wheels moving at speed. The Jeep, Nick's car, is skidding forwards into the darkness, already gone.

'Where on earth is he going?' she says, flicking her brights, illuminating nothing.

'Mom!' My voice escapes my throat at an odd angle. The sirens are real now. I can hear them, can imagine their blue-and-red glow. 'We need to go, Mom.'

'Shouldn't we—'

'Just go!' She turns the key and slams her mud-caked foot on the accelerator. The wheels make a grinding sound as we leave the soil of the verge for the smoothness of the road.

# FRIDAY

14:32

## Sebastian

*Table View*

The image in front of me is a visual platitude – a postcard. Blue-grey, flat-topped mountain, flanked by twin peaks, all blanketed in a thin tablecloth of cloud. This is not Cape Town. I should be looking directly up at the mountain, or down from it, or sideways at it. It should fill the frame. I'm too far north for comfort. Charley leans against the heat of her car, on her phone as always.

'Come the fuck on, Seb,' she says, looking up. 'We have to be there in an hour and we still have to check the light.'

The sea air wends its way into my nostrils as I ready myself for our usual argument. Time. We are always bickering about how much we have left. Time is money, as they say.

'I need to see it's there.' I retrieve the crumpled square of paper from my pocket, check the code again.

'It's *there.* They sent me a picture. I forwarded it to you.'

'That's not a picture. That's an *artist's impression.*'

A sigh. 'Get on with it, but be quick.'

I press the code, hear the requisite *beep beep beep* and watch the metal curtain rise.

'Happy now?'

I pull back the dust cover. *Happy* doesn't quite equal the feelings rippling through me. I can hardly believe I have been trusted with this gleaming piece of luxury machinery, shipped from Germany under cover of darkness. Its surface feels alive. I can see my reflection distorted. I look older than I feel. I should shave.

This car, and how *I* will capture it, is my ticket. Think sweeping, majestic aerials, tightly crafted close-ups, shimmering night shots lit with giant sun lamps. We're spending the budget. In less than a week, this car – which no one but a handful of execs and I have seen – will be gliding along the contours of Table Mountain, a tattooed hero at the wheel. He will circumnavigate beaches, forests and vineyards – an imperfect circle – before returning to where he started. Crisp white titles on a black screen will read, 'Besitze die Straße … Lebe die Reise … Fahren Sie den Moment.' *Own the road. Live the journey. Drive the moment.* The car is finally here. Now all I need is my leading man.

I close the door to the storage unit and return to our air-conditioned cocoon. Charley likes to drive. I don't mind being driven; it gives me the opportunity to think about my angles, work out some of the technical aspects of next week's shoot.

I close one eye, make L shapes with my hands and watch the scene unfold through my side window, pretending this is new. Charley is thinking her own thoughts.

As we reach the city centre, mountain looming above us, ocean now behind, I'm reminded why so many commercials and films are shot in my home town. Cape Town is a stand-in, an understudy, and, unlike the rest of the world this time of year, the light is always on.

The suburbs of Cape Town are beads on a string – a necklace hanging from the slopes. The city centre – spiky, gleaming reflective surfaces – that's the clasp. Crop out the mountain, it could be New York. Pan in closer, central London.

We move south along the coast through the streets of Green Point, the wide mouth of the stadium and Sea Point where waves crash against the rusted railings of the promenade. Palm trees cast geometric shadows on apartment blocks. A cubist impression of Cannes or Los Angeles.

At the foot of Lion's Head, we slide through Bantry Bay and Clifton – four perfect pearlescent replicas of remote islands. Clifton gives way to Camps Bay. Neon signs face the not-yet-setting sun as they would on Miami's South Beach or Santa Monica Boulevard. Buildings give way to pure mountain rock. The Twelve Apostles hunch over the Atlantic. Ocean to the right, rock to the left. If it were nighttime, this would be where we'd flick on the brights.

Hundreds of car commercials have been shot on this stretch. You've probably seen one – you just didn't know it was *this* road. It could be Monaco, or the Algarve. Road closures are a bitch, and permits are a nightmare but, in fairness, someone needs to pay for the gabion cages and steel nets to stop rocks from tumbling onto the road.

The smooth tarmac leads to my neighbourhood, Llandudno: clapboard houses and glass compounds jut out at angles towards the glare of the ocean. It's Malibu, without the celebrities, and no key is needed to access the beach.

We pass the turn-off to our house, down Suikerbossie, the steep hill that has become the source of more than a few of my speeding fines. We dip into the valley. The light changes, as does the mood. My attention is drawn to the vastness of Chapman's Peak – the unreal colour of the sea – and then, as though it's the first time I've seen them, I marvel at the silver shacks of Imizamo Yethu. Thousands of makeshift houses stretch up as far as you can see and gravity will allow. Electricity cables weave between washing lines; giant satellite dishes balance on every zinc roof: eyeless alien life forms on a dystopian lunar colony.

We snake past the township. The trees begin to thicken. It starts to drizzle. The road gets very winding here and signs suggest we take the bends slowly. Hout Bay is the Borneo jungle, or the Amazon rainforest. Our car climbs higher up the back of the mountain. At Constantia Nek, a traffic circle sits like a cameo on the décolletage. If we were so inclined we could park at the foot of the mountain, take a hike up its slopes, or veer slightly to the right and choose one of two roads that lead down into the exclusive valley suburbs of Bishopscourt or Constantia.

'Let's go through Constantia,' I say.

Charley's hands slide smoothly over the steering wheel. The mountain is now on our left. A perfect patchwork of vineyards stretches down towards the False Bay to our right. It is Napa County or the Hollywood Hills. The Constantia Wine Route is one of the oldest parts of Cape Town, as evidenced by the 200-year-old trees lining the roads. I draw breath as we pass the driveways of English-country-style houses in cul-de-sacs whose names evoke summer smells: Avenue Provence, Rose Way, Meadow Lane, Alphen Drive.

Trees become traffic lights – or robots, a fact I've had to explain to more than a few of our foreign clients. The lights are red. A one-legged man approaches Charley's open window displaying a toothless smile and a cardboard box of ripe fruit. Charley's finger curls around the button to close the window. I see her suppress a smile as he shouts through the glass, 'Where the lady goes the mangos!'

The lights turn green. Now we're on the M3, meandering towards Kirstenbosch National Botanical Garden and the fortress-like, ivy-covered facade of the University of Cape Town. The clouds are heavy in the sky. The windscreen wipers increase their metronomic sweeps. Moments later, the greenery on the slopes gives way to burnt trees (evidence of recent fire) and dry grass (evidence of recent drought). Frame out the highway and it's an African wilderness complete with mountain zebras and wildebeest. I take it all in through the streaks of rain on my window. The sky becomes still, clouds thin.

The dry peak of the mountain towers above Hospital Bend, a curved ribbon of highway that hugs the building where the first successful human-to-human heart transplant was performed. Now known as Nelson Mandela Boulevard, the road brings us seamlessly into the industrial district: Salt River, followed by Woodstock. Ad agencies, factories and just-built micro student accommodation. We're back at the clasp of the necklace, skyscrapers reflecting the last rays of afternoon sun. The journey has taken us through two separate weather conditions in less than an hour.

Now, how to tell it in thirty seconds?

The casting studio on the outskirts of town is a tiny, air-conditioned space that makes my eyes feel dry. Anxious models and actors sit in orange plastic chairs, unsticking and re-sticking numbered labels to their chests. Been there. Done that.

'Number fifty-five!' yells our casting director. In the decade we've known Angus, his beard has gone from slate to silver, but his Metallica Tour T-shirt has held up remarkably well. Charley has been nodding off the whole afternoon. I worry about her lack of sleep; it's worse than it was after our kids were born. That first time, after Katie's arrival, Charley didn't sleep for four days straight. Her teeth chattered, hands shaking as she caressed her face, marvelling at the strange woman in the mirror. She told me she felt that if she slept, Katie might die. She knew it was illogical, but some primal force told her rest was not as essential as our daughter's survival. Eventually, I had to hold Charley's head firmly on her pillow with the flat of my palm, promising I would watch over them both, until the shaking subsided and she disappeared into sleep.

When Leo arrived two years later, she let him curl in between us in our bed, until she became convinced one of us might suffocate him if we turned over in our sleep. Leo was inconsolable, as if picking up on his mother's intrusive thoughts. In the dead of night Charley would pace the hallways. I would find her asleep on couches and stairs and rugs. She told me she needed to stay awake, like a hammerhead shark.

This time, four years later, she tells me she can't understand the purpose of her wakefulness. Charley doesn't do anything without good reason. She's even started taking the CBD oil her mother sent her. Deirdre swears by any newfangled, New-Age potion to make you feel and look better. Sometimes Charley thinks her mother (who is pushing seventy) looks better than she does. I told her it's because she is single and no longer has children under the age of seven. She raised her eyebrows and that was the end of that conversation.

Today I am wearing my new spectacles, the red-framed ones. Charley is the only person who knows I don't need them. She knows I want to be the sort of director who wears red-framed glasses, slightly too small for my face. She thinks it makes me look just the right side of eccentric. Not quite Pedro Almodóvar, but close enough.

Charley walks back into the studio from the toilet. I have one of the arms of the spectacles in my mouth and I'm squinting at a laptop, nodding my head furiously. I am agreeing with The German Client who is, at this moment, patched in from Hamburg. While he talks, my mind can't help but regard his existence, this man in his glass cube, snow falling dramatically down floor-to-ceiling windows, as we parade a digital conveyor belt of tanned, tattooed specimens for his consideration.

'What do we think of this guy?' I whisper to Charley. We are behind a two-way mirror. I've learnt the hard way, the space is not completely sound-proofed. She looks up at the model, who smiles broadly at the camera as if his life depends on it.

'Hey! I'm Keith, I'm twenty-seven!' he says.

'He's a bit young,' she mouths, gesturing to her biceps, 'and not enough tattoos.' Charley has always been decisive. It's one of the many qualities I love about her.

Keith is now brandishing a disembodied steering wheel. He grins like a child wielding the controls of a bumper car. His tattoos are subtle. I have more ink on my arms, I note with pride. I'm not the right age group, though. The German Client wants *young*.

'Do you have a licence?' says Angus.

'I do, sir. And a motorcycle licence too.'

'And have you done any competitive car commercials?'

'No, sir!'

'Right. Thanks, Keith. We'll be in touch.'

By 5 p.m., eight men have come and gone through the confines of the thin casting-studio walls, narrowed down from 135 the week before. The German Client has his heart set on a Brazilian whose right arm boasted an impressive seascape sleeve, the waves undulating gently as he contracted the muscles in his bicep. 'It sends the right message,' says The German Client.

I nod and nod as is customary. Charley yawns, opens and shuts her eyes, windscreen-wipering her corneas to clear the sleep that threatens to overtake. And then she shakes herself into consciousness before she says, 'We'll need a release form.'

'All sorted,' confirms Angus, unhitching the camera from its tripod.

'For the tattoo?' says Charley, straightening the lapels of her blue blazer, rearranging her new haircut, reminding him who is in charge, who is paying for everything.

'I'm sorry?"' he says. The skin around Angus's eyes crinkles in confusion.

'The tattoo artist needs to sign off on us using the tattoo in the commercial. It's his artwork. He could sue us if we don't have the proper permissions.' And then, because she can't help herself, 'I thought this would have been obvious?'

Angus searches his teeth with his tongue.

That's my wife — always a stickler for the details. But, while I smile inwardly with pride, I chew on the arms of my useless red frames. If the client doesn't get his first choice for leading man, will that make him less likely to acquiesce to my creative whims?

'You're joking,' says The German Client through the speakers of the laptop.

'I am not,' says Charley, matching his tone.

Angus is already on the phone to the Brazilian's agent. The German Client is put on hold, the laptop closed while Angus whispers that the Brazilian was inked when he was drunk. He thinks he was in Belgium but can't remember the name of the tattoo parlour. He thinks it may have closed down.

'Brilliant!' I say. 'No chance of us being sued then.'

'Seb,' cuts in Charley, her eyes connecting with mine. 'We can't take a chance. Remember what happened *last time*?'

I feel the tips of my ears redden. The beer commercial in the art gallery. How could I forget? I had accidentally included one of the artworks in the final edit. An entirely black canvas – a black square. Surely, no one could lay claim to that? The artist had spotted his work and accused the brewery of profiting from his art. He settled at roughly half the price of what the whole commercial had cost to make. It was an expensive mistake — and one we are still paying for. We are still paying for everything.

'We'll have to go with fifty-five …' says Charley, brushing imaginary lint from her jeans.

'The guy without the tats?'

'Yes. It'll cost us less to hire a make-up artist to do some sort of sealife-esque scene on his arm than it will to buy the other guy and his tattoo artist out anyway. They're similar. Besides, he had a good smile, don't you think?' Assuming the sale. She is so beautiful, so clever, so in charge. She rolls her eyes at me behind the monitor. Her bracelets jangle as I put the idea to The German Client in my most obsequious tone. In his office, The German Client nods, sips from a bottle of mineral water, and says, 'Yes, yes. Okay. We see you Monday.'

# FRIDAY

18:45

## Charley

*Bree Street, Cape Town* CBD

The restaurant interior is uniformly black. Conversation a dark hum, punctuated occasionally by the hiss of a cooking steak or the shout of an impatient chef. The air is thick with notes of other people's perfume.

'You have a reservation?'

We follow an aftershave to a table set meticulously for six. The host scrapes back a chair. No one pays me the attention I thought the scrape might have stirred, and some part of me is disappointed. It's been a while since I've worn uncomfortable matching underwear, drawn dark lines across my eyelids, applied lip gloss I will need to reapply (and probably won't). These preparations already belong to a different era.

I have a theory: self-perception ossifies at twenty-eight. My mother agrees with me. My husband will not accept he is forty-one this year. I'm still *in my thirties* but I like to believe my new Eighties-inspired haircut makes me look like a twenty-eight-year-old Lady Diana, although the hairdresser referred to it as 'The Lion', which I have no objection to. Anything but a mom bob, I said.

Franky arrives alone. 'There she is!' I say, hiding my suspicions. She squeezes me for longer than necessary, aware of other diners casting their eyes over her small frame, silver knitted dress, her tousled, French-girl hair. Our embrace becomes a dance, a communication via osmosis. My eyes juice from the pressure of it.

'Love the hair!' she says, pulling away. Her hands grip my shoulders. 'What else's new?' She's manic and smells incongruously of the cheap coconut-scented air-freshener of her recently departed Uber. There's something disturbingly false in her mannerisms, more so than usual.

'Let me have a go!' says Seb. He pretends to force his way into Franky's arms, flexing his tattoos. 'Five years, hey?' he says with a smirk. Seb and I have been a couple since we were teenagers. I've known Franky since before we were teenagers. She will always win.

Seb pushes his long hair off his face with a leather-bangled arm. As we return to our seats he picks at his T-shirt as if preventing it from sticking to his skin, 'It's hot in here, no?' He nods at the waiter, who has materialised with a bottle of red. 'Where's Nick?'

'Playing golf with Adam,' says Franky.

'On his anniversary?' Seb swills his glass, takes a tentative sniff. He taps a beringed nail-bitten finger to his lip. 'Excellent bouquet. I'm detecting gooseberry, wet grass and maybe just a hint of cinnamon?'

I feel my eyes roll as I make what I hope are apologetic gestures to the waiter. Franky is making attempts to regain my attention. 'You know Nick and Adam and their bromance!' Her laugh is jagged. 'Who am I to stand in the way?' She lines up her cutlery, straightens the menu. Franky is at the head of the table. I sit to her left. Seb is to my left. Nick's empty chair pulses with absenteeism to her right.

'Is your mom not coming?' I say, trying to make the question sound neutral. Before Franky can answer, a throaty Spanish accent drifts towards us: 'Who's having a bromance?'

We all rise from our seats to greet Maria, chairs scraping. Heads turn. She tucks a tendril of dark hair behind her ear and bends at the waist for European kisses. Even without heels she dwarfs her husband. He hovers on the periphery, waiting for his wife's entrance to come to its natural conclusion. Adam's oversized spectacles, greying beard and tight curls give him a professorial aura. He looks exhausted by the time he sits down beside the empty chair reserved for Nick. The lamp shades suspended above the table swing from all our movements. Twin circles of white light shift on the table's atramentous surface like spotlights searching for the evening's headline act.

I don't know Adam well, but I suspect he isn't partial to restaurants of this ilk – all the darkness and pretension. Waiters who linger probably make his eczema bloom. I notice him baulk as Seb leans across the table in an attempt to fill his glass with red wine. Adam shoots his thick fingers across the rim, musters an apology, orders a beer.

Franky jumps. 'How do you do that!?' she says, holding her hand over her heart. Nick has arrived, sliding in the door behind Adam like an unseen shadow.

'What?' he says, smiling broadly and giving a general wave to the table that says, *I'm not going to kiss and hug every one of you, I'm going to focus my attention on my wife.* He's so fucking confident. Franky and Nick kiss appropriately. I drink wine.

Five years ago, to the day, the people seated around this table (and Franky's mother) witnessed Nick and Franky's marriage. It was a small legal ceremony. I wore a yellow dress. Franky wore a green one. I can't remember what Nick wore. His clothes are not the thing people remember about him.

'Sorry we're late,' he says, flashing air-quote dimples. 'Have you done something different with your hair?'

'Good game?' says Seb before I can provide a suitable response. Seb leans back in his chair, hand cupped protectively to the back of my neck, readying himself to pretend to know the difference between a bogey and a par.

'Well …' begins Nick, launching into a story directed mainly at Adam, about which shots they could have played better. Franky nods in all the right places, pats Nick's hand, only once stealing a glance in my direction. I stifle a pretend yawn and we giggle. I feel younger still.

It's apparent Maria still has to strain to keep up with English conversation. She plucks the lemon from her glass and sucks it briefly before asking Seb her usual question: 'What *arechoo* working on right now?'

'I'm directing a car commercial,' he says. 'The new Mercedes?' Maria nods in false affirmation. To the casual observer, Maria looks the most sophisticated of us all. She's a former model, a stay-at-home-mother-of-three who dabbles in sculpture – and she's the only one here who *is* twenty-eight.

'It's top secret, not supposed to talk about it, but—'

'… you are anyway!' I say, giving Seb what I had intended to be playful clip on the back of his head. My fingers smart from the unexpected force of it. 'A few glasses of wine and you might say things you aren't supposed to say.' For the benefit of the rest of the table I say, 'May I remind you, *I* am the executive producer on this job and I will make sure our client's wishes are not compromised.' He looks up at me like one of our children. Leo's eyes, Katie's chin. 'Oh, go on then …'

'So, it's a guy driving on a lonely coastal road.' He leans in as if sharing gossip or a ghost story. 'Only he's not the typical "guy in a car commercial" – you know, the "silver fox".' His performance seems to be directed exclusively at Maria. 'The German agency wants it to be, like, a young guy, lots of tats … that sort of thing.'

'Yes,' interjects Adam, 'because tattoos are always a sign of wealth and privilege these days.' He raises his substantial eyebrows in my direction. I return his smile. Adam is skint – always has been, always will.

Steaming works of miniature culinary art are placed in front of each of us with a flourish. The waiter asks if we'd like a description. I indulge him. Everyone else continues their conversations. While he speaks about prawn foam and jus and where exactly the lamb shank was reared, I speculate about our waiter's personal life. An Economics student, I imagine, or a winemaker's son. He speaks confidently, but with relative disinterest, and without showing his teeth. Are those braces I see, catching the light?

And what does this waiter make of us? Has he guessed that Seb and I are the wealthiest couple at the table, despite the fact that my husband has holes in his shirt? Has he deduced that Adam, a failed software designer, is Nick's longest-serving friend, and Franky mine? Maria and Seb are the links at the end of that chain, but with their polished skin and dark hair, could they not look a more appropriate couple? I wonder too if he's worked it out: of all the women seated here, Franky is the only one who isn't a mother. Is it me, or does she look younger than the rest of us?

By the fourth course, I've forgotten I was so tired. Franky has overcome her social awkwardness and is talking to Adam about his skin complaints. 'How long have you had eczema for?' I hear her say. 'Do you think it's genetic?' Nick interjects, citing an article he's read. Adam nods, concentrating the bulk of his attention on his food. He takes a swig from his second beer.

Franky tells me about her latest assignment, the copy she must write for a skincare client's foray into the haircare market, how stressful it all is, how she's feeling uninspired. I feign interest. 'You seem … I don't know, different,' I say, narrowing my eyes.

Nick comes to her rescue, as always. 'How old is Katie now?'

'She's six,' I say, 'going on thirteen. Leo is four. God, the "terrible twos" are nothing compared to the "fucking fours".' I throw back my wine as if to punctuate my well-rehearsed remark. I'm hitting my stride now. But, I note with annoyance, as I start to explain the exact nature of Leo's tantrums, Franky has tuned out of my performance and is instead picking up on the one at the other end of the table. Seb is making invisible titles in the air with slow-motion jazz hands.

'Own the road … Live the journey … Drive the moment.'

'Wow,' says Maria, 'that's … that's so powerful?'

'I know, right?' Adam's attention is focused exclusively on chewing, swallowing, sipping. When his plate is clean, I hear him give Nick the details of his new project.

'Yah, it's all about leverage and the optics of it, but getting the framework is the thing … If we get the account, we're talking huge bonuses all round, which is … you know … kind of what we need right now.' Nick moves his head in sympathy, rubs his stubbled chin.

'So which one are you?' says Franky, squeezing my knee under the table.

I finish the last of my seared tuna, dab my mouth with a napkin. 'Which one am I what?'

'Are you The Rose or The Gardener?'

She must be drunk, quoting our shared psychologist. I'm not drunk enough. I take a sip of water, buy myself time. She presses on.

'In all relationships there's a rose and a gardener. Which one are you?'

She knows the answer. There's some sort of point to be made, although I'm not sure why she chose this moment to make it.

'I'm the gardener for sure!' says Adam, covering his lips with the back of his hand – a half-hearted apology for a belch. At the opposite head of the table Maria is a drooping rose, head resting on her hand.

'I'm not into gardening,' says Nick, patting Franky on her left thigh. I suspect he has no awareness that my hand now rests casually on her right thigh. She shifts in her chair, as if to expel us both.

'*I'm* the gardener,' I say, 'obviously.' I give Seb a pointed look and he returns a wink. He's still so handsome when he smiles – the actor I fell in love with.

Nick finds his moment, clearing his throat and raising his glass. He makes eye contact with a waiter. I see panic rise in Franky's throat, her pulse under the skin of her neck. The smile drains from her face. I reach for her elbow as if to steady her. Her hands grip the sides of her chair.

'To my beautiful partner in crime,' says Nick. 'The one who looks after me, for better or for worse. My rose *and* my gardener – my best friend.'

'Steady on!' I say.

'Nice one!' says Adam.

The rest of the table makes a collective, positive-sounding murmur that falls just short of a cheer. Other diners briefly pause their conversation to tune into ours. I feel Franky's muscles relax under my grip. Our waiter arrives with some sort of deconstructed chocolate dessert. *Happy 5th Anniversary* is written in looping cursive red jam on the plate. I dip my finger in the curve of the five. It tastes tart.

'You know what we should do?' I say, sensing the end of the evening. 'We should go dancing!'

'I'm in,' says Adam, tipping the neck of his bottle towards my now empty glass. Maria's long neck angles towards the door. She fiddles with the charm on her necklace.

Franky asks for the bill.

'It was my idea,' she says, fishing her card out of her clutch.

'Already taken care of,' says our waiter, hands behind his back. Nick shrugs and I watch her kiss him on his beautiful, sandpaper cheek.

The six of us soon find ourselves in the basement of a newly renovated Victorian speakeasy that, I'm told, once housed a cold-storage facility. Nick reclines in a red velvet booth, his eyes on me while he pretends to listen to Adam. Adam leans towards him, trying to make conversation over the music. He stabs at his chest with a finger. *What about me? What about how I feel?* he seems to say. Nick moves his head up and down, although I'm fairly certain he can't hear anything Adam is saying.

Seb is engaged in an equally animated discussion with the barman. He laughs, orders another drink. Maria has excused herself with more argan-scented kisses, saying she must relieve the babysitter. Franky and I are in the middle of the intimate dance floor. Her hands are surrendered, freshly shaved underarms pale and vulnerable in the fluorescent lights. Her silver dress glitters. She is alone in a private reverie, eyes closed. My eyes are only half-closed; I can see the white reflections of the disco ball's facets across my friend's face. My new hair flicks across my vision as my neck muscles twist in time to the beat. *This will hurt tomorrow*, I think. My hips, legs, arms and shoulders move fluidly, propelled by some transcendent force. I can feel eyes appreciating me. The pulse of the base reaches the empty cavities of my body. Stevie Wonder is encouraging me not to worry. I find myself mouthing his words – a mantra. No need to keep worrying. About anything. Not work, not money, not parenting, not getting older. Everything works out in the end, doesn't it?

# FRIDAY

23:12

## Franky

*Bree Street, Cape Town* CBD

'Why aren't you drinking?'

Her tonic-scented breath is hot in my ear. She leans back, inspecting me, plucked eyebrows twitching. 'Oh don't tell me you're up the duff!' I blink at her. 'You are! You are up the duff, you crazy bitch!'

I look at the ceiling, a firmament of light emitting diodes, tears threatening to spill. *Size of a grape*, I think. *Say nothing.* Nick is at my side, ready to make a quip that will throw her off the scent. 'If anyone's crazy in here, it's you, Gabby!' he says.

Gabby is my art director. We're an arranged marriage. Although, as it happens, I had not known she would be here tonight. I spend an impossible amount of time in her presence; I'd rather not see her socially. She looks momentarily stung by Nick's comment. My throat constricts as I remember how she had announced her own pregnancy at the office last summer. She'd graciously accepted the hugs, the congratulations, the name suggestions and the unsolicited advice. When she didn't show up to a presentation a few days later, we all knew. A carefully worded send-to-all from her boyfriend confirmed, *These things happen*, followed by a lightning emoji and a pulsing heart. No, I would not subject myself to the extra pain of that. The twelve-week milestone is there for a reason. Nick hands me ginger ale in a champagne flute as instructed. Gabby's attention is diverted elsewhere.

I have already said my goodbyes to Charley and Seb. I'm grateful they left early. Normally it's impossible to get Charley off a dance floor. Even in her inebriated state, she snapped into focus when the alarm on her phone buzzed in the pocket of her trouser suit. Tomorrow they're finalising locations. An early call time, she said. She hotfooted over to the bar and practically dragged Seb away from his unfinished drink. Charley is so in charge of her relationship. I would never speak to Nick the way she speaks to Seb. Maybe it's because they work together, or because they've been together forever. Deep down, we're all a little afraid of Charley.

My mind wobbles. If Charley had heard my exchange with Gabby, her suspicions would have been confirmed and my secret would be out before its time. Charley would not have taken well to the deception. We tell each other everything. She would have been annoyed with me and then pretended not to be, just enough for me to know I had broken our unspoken contract.

Not telling Charley is a test, a challenge, a superstition. If I can make it to twelve weeks without telling my oldest and dearest friend, I have proved my strength of character and the universe will reward me. Besides, what's the point in more people being disappointed if it doesn't go to plan? Not telling Charley is as good for her as it is for me.

Charley and Seb have been gone for more than an hour now. I've been dancing alone and it's liberating. I connect with the rhythm in a strangely passive way, like my body requires less energy to dance than it does to think. It's not easy to dance *and* think catastrophic thoughts.

Nick has bumped into a Dutch architect he once worked with. I shook his hand vigorously, but his name drifted over my head. Amsterdam Guy, we'll call him. The two of them are now enmeshed in a conversation involving lots of hand gestures approximating columns or other weight-bearing structures.

Adam left about twenty minutes ago, saying he would order an Uber. Earlier Charley and Seb had offered to share theirs with him, but he waved away the suggestion. Charley couldn't hide her relief. Adam seemed relieved he could continue his conversation with a girl at the bar – blunt fringe, cheap-looking red leather jacket. She was laughing at everything he said. The man next to her made half-hearted attempts to conceal his irritation.

I swallow the last of my ginger ale and remind myself how lucky I am. I can dance as late as I want. No babysitters for me to relieve yet. But my shoes are killing me. As I shift in next to Nick, I watch him retrieve his phone from his pocket. 'Who is it?' I say, struggling to make myself heard over the deejay's new choice. Nick's face takes on the ghostly blue of his phone.

'It's Adam. Five missed calls …' He holds my gaze in silent understanding.

He says goodbye to Amsterdam Guy and I follow him up the stairs to the street. The wind cools the sweat on my face. A cherry-coloured Lamborghini slows unnecessarily outside the entrance to the club. A barefoot boy negotiates his way around the slowing car, asks us for coins.

'Lady! Lady! Something for me!' The boy spits onto the pavement as we avert our eyes. I close my jacket inside my folded arms, tilting myself backwards and forwards on my wedge heels.

'Adam? Hey, buddy, what's ...' Phone to his left ear, finger in his right.

I strain my ears to hear Adam's reply, but the Lamborghini's roar and the hum of the wind are too loud. The boy is shouting obscenities at another couple who are crossing the road towards the club.

On the walk to our parked car, Nick explains that Adam has been in some kind of accident. Adam thought he was okay to drive but now he realises he wasn't. Clearly the Uber suggestion had been ignored. Nick has had two glasses of wine washed down with a five-course meal, followed by coffee and water. Technically he's over the limit too. I sense now is not the time to bring this up. High-profile DUIs have been headline news of late. *Zero Tolerance* is the catchphrase the City has come up with. I feel certain I could have come up with something more motivating. *Zero Tolerance* is a sugar-free energy drink.

'How did he sound?' I say as we climb into Nick's car, wind whipping my hair. I try to make my voice steady; no need to panic just yet. Nick knows – I am always ready to panic, my thumb figuratively (and at times literally) hovering over the red button of our gate fob.

Nick grips the steering wheel at ten to two while he relays the conversation: Adam is somewhere on the winding road that snakes towards Constantia Nek from Hout Bay, in the valley. 'He sounded tired, like he'd just woken up. He just kept saying, *Please don't call Maria. Please don't call Maria!* before his phone went dead.'

I remember Maria's curt goodbye. Her tight smile as she made her excuses.

Adam said it was dark, not many landmarks, red-and-white chevrons in the road indicating a sharp bend. I know that bend. I've driven it many times myself – on my way to my mother's house in Constantia, painfully slowly, while a taxi hooted its disapproval behind me.

'Did he call an ambulance? Should we?' I say, my imagination editing a montage of horror crash footage. Nick makes a *pffft* sound that could have come from his mouth or his nose or both. I let the silence settle before I ask my next question.

'Which way around the mountain did he go?'

'Oh fuck,' says Nick. I take in the perfect profile of his face, wounded that my questions seem to annoy him so much. I want to be helpful, I want to show him we're a team. For the second time tonight I feel the threat of tears. I turn my attention back to the road and through my now blurred vision I see what looks like a carnival at the end of the Camps Bay strip. Of course, it's not a carnival – it's a roadblock.

'Do you want me to switch over?' I say, adrenaline jump-starting my heart. 'I could get in the driver's seat?' The roadblock is just visible on the horizon.

'No, I'm fine. We're fine. It's fine.'

Could Adam have gone the other way around? His and Maria's home in Hout Bay is equidistant whether you travel on the M3 from town around the back of the mountain or take the coast road around the front.

'He must have taken the M3,' says Nick, running his hand down his face.

'My mom could get there before us,' I say, making the statement sound like a question. The clock on the dashboard reads eleven thirty. My mother would know what to do. I am suddenly desperate to show Nick I am on his side, as I always will be – no judgement. Our car joins the queue that will travel through the roadblock. The ocean is a black expanse to our right, the moon's reflection a messy configuration of jagged parallel lines.

'Okay,' he says, eyes boring into the car in front of us. He's calculating, making decisions. I can practically see the neurons firing. At least my phone call will be a distraction from thinking about what's about to happen. After five rings, my mother answers with the three words everyone uses when they get a call after 10 p.m. 'Yes, Mom. We're fine. Sorry to call so late ... We're fine.' I repeat myself to ensure her calm compliance. 'It's Nick's friend Adam. He's had a minor accident. He called us from the side of the road. He's in Hout Bay, on the bend opposite Phantom Acres ... Yes, that one.'

My mother's voice takes on a determined 'can do' energy. She will do this for us. She is five minutes away. We're possibly twenty to thirty depending on how long this roadblock will take. My mother will get into her car and drive to the scene to establish what has happened. I thank her, twice, and hang up. 'She's on her way,' I say. Nick reaches over and places his hand on my thigh. I close my hand over his. As we approach the front of the queue, a police officer in a hi-vis jacket waves us past with the flick of his torch. I try to imagine how we must look to him. Not teenagers out on the town in one of our parents' cars. Not a taxi over capacity on its way back to Imizamo Yethu. We're an average couple from Green Point, responsibly celebrating our fifth wedding anniversary. Nick picks up speed. I didn't realise I'd been holding my breath. I steady myself with one hand on the dashboard as he takes the corners of the unlit coastal road at an uncomfortable speed. We drive the rest of the way in silence, my toes curling inside my shoes.

# FRIDAY

22:35

## Sebastian

*Llandudno*

I want to have sex. My wife is asleep. I'm too drunk. I knew when she started taking her make-up off, as soon as we walked in the door, all hope was gone. I had to pay our babysitter, relieve myself of the last few notes in my wallet, call an Uber, let her out. By the time I made it back upstairs Charley was fast asleep. Oh well. Maybe in the morning before her alarm. She is snoring gently. Red wine does that. Her new haircut juts out at odd angles. I'm not sure if I like it. It'll grow – or it'll grow on me. Time to re-edit the evening. Maria. God, that women is gorgeous. I don't trust her, of course. I can see the way she looks at me, the way she asks me question after question with her eyes. It's a performance for her husband. Could it be some sort of foreplay? Adam's such a weirdo. And as for Nick, God help us – what a bore. Fucking engineers, man – buzz-kills. Wait, I don't want to think about Nick, I want to think about Maria. I wonder what she's like in bed. I wonder if she and Adam actually have sex. They must have to get those three kids. The thought of them together repulses me. Man, I'm tired. I wonder if the recce will go well tomorrow. I hope the permit comes through in time. Fuck, what if it doesn't come through in time!? No, that's not my problem, that's Charley's problem. She'll fix it. She fixes everything. My wife. I love my wife. I love my children. I'm a pretty lucky guy when you think about it. I wonder if this commercial will win me an award? I wonder if …

# SATURDAY

00:08

## Franky

*Sillery Avenue, Constantia*

Adam is on his back in my mother's gated driveway. Ash-coloured curls frame his pale porcine face. His eyes are closed and he's laughing, a British holidaymaker reclining on a pebbled beach. My shadow makes a strange shape across his body. I can see my mother itching to say something, but she thinks better of it, shaking her head as she makes her way towards her lit front door. Manicured salt bushes stand to attention on either side. 'I'll put the kettle on,' she sighs.

Nick's arms are folded. He is not laughing. The ornamental stone fountain behind him makes him look like he's wearing a crown.

'What were you thinking?' I say. 'You drove him away from the scene of a crime!'

'A crime?!' His voice is an octave higher than usual. 'Let's not get dramatic. It was an accident!'

'He's drunk!'

'So?' says Nick, petulant.

I inhale the night air, attempt to regain my composure. In the six years we've been together I have never raised my voice to him – not once. I'm in as much of a state of shock at this as he appears to be. I try a new voice, slow and enunciated, accentuating my own hyper-sobriety. 'He was driving *drunk* and you drove him away from the scene of an accident. That's illegal. You have broken the law. *We've* broken the law and now my mother is involved.'

'Oh, please!' He's singing with disbelief now, spittle caught in the outside lights. 'There was no one else involved. And, what' – nostrils flaring – 'do you think the cops would have done when they arrived?'

'I'm so thirsty …' croaks Adam from the ground beneath us. Nick helps him up. Adam stumbles into him and pats his back.

'Thanks, bru,' he says, suppressing a burp. 'I just needed a little lie-down. I owe you one … no two, I owe you at least two.' He's laughing again, holding up his two fingers in a peace sign before addressing me directly for the first time. 'Franky! Why you look so mad?' A clown's face of forced distress. Surely the shock of the accident should have sobered him? I shudder to think of all the souls he shared that twisting road with. My ears are pricked as I wait for the sirens to find us.

'Come inside,' says Nick, eyes imploring, composure regained. He is a grown-up again, his forty-one-year-old self. The inside of my chest burns.

As my mother's Mercedes caught up with the red eyes of Nick's Jeep, I felt the distance between us grow. I knew instinctively his route would most likely end up at my mother's house – the closest safe haven – but I was at a loss as to why he thought it necessary to cover our tracks. He followed roads off Constantia Nek, then back on again, down Rhodes Drive, up Southern Cross instead of taking the quicker path around the circle. What was his plan? Was he giving himself time to think while the sirens screeched, their cries moving in and out, at once closer then further away?

Now their sound has all but faded as I watch the backs of my husband and his oldest friend move towards the double door of my childhood home. *Who are these people?* Nick, *my* Nick, is on someone else's side – not mine. This feels like betrayal of the highest order.

I stay in the driveway, pacing to keep my mind from freezing. The gravel crunches obediently under my wedges. I must argue effectively like I did when I was first speaker of my high-school debating team. *Should euthanasia be legalised?* 'No' was the answer I pulled from the blue velvet drawstring bag, although my mind had instantly said 'Yes' (after I'd looked up what euthanasia was). 'Webster's Dictionary defines euthanasia as …' Charley was third speaker. She would handle the rebuttal. She knew how to defend. 'The opposing team seems to have made the assumption …' she would say, drawing out syllables, fingers poised liked spiders on our table, '… that assisted suicide is murder.'

Mostly, in this moment, I'm struggling to identify who it is I'm trying to protect: myself, Nick, my mother, or is it all the imagined people who could have been affected by Adam's reckless behaviour? My intelligent, charming, husband, whose engineering brain is so accustomed to making clear, calculated decisions, somehow now complicit.

What *would* have happened if the police had arrived on the scene before us? Once they'd established Adam wasn't physically hurt, they would have breathalysed him – even though it would have been obvious he was drunk. They would have bundled him into the back of a police car, as one might dirty laundry into a washing machine, door closing with a satisfying thump. Job done. Wasn't that a fair price to pay? He had endangered other people's lives, not least his own. Who were we to get involved? What if he'd been coming towards us on the other side of the road? Would we be so forgiving then? No one else was hurt – but they *could* have been. Isn't that reckless endangerment?

Then I remember the story that made headlines last week: *Suicide After Prison Rape* were the words that leapt off the page, impossible not to keep reading. *Man in jail for running a red light, leaves behind wife and three children.* Was this the story at the forefront of Nick's mind when he hustled Adam into his car and fled? A white-collar crime? A vigilante protecting a friend from a flawed justice system?

I'm aware I am spinning myself in circles now, pacing around the fountain, looking at topiaries in the moonlight and wondering how my mother manages to keep them so well maintained. Simultaneously, I contemplate why exactly I have so much unexpressed rage. And, as if to prove my mind is capable of all these unrelated thoughts and more, I am also mulling over the thin crevice of circumstance that separates *here* from *no longer here*.

'Come on, sweetheart ... I've made them both coffee. It's cold outside.' My mother's voice induces tears. She wraps me in her arms, a physical as well as mental pulling together: brown paper around a bunch of errant wildflowers. With my heels on – she's much shorter than I am – my chin rests near the crown of her head. She smells of Molton Brown, white wine and woodsmoke. I follow her inside, ready to debate my position – like the criminal lawyer I am not.

# SATURDAY

00:15

## Franky

*Sillery Avenue, Constantia*

Nick has a solution. Adam is in the bathroom. I am seated at my mother's patinated kitchen table. A silver champagne bucket of roses blocks my view of Nick. I am using all my willpower to stay open-minded. I fiddle with the tag of my cooling mint tea.

'Tomorrow morning we drive to the police station and Adam turns himself in,' he says.

'You mean *we* turn ourselves in?' I am trying to keep the sarcasm from my voice. I feel Nick's stare through the foliage. I look down and imagine his clenched jaw.

'No,' he says slowly. 'Technically, we have twenty-four hours to report an accident. I will drive him there in the morning. He will walk into the station and explain that he had an accident last night, the cops were delayed, he was unwell and had called for medical assistance. A passer-by stopped to help him and took him to the hospital. His wife collected him and now he would like to help locate and retrieve his car, sign paperwork, get a case number. The end.'

'What if someone sees the car between now and then?' I'm trying less for derision, more devil's advocate, but Nick's tone tells me I have failed.

'They won't, it's too far down. You'd need to be looking for it.'

'But my mom called the police!' I can't help myself. 'They will be looking for it.' I am throwing my mother under the proverbial bus with this statement, but Nick and my mother aren't normally the best of friends anyway. Rather that than Nick thinking *I* might have called the police – which I would have, given half the chance. Nick squints at the ceiling and chooses not to respond. I try another question, consciously relaxing my jaw and the muscles around my eyes. 'How do you think Maria will fit into all of this?'

'I'll give her a call now and explain what happened.' He nods, agreeing with himself. 'She'll understand. Adam can stay at our place tonight and I'll drive him through early in the morning.'

It has been decided. The toilet flushes. Adam returns, sniffing his hands.

'Silvia, this Molton Brown stuff is amazing. I could eat my hands!'

My mother smiles despite herself. I glare at her and she suppresses a yawn. She has been uncharacteristically quiet, eyeing Nick and me over the rim of her teacup.

'Well, this has all been lovely,' she says now. 'But I think it's time you lot cleared off.'

'I think we should call a lawyer,' I say, still avoiding eye contact with Nick. 'What about Dad's old friend, Abe or Gabe or what was his name?'

'Swersky?' she says. 'He's long retired, love. You know if your father was alive today he'd be seventy! Hard to imagine, isn't it?' Her eyes well up. At the mention of my late father I feel the familiar constriction in my throat. The irony of a surgeon suffering a heart attack while performing heart surgery was not lost on anyone, least of all my mother. Emotion is still raw on her features.

'Mom,' I say, feeling fatigue surge through me in the wake of the adrenaline, 'you must know a lawyer.'

'I know one!' says Adam, animated. I met him tonight. 'Wanker.'

'What was his name?' asks Nick. I take his intrigue as affirmation. Relief waits in the wings.

'Dane, or Wayne or Shane? Shane, yah, Shane. Dating Susie Winchester, the chick who works at the front desk, with the fringe? Older. Too old for her. Tinder … I think they met on Tinder.' He yawns, not covering his mouth.

'Right!' I say, rising to my feet. 'Nick, shall we …?'

Nick is up, his hands on the back of an antique wooden chair. I'm struck suddenly by his physical strength, the muscles in his forearms straining, navy-coloured eyes brooding, dark hair I can run my fingers through. All at once I want to drop Adam at home, somehow find the funny side in all of this, wake up tomorrow and realise it wasn't *such* a big deal after all. Haven't we all driven a little tipsy before? Wouldn't we all want to be rescued in that situation, not least by someone we trust?

But the stone that lodged itself in my throat at the mention of my father has now deposited itself in the pit of my stomach. I have a feeling our argument will not end here, and I'm suddenly afraid of what we might say to each other when we're alone.

'I think I'll stay here tonight,' I say.

'No, you bloody won't!' says my mother, eyes desaturating. 'I'm exhausted! Get home, the pair of you. It'll all be better in the light of day.'

In the car, on the way home, there is silence except for Adam snoring in the back seat. The police didn't find us after all. This isn't a film where there's an all-seeing electronic eye on every corner, capturing hi-res images that can be enhanced and cross-referenced in some underground nerve centre. I feel like a child who has forgotten what I was sulking about, and then I remember the upside-down creature at the foot of the forest, its dull metallic abdomen exposed. I wonder if anyone has tried to right it yet, as I would if I found a ladybird on a windowsill – dead or alive.

This time, we take the less scenic route through the city, yellow-and-black squares stacked to the sky. How many are having arguments, making love, spooning ice cream, cleaning up after a dinner party, or working online with a client or colleague in a different time zone? How many are looking out of their windows, contemplating the lives of people like us sliding along the highway in our silver boxes, secret itineraries locked inside our skulls? We approach the final stretch of highway; I tentatively reach out to touch Nick's thigh. He puts his hand on mine but does not squeeze. Inside me, I imagine a kick and as I do I find myself saying, 'I love you.' As we draw up to our Art Deco apartment in Green Point, our giant child in the back seat and our minuscule one curled up inside me, Nick sighs and says, 'I love you, too.'

# SATURDAY

06:05

## Franky

*Ocean View Drive, Green Point*

I must have forgotten to take my contact lenses out. My eyes are dry and scratchy, the edges of my vision blurred. On the bedside table the vague outline of two tiny, shrivelled plastic husks confirms I *did* remember to take my lenses out. I blink rapidly to dislodge the offending object, dab my eye with a chipped fingernail – a watery, stinging sensation, followed by a burn. Maybe if I cry, whatever it is will wash itself out. Crying comes easily to me these days. Perhaps I should summon a sad thought. The sadness lodges in my throat. I blink again and dab. Finally, a perfect blob of mucous detaches itself from the corner of my eye to the skin of my fingertip, and to it clings the decapitated leg of a small spider. Satisfied, I flick the false eyelash onto the carpet, wondering if I should have made a wish.

I rest the flat of my palm on the base of my belly, softly recite my morning prayer.

'Please. Please. Stay where you are. I don't know you yet, but I know I will love you and I will do whatever I can to keep you safe. Please just … stay there.'

The apartment is silent but for a faint hum of traffic. High ceilings and wooden floors absorb the sound of sleeping men. Nick is facing away from me. I imagine Adam sprawled on our purple velvet couch, mouth open, his hand in his pants, the sun through the blinds painting stripes on his damp forehead.

Dread surfaces. And then I remember: we have a plan. All is well. Maria accepted the idea with characteristic European flare. 'Ai, ai, ai!' her disembodied voice squeaked through the speakers of Nick's phone last night. She's been with Adam for a decade. This was no great surprise, no great disappointment, but, even through the hiss and crackle of the line, there was the unmistakable tone of bitterness. 'Tell him I'll call him in the morning,' she said with finality. An ominous warning, like a summons to the principal's office. I felt for her, this younger woman I had known for so long yet did not know at all. We had little in common, not least the fact she had three children. Perhaps my situation would change that. Would we relate better to one another once we had shared our lack-of-sleep stories and our teething dramas? Would she sweep in and become my mentor, or sit back and delight in my failure?

I am fully awake now, marvelling at how little sleep I've had, wondering if I should try to fall asleep again, when my phone vibrates on the bedside table. *Too early*, I think. It must be my mother. It could only be my mother. I reach for the phone, careful not to upend a glass of water that ripples with each new vibration. *Unknown number.* 'Hello?'

The words on the other side don't make sense. I press my ear closer to the warming screen in the vain hope that meaning will follow if the words are repeated or spoken louder.

A man's voice, not speaking clearly. 'She's gone.'

'Who's gone?' I say in a whisper, so as not to wake Nick.

'Charley's gone.' It's Sebastian. I recognise the way he says her name.

'Gone where?'

'She's fucking gone!' he shouts. I pull the phone away from my ear as the line goes dead.

The sensation starts in my fingertips, moves through me, down my arms into my torso and my legs, resting near my pelvic floor, *my grape.* My tongue becomes a foreign object in my mouth. I am retching and running, emptying the remnants of last night's ginger ale into the toilet bowl. I am fascinated by the bath mat next to the shower, its soft surface, its pale cream colour. How could I not have noticed it before? I reach out to touch it, stroking it like I would the fur of a small animal, waiting for my brain to catch up with my body, or the other way around.

'You okay?' comes a voice from the bedroom. 'Frank?' Nick squints in the early morning light, raises himself up onto his elbows. 'Shit! My alarm didn't go off!'

My throat is raw, a headache sprouts at my temples, my stomach feels bruised, and the pins and needles have moved to my toes. 'Sebastian just said Charley's … gone?'

'Gone where?'

'I'm not sure I … He sounded weird … I'm finding it hard to … breathe …

Something must have happened.' In this moment I long to be back in bed absent-mindedly pulling an eyelash from my eyeball. The day had seemed a blank slate. In between all the thoughts of last night I'd thought about breakfast, perhaps a trip to the antique shop. Another Saturday like any other, despite the aftertaste of last night's argument still on my tongue.

Nick is up on his feet, moving around the room, muttering to himself. His phone was plugged into the charger – but the charger was not plugged into the wall socket. I am certain now I must have misheard Seb. Once Nick charges his phone he will confirm that whatever I just heard Seb say is something entirely different to what I imagine it to be. I am both blessed and cursed with a too-vivid imagination. My mother constantly reminds me of this. She gave me this imagination, for Christ's sake.

I saw Charley last night. She can't possibly have … gone. Even as I think these thoughts I see the irrationality of my argument. Does Seb mean 'gone' as in 'away' or 'gone' as in 'not with us any more'?

I stumble from the bathroom back to the bedroom, sit on the edge of the bed. Perhaps if I keep still, nothing else will happen.

'Give me your phone.' says Nick. He's now fully dressed, emerging from the bathroom in a cloud of deodorant.

'Why … are so many things going wrong?' I say, aware of the drama curdling my voice.

'Don't start that again. I'm sure there's a reason.'

Last night's argument had been real, had frightened me more than anything – the possibility of us not thinking the same way, the idea that we had real differences, irreconcilable even. Now this. This. What is *this* exactly? My brain flips through the possible scenarios at warp speed while my body refuses to move, everything clenched and holding on to the present reality of incomprehension.

'I'm sure there's a logical explanation,' says Nick. 'I have to go to the police station with Adam as early as I can, hopefully before anyone notices the car. Keep your phone on. I'll charge mine in the car.' He throws my phone back on the bed. I note he doesn't kiss me.

In the lounge I hear Nick say, 'Come on, champ! Up and Adam, Adam! Let's do this thing …' Adam moans, 'Do what thing?'

Everything slows. I lean back against the pillows and call Charley.

*You have reached the voice mailbox of …*

Something's not right. I call Seb on his mobile. The line rings, then cuts off. The screen declares, *Connection failed.*

I try again and again, panic rising with each electronic denial. Nick is back in the room, kissing my forehead. 'Don't panic, love,' he says. 'She's fine. He's probably coming down from something. You know him.' I try to hold onto his forearms, make him stay with me.

'Should I come with you?' I say.

'No, let me do this.' He's rushed, tying his shoelaces at the foot of the bed.

'Call Maria for me if you can. Tell her he'll be home soon. Just going to get a bucket of coffee in him and we'll be right as rain.'

'Guys!' shouts Adam from the lounge. 'What the hell?'

'I have to go,' says Nick, a toothpaste-flavoured kiss on the lips this time.

I am stuck in place. As the door closes behind them I hear Adam's retreating voice: 'What the hell are you on about, man? Seriously …'

'I'll go over everything in the car …' Keys jangle, the door slams, footsteps recede down the concrete steps to the street.

I am alone. We are alone. I slide off the edge of the bed and try to keep the anxiety coursing through my body to a low hum, so as not to contaminate *the grape*. I dress without looking in the mirror, but while I brush my teeth I search the brown flecks in my reflected green irises, trying to pin myself to the present – to what's real and not what I imagine.

The sun is already high in the sky as I leave the house, Saturday-morning beach traffic snaking its way up the street outside. On the drive to Charley's house I call my mother.

'Francine? Is everything okay?'

It's not like me to call this early. I imagine she's already been up watering her roses, paper spread out in front of her, black coffee in a china teacup.

As I relay the contents of Sebastian's garbled call, my mother remains silent – so silent, I think I may have lost the connection. 'Mom? Are you there?'

'That *is* odd,' she says now, shaking out the paper as if distracted by the morning's other headlines.

'I'm driving to Llandudno now. I'm sure everything's fine, or not, but you know, just wanted to let you know I'm going there and I'll call you when I'm back. Nick's already gone with Adam to the police station in Hout Bay to do … you know, what they think is best.'

'I bet he was worse for wear this morning!' she laughs. I'm annoyed at her jovial yet nonchalant tone. Why does everyone always assume I make mountains out of molehills? What if this is an Actual Mountain this time, and no one is taking me seriously?

I have reached the outskirts of Camps Bay. Sunlight reflects off the ocean and hurts my eyes. There is no evidence of the roadblock we passed through last night. The Twelve Apostles loom large on my left, the ocean froths like an overboiled pot to my right. It's at least a fifteen- to twenty-minute drive between my house in Green Point and Charley's in Llandudno. My mother's house is the same distance from there if I continue through Hout Bay over the Nek into the Constantia Valley.

'I'll come and see you afterwards,' I say, injecting positivity into my voice, before ending the call. I turn on the radio to drown out my thoughts. It's the classic station, the one I use to calm my nerves in traffic. The road twists and turns. Cars appear in my rear-view mirror; their drivers make aggressive hand gestures out of their windows before overtaking. My knuckles glow white on the steering wheel.

The drive is dotted with places where you could take a post-able picture, or buy shells you couldn't possibly find on your own. Sharks made of beaten metal lie alongside wooden giraffes with comically elongated necks. A temporary relief surges through me as I reach the newly installed traffic lights that demarcate where I can turn off the mountain pass to Llandudno.

The road dips like my stomach as I turn down towards Charley's impressive house, a Frank Lloyd Wright-inspired glass cube. It's the last one on the street, set against the mountain and flanked by smooth prehistoric-looking boulders. A few years ago, Seb shot a commercial in this house – before they made an offer. The view over the ocean was breathtaking, if not blinding, just before sunset.

On this occasion, it is not the view taking my breath away, but rather the sight of too many cars parked outside. Surely parking for the beach isn't in demand this early and this far from sea level? Could Seb and Charley be having some sort of early-morning party we haven't been invited to? Could it be one of their kids' parties I've forgotten about?

I see a police car parked haphazardly on the curb. I open my window, letting in the sounds of electronic bleeps and garbled voices coated in static. I turn off the engine. The music stops and the fear rises anew.

# SATURDAY

07:14

## Sebastian

*Llandudno*

I am staring at the screen of her laptop, willing it to reveal the code. The screensaver is the view from our bedroom balcony: an ocean at sunset, cheesy, but true.

There is a low murmur around me. A strange mix of familiar faces have gathered, forlorn. There are offers of tea. Windows are stared out of. People visit the downstairs bathroom, blow noses too loudly. 'If there's anything I can do …' they mumble.

Her birthday. My birthday. Our kids' birthdays. Her mom's birthday. And I'm locked out. Determined not to take my swollen eyes off the screen, I find a pen and write the possibilities I will insert when enough time has elapsed. Her best friend's name. Our cat's name. My name and her name combined. Our address. Our last holiday. Her favourite food. Someone is patting my back, telling me to give up. I shake them off, annoyed. They can't possibly understand. I'm embarrassed. I feel judged. And yet, below the surface, there are other more urgent emotions in need of my attention. I push them aside, a slew of emails I will open later.

My wife is … gone. The policemen I opened the door to six hours ago informed me it was an accident; no other cars involved. Her car collided with an oak tree on Constantia Nek road. Nothing could be done. Case opened. Would I like to take down the reference number? I have not accepted, and will not accept, these arbitrary statements. That said, there is an area of my brain that recognises getting into her computer is of the utmost importance to my survival. I need to find out about the permits for the shoot. I'm not the one who does the payments; I don't know who we pay and when we pay them. I need to pay the bond, our staff, the phone bill, the school fees, the gardener. I picture myself googling *Why did my wife leave the house after I fell asleep?*

'Daddy, will Father Christmas still come?' Katie, our six-year-old, slides in next to me, curling her small body under my arm. She is crying, but her expression is no more fraught than when she stubs her toe. Her emotions are temporary. She is less confused than I am. I should feed the children. Yes, but no. That task is not as important as the one at hand. I am allowed another chance. I stab the keys, retype her birthday into the password block. Perhaps I made a mistake the first time. I'm not thinking clearly.

'Let's get you some breakfast, Katie. Then we can write a letter to Father Christmas, yes?' says Joy, ushering Katie away in her soothing Malawian tones. I have tried to learn Chichewa out of respect for the many wonderful Malawians responsible for the day-to-day running of our lives, and I find it always cheers me up when I say, 'Muli bwanji?' (How are you?), but I still struggle with the reply: 'Ndili bwino, kaya inu' doesn't roll off the tongue. And besides, today – today – *I am not fine.*

I let Joy take the children and try to remind myself why we have gathered on this Saturday morning. It's nobody's birthday. No cake, no decorations. Charley's mother isn't here yet, but she will be soon.

I stand, blood rushing from my head. I must shower. That will make me feel better. I'm vaguely aware of people issuing commands, offering help. The wi-fi of my consciousness is down. I cannot pick up any signals. I cannot connect to other people's instructions.

*Dead. Dead. Dead*, I think. What a bizarre word. The 'e' and the 'a' sandwiched between two Ds, squeezing the life out of them. Under the spray of water I sob, uncontrollably and with a sing-song cadence. My former drama lecturer would accuse me of being too over the top. 'It's not real enough,' Mr Potgieter would say, hands flapping. 'Tone it down, make it smaller, more real!' But I'm howling now, cartoon sobs. My wet hair is seaweed on my face. I'm suffocating. I don't want to be in my skin. I want to evaporate with the steam in the shower. My mind scrambles for the password that will release me, restore the day ahead.

A gentle knock. I turn off the shower, wrap myself in a towel and open the door, just a crack. Franky looks into my eyes.

'She's *dead*!' I say, trying the word.

'I know.' She reads my eyes like a teleprompter.

'Like, actually *dead*.' I am acutely aware that I sound like a crazy person. The director in my head reiterating, *This scene isn't ringing true. Would a person say that?* She hugs me fiercely. I'm wetting her shirt. I feel bad about this. We cling to each other and it's wrong. My head is a helium balloon that wants to escape to the atmosphere above. I need to extract myself from this woman who is not my wife. 'Do you know what her laptop password might be?' I say, hopeful. She regards my non sequitur with a mixture of pity and tolerance.

'I'll give it a few tries.'

When she's left the bathroom, I stumble to the bedroom, wrap the towels tighter around myself and collapse onto my unmade bed. Someone is in the room with me. Someone is handing me two oblong pills and one round one, blue and impossibly small. I am Alice in Wonderland, I am the Mad Hatter. I will eat whatever this person gives me. I must make myself smaller. I must shrink to the smallest size I can possibly be, so I can fit through the keyhole.

# SATURDAY

11:32

## Sebastian

*Salt River*

The woman sitting opposite is crying, which seems vulgar. Beneath her sobs I can still hear cars carrying people where they need to be, urban birds calling to one another, and the hum of something unseen and electronic. This place feels like a post office, or a room you might visit to renew your passport. Posters on the walls explain the importance of keeping your belongings close to you at all times. There's a framed photograph of a former president staring at us in blissful ignorance. An unloved plant droops melancholic in the corner.

This is not a place you would expect to find yourself on any Saturday morning, let alone at the height of summer, and yet *here we all are!* in this institutional and surprisingly unclinical setting – waiting to identify people we are uniquely qualified to recognise.

The woman clutches a tissue in her left hand and sniffs loudly. Her hair is matted on one side and the creases in her clothes suggest she has slept in them. A man next to her rubs her back in circular motions; a kind, grey face set in a large frame. The woman is making strange sounds like my son post tantrum. Her open mouth suctions her bottom lip and the rest of her face twitches as though she might at any minute resume her crying or punch the man next to her square in the face. I find myself wondering what specific tragedy has brought her here, before remembering it's my own tragedy I should concentrate on. Already, I want to forget.

'You … okay?' says Franky in a whisper, offering her own perfunctory back pat. I'm hyper aware of her touch. It makes me flinch but I try not to show my discomfort. I try to decipher her state of mind. Her eyes are bleary and pink, early-morning emotions evaporated in the air-conditioned room. She looks like I feel, but more hyperactive, perhaps unsure of what particular role she is expected to play. Her knees jiggle up and down. She tries to tame them with the palms of her hands. Her wedding ring catches the stark overhead lights.

She offered to come with me for this, the first most unthinkable of tasks. My mother also offered, my father too, but I wanted someone with me who knows and loves Charley like I do. Charley's mom lives in Johannesburg. She's probably packing for her visit, spritzing herself with overpowering perfume. The thought of dealing with my mother-in-law on my own fills me with another sort of dread.

Cancelling phone contracts, dealing with insurance, issuing statements: these are the things Charley is good at – *was* good at. She is my producer in both work and life – I, the egotistical commercials director, always pretending to know what I'm doing, pinching the bridge of my nose in concentration, or creative contemplation; Charley sweeping in to make my imaginings fit the brief and the budget. I like to think we are a team, but I know she does all the work.

Perhaps when we are called, I will ask Franky to step forward. She could do it without me. She's known Charley since school, at least a third longer than I have, and yet the desire to see my wife is so powerful, I am certain I would tear down a wall with my bare hands to see her. Even if I'm not sure if it is in fact my wife in that refrigerated room at the end of the corridor. What a relief that would be. 'It's not her!' I would shout, laughing and crying at the same time. And then, perhaps, I would wake, groggy with sleep, turn to my wife, kiss her coconut-scented shoulder and say, 'Good morning.'

Believing this is indeed a very real possibility, I now want to jump up, tuck my hair behind my ear and say, 'Well, I must be going now!' But on some extrasensory level I know I am not one of the people who gets to be carried away from this scene – not now, and, I fear, not ever.

I remember reading something that said at first it's like a boulder you must carry, and eventually a pebble in your pocket that you thumb on most days. But this is not grief, this is disbelief. I will not grieve. Why would I when there is no actual evidence that my wife is dead?

'Mr Hastings ...'

A man with a clipboard is summoning me. Francine's face crumples and tears flood her cheeks. Her hair is piled on top of her head – a bird's nest of blonde indignation. I'm annoyed she's clearly not of the belief that the woman in the room at the end of the corridor is anyone other than her best friend. Why can't she at least pull herself together, for me? Charley would have.

We walk down a corridor, nothing like the place I imagined it would be. I have driven past this building a hundred times and never pictured the horrors inside. It's not signposted. No one would know this is the end point of every tragedy in Cape Town. This is the full stop, the literal cul-de-sac of existence, this unremarkable brown-and-beige linoleum hovel. It is dark, even as the strip lights flicker, and I am certain this is what hell feels like. A square of blue sky just visible through a closed, too-high and illogically curtained window mocks our activity. As we reach the door, Franky hesitates, frozen. I refuse the hand she offers – almost angry – and move into the room after the man with the clipboard. My wife is asleep on a table.

# SIX YEARS AGO

## Franky

*Alphen Hotel, Constantia*

'Mom, this is Nick.'

'Pleased to meet you, young man. I've heard a lot about you.' For a moment, I think they might hug. She proffers her hand and Nick cups both his around hers, adding a clerical bow. It's excruciating.

'All good things, I hope,' he smiles, dimples beneath one-week-old stubble.

'Yes, well …' she says.

My mother is a bear. Nick is a bird. I am a rabbit. My mother will bite. Nick will escape through the window. My body pulses with the effort required to keep still.

The restaurant I have chosen is nestled under ancient oak trees. Squirrels dart up thick trunks, their bodies camouflaged against the bark. Only the silver halo of their tails gives them away. We absorb ourselves in the menu while I reconsider possible conversation topics. Why am I so desperate for my mother and my boyfriend to like each other? I am thirty-three; Nick is thirty-five, perfectly suitable. We're all grown-ups here, aren't we?

'I'm so sorry I am not able to meet Franky's father,' says Nick, pausing to accept a beer from the waiter. 'He sounds like he was an amazing man.'

My mom fashions her mouth into a half-smile. 'Do you have parents?'

'Of course he has parents, Mom! Everyone does!'

She shoots me a look. My laugh echoes in my head.

'They're both …' he says, cautiously. 'My father passed away a long time ago. My mother is … she's not well. She has Alzheimer's and dementia.'

'Oh, I am sorry to hear that.' My mother places her hand on his. I feel a rush of joy, followed immediately by ossifying fear.

'It must be so hard,' she says.

'She's in a care facility.'

'Oh, God forbid. Do you visit much?'

'No.'

I cut in. 'Mom, she's ill, we … I want to visit her … but Nick says it's more complicated—'

'Franky tells me you were an art teacher?' says Nick, holding my hand under the table. 'Do you still paint?'

My mother waves away the suggestion. 'I'm hardly an artist. I like to get creative every now and then. It's good for the soul. High-school children can be so tiresome – all those hormones and confused feelings. I've thought about teaching an adult class, but I prefer my own company.'

'And you don't …' he hesitates, '… have anyone else … in your life now?'

My hands clamp the chair beneath me. I let my tongue fall to the base of my mouth to prevent myself from answering for her. My mother gives Nick a long, cool stare.

'When Graham died I lost my best friend. I will never be able to replace him.' She sighs, avoids eye contact with us both. 'Most of my friends are dying or dead. It's a terrible business.'

'Mom, Nick's working on engineering plans for the gallery refurb at Company Gardens.'

'I hear you and Francine are thinking of moving in together?' she says, ignoring my segue. I feel responsible for, and unable to control, them both – this large stubbled man, this paper-thin woman. This bird, this bear. She eyes him cautiously, irises becoming paler, although it could just be the afternoon light.

'We're not sure yet,' he says.

My stomach drops. Is he having second thoughts?

'Yes, it's important to be sure.' says my mother. 'You learn a lot about someone when you move in with them. Towels on the floor!' Her eyes sparkle. 'It's a good way to size someone up. Francine was always untidy as a teenager. Her father used to tell me, "Just close the door, Silvia. Close the door!"' Her laugh is as delicate as a Christmas ornament.

Nick's laugh is deep and sincere. 'Well, I'm kind of a neatness freak,' he says, giving my hand another squeeze.

'So, he doesn't like his mother,' she says on the phone that night. 'That's telling.'

'Mom, they have a different relationship …'

'If you even *think* about putting me in a "care facility" one day, you've got another think coming.'

'Mom, it's different. I mean—'

'Go on.'

'When Nick was a kid, his mom tried to …' I struggle for the appropriate euphemism, settle with the clearest, '… kill herself. He's never forgiven her.'

'Oh goodness,' she says. 'That's dark.'

I blow air through the receiver.

'And *are* you moving in together?'

'I think so. It's been three months, so …'

'He's very handsome,' she says. 'If you like that sort of thing.'

# SIX YEARS AGO

## Franky

*Somerset Road, Green Point*

'Hey, I'm Franky.'

He gives me a bear hug.

'I'm Adam, obviously!'

Nick's laugh is unfamiliar.

'So this place is cool, hey?' Nick sounds like someone's dad when he says this. We're on the balcony of a bar in Green Point, watching the cars slide along Somerset Road. There's a mild smell of garlic butter and seafood from the restaurant below.

'I'm Maria,' she says, leaning in for a double kiss. She smells freshly showered, her hair slightly wet, skin warm. She is as beautiful as I imagined she would be.

'So, nice to finally meet you guys.' *You guys?* My voice has become childish.

Adam and Nick are sharing a joke Maria and I are not privy to. Nick is laughing so hard he feels the need to shield his eyes with his hand. I've never seen him laugh like that before.

'Nick tells me you work in advertising?' She clutches a sparkling pink drink with chocolate-coloured fingernails.

'Yes!' I say. 'And you're a model? Have you done any local commercials? Could we have worked together?'

'Oh, God. A lifetime ago,' she says, throwing back her head, a slight roll of the eyes. She holds up her index finger pressing pause on our conversation before addressing Adam. 'Adam, baby, please don't drink too much, okay? I don't want you to be snoring tonight.'

She pronounces his name *Aa-dumb*.

'I have two babies, right?' she says, returning to me. It takes me a while to realise she's not talking about her actual child and Adam. 'One on the way. Can you fucking believe it?!'

'No, I can't,' I say, taking in her flat stomach, her boyish frame. I can't help but feel she must know so much about me already. How much has Nick told Adam? How much has Adam relayed to Maria? The questions we ask each other ring false. I'm desperate to make a proper connection.

'I like your hair,' she says, touching the end of my ponytail. 'You did any modelling before?'

'Me? Oh, God, no!' She's flattering me. I take the bait. 'I've made a lot of commercials, though. They still like us old wordsmiths to get involved in the casting process. I'm sure you must have been on one of my casting tapes back in the day!' *Back in the day* – really?

'Frank, what do you want to drink?' says Nick.

'I'll have what she's—'

'And this one!' says Maria, her arm reaching around Nick's neck in what I take to be a sisterly stranglehold. 'He's so handsome, no? But he has a boring job like *Aa-dumb*. Engineering. Almost as boring as software. Who cares, right? Tell me what *you're* working on?'

'Oh, I'm … it's pretty boring.'

'Tell her, Frank. Tell her about the dog food thing,' says Nick without sarcasm.

'Oh, no, it's … it's lame, I …'

Somehow I know this woman will only pretend to be interested in the commercial I'm shooting next week, the identical twin toddlers we've cast to play doting pet parents.

'How long have you been in Cape Town?' I say as Nick retreats to the bar. It's beyond me why I keep asking questions I know the answers to.

'Oh,' she screws up her exquisite face, mentally calculating. 'Like, four years now.' She looks wistful, distracted. She gives a wave to someone who has walked in behind me. I turn my head, but it's not clear who the wave was for.

'Do you go back much?' I say. 'To Barcelona?' I've let slip I know where she's from. Nick hands me an identical-looking drink to Maria's.

'No! Have a real one, baby girl!' she says. 'You don't need to have this boring stuff I'm having. It's okay!' She takes the glass out of my hand, walks over to the bar. The barman gives her a wink in lieu of payment. Maria has her own currency.

'I don't get on with my parents,' she says, handing me a taller-than-average glass of champagne. I'm momentarily confused before I realise she's answering my last question. 'You know, they're not impressed about me having a baby as a teenager.

Even though my mom she was a teenager when she had me. So hypocritical, right? Do you want kids?'

'Oh, I … it's not something I'm thinking about right now.'

'Yeah, you know what – if you want my advice, make sure you have enough money. Do what you need to do, girl, because when these babies come, it's all about them. No more you.'

'What are you two talking about?' says Adam, sliding an arm around his wife's waist.

'Oh, how you say, the birds and the bees?' she laughs. She has to look down slightly to look him in the eye.

'It's early days,' I say.

'Yeah, get a TV instead,' says Adam, winking at his twenty-two-year-old wife. She rolls her eyes. They are an odd couple. Adam is wearing a grey hoodie and camo shorts. Maria's ensemble is all black; a silver cuff on her tanned arm catches the light like the blade of a knife.

Nick returns with more drinks. 'Cheers,' he says, raising his beer. Adam reciprocates. Maria raises her pink drink. I lift the glass of champagne. 'My family!' says Nick.

Maria makes an 'aahhh' sound. The three of them huddle together, Maria's long olive arms around both men. I find myself on the outside of their soft triangle, smiling manically. I tip back the champagne, feeling the bubbles explode on the tip of my nose.

# FIVE AND A HALF YEARS AGO

## Franky

*Ocean View Drive, Green Point*

He squints into the middle distance. He doesn't wear glasses, even though he should. Right now he's not squinting because he's trying to see something. He's squinting because he's had enough of this conversation. He's pretending his attention has been caught elsewhere. He is so like my father in this moment. I blink to banish the thought.

There are times I wonder if the ghost of my father had some role to play in bringing this man into my life. Some existential string-pull so I would be taken care of in his absence. There are striking similarities between them, which my mother denies, or can't yet see: the sureness, the calmness, the ability to see things for what they are and not what I might imagine them to be. And, like my father, he could vanish at any given moment.

We're in our pyjamas, sitting on the end of his bed. I can tell he wants breakfast, but the thoughts in my head are too big and I need to let them out to make space for myself. One of the self-help books on my bedside table purports that women need to be listened to to feel heard, and men need to have sex to feel heard. I grab his hand and squeeze it once, bring it to my mouth and kiss his fingers. He kisses my hand back, his blue eyes over my white knuckles. I feel relieved again. He won't fly away just yet.

We've only been together for four months but already I know this: Nick doesn't wear a watch, or rings, or adornments of any kind. He's fastidious about his shoes and his socks. He needs to know how things work and why they work. He must take things apart and examine them. He is patient – ridiculously, annoyingly, infuriatingly patient. But time is irrelevant to him. He likes numbers, measurements, calculations, but time is one number he can't quite connect with.

'We need to go!' I've been known to say, 'They'll give our table to someone else!'

He laughs. 'No, they won't, and so what if they do ... We'll go somewhere else.'

He has an ability to filter only the important information. He asks questions because he wants the answer, not because he wants to make conversation. He always tells the truth, no matter the consequence. A does-my-bum-look-big-in-this type question will illicit an I-prefer-you-in-the-other-one type answer. You can rely on him for this. He's easy to love, but not always easy to please, and, for reasons I'm still unsure of, I want so badly to please him.

He stands and closes the door of his cupboard. It smells mildewy. I wonder if I should clean everything. Would he appreciate it? Probably not. He doesn't like it when I move his things. He leaves slips of paper, golf tees, small spiral coils – which could be the metal parts that connect with a battery – on the mantelpiece, the kitchen counter, next to the bath. Each time I see these items it infuriates me. Despite what my mother may think about my teenage self, I like a house that is orderly and smells vaguely of fig or vanilla. Turns out Nick is far from a neatness freak – except when it comes to his shoes and his car. He does a complicated dance after surfing and expects everyone with him to do the same. When I hop into the car with sandy feet, he sighs and says, 'Babe ... your feet!'

'Sorry!' I say.

When he can see how hurt I look, he says, 'It's not such a big deal.' Although I sense it is. When I annoy him, I swallow my own anger and try to decipher in what way I can change my behaviour to make him stay. The slightest sign of danger, and he will be gone – like *his* father was. History repeats itself, after all. And then there's the story he told me about his first girlfriend, Heather.

I've been exploring this a bit with Charley's psychologist. I realise that when Nick shows any kind of displeasure towards me, I'm transported back to my childhood. My mother ignored me if I did something wrong. Not for hours, mind you, but just long enough to make me wonder if she still loved me. I would spend ages working out what the infringement was and then try to correct it as soon as possible so she would love me again. 'I'm sorry, Mommy.' Those were the magic words. Her face would soften and she'd open her arms to me. I learnt early on, saying sorry is a way out of most things – even if you don't mean it. Sorry just means *I didn't mean to make you cross. Please can you stop being cross and go back to loving me again?* When I tentatively brought this up with my mother she said, 'Oh please! That's right – blame the parents for everything! I always loved you; you know that. Children need to learn somehow – it's not as if I hit you!'

Nick and I have had a few quarrels. They always end with me apologising – usually because I'm afraid he'll see me for who I am. *I didn't sign up for this,* I picture him thinking or saying. So, admittedly, it's odd that I feel the need to push him on this particular subject.

'Please,' I say. 'I think you should visit her. She's still your mother.' Nick makes a *pffft* sound. I am in possession of only a handful of facts. Her name is Gwen. She must love him. He doesn't see it that way, or rather, he doesn't *feel* it that way. He loved his father. His father had an affair. His father said he felt unloved. In turn, his mother said *she* felt unloved. He was their fourth child and the love was spent along with the money for new school shoes.

Nick tells me the three words he remembers her saying most, all throughout his childhood, his teenage years and young adulthood, were 'Have you eaten?' He had stories to tell, adventures to share, but she shook her head, dipped the mop back in the bucket and asked again if he was hungry.

My mother, on the other hand, was not much of a cook. We had a cleaner. We ordered in. She valued creativity, imagination and magic above all else. One of my earliest memories is of her waking me in the middle of the night, of her high-waisted jeans and the fabric of my blue terry-cloth gown between my fingers. She whispered a commentary of what was about to happen as she took me up the dark gravel driveway into the moonlit street. As we turned the corner towards the Constantia common, we saw a field of people holding candles, singing carols – the Real Father Christmas among them. I gasped a four-year-old's gasp.

Nick's mother wasn't concerned with such frippery. Or was she? I wasn't there at all the Christmases and birthdays he must have had. My father was a surgeon. We had money. Nick's father worked for the council. Money was in short supply. Perhaps his mother *had* been attentive and kind and caring, but his memory had been eroded on the day she plotted her escape.

He told me he had watched her from the doorway. She had slumped on her bed, let the empty plastic pill bottle fall from her hand – as if purely for dramatic purposes. He had watched it roll across the floor, stopping at his twelve-year-old feet in their too-small shoes. She was forty. Her wish was not granted. Instead, the universe defied her and gave her three more decades – with the last five years a jail sentence of Alzheimer's and dementia.

*

We enter the forgettable building. My nostrils register the smell of boiled vegetables. This was my idea. I can only see things from my limited perspective, one dominated by my unquestioning devotion to the woman who wished me into existence.

Gwen is weak and disorientated. Her hair is bright white against her sunken skin. She says she is sorry she can't remember our names. For some inexplicable reason she offers us ice cream. 'I know you,' she says to Nick. His eyes fill with defiant moisture. He excuses himself from the room, mumbling about the need to put the roses I had made him bring into water.

I stare at the smiling stranger in front of me. I can't decide if I regret making him see her or if I should congratulate myself for bringing them together. I return her smile.

'You're a lovely girl,' she says.

Do I have a right to be flattered? Whose side am I on? What am I looking for here? Is it good to know he has some depth of feeling for his mother? Is it anger? Is it sadness? Or, perhaps, some potent version of the two? When Nick returns to the room, sniffing sharply, his mother tells him not to cry before adding gently, 'I must get you something. You look hungry.'

During the car journey home I know it's best not to draw attention to the uncharacteristic emotion that has ballooned inside him. So, instead, I say, 'Do you want children?'

He says, 'Do you want to get married?'

I'm not sure if this is a question or a proposal. Either way, I say, 'I thought you'd never ask.'

# THIRTY YEARS AGO

## Franky

*Main Road, Rondebosch*

'You know there's no actual tooth fairy, right?'

'What do you mean?'

'I mean it's just your mom, or your dad. My dad's dead. So it's probably my mom. She's over it, though.'

'Oh. I thought—'

'How many teeth have you lost?'

'Six, I think.'

'I've lost nine – wanna see?' She lifts up her lips and shows me her gums.

'Is it true your mom is Mrs Allen?'

I don't like this question. 'Mm. She's moving to the high school next term.'

'Are you good at art like her? You haven't even started yet.'

'Not really. I like writing stories.'

'Me too!' she says. 'Hey, can I borrow some of your ink? Mine's spilt.'

'Sure … What are you drawing? It looks kind of … scary,' I say.

'It's a monster drowning in a river. My brother died, and my dad.'

'Oh.'

'It's okay. I was, like, three; he was like two or something. I don't remember him. My mom does though, obviously. I think that's why she's over the tooth fairy thing. She's over a lot of stuff. Your mom's cool, though. Does she still do the tooth fairy?'

'Well, I thought … I think there *is* a tooth fairy. My mom's not good at lying, so I think I'd know. I'm Franky, by the way.'

'That's a boy's name! I'm Charlotte.'

'Cool. I'm Francine. My dad called me Franky when I was baby. Hey! You could be Charley?'

'Only if I can call you Frankfurter!'

'You're funny.'

'Thanks.'

# TWENTY YEARS AGO

## Sebastian

*Dean Street, Newlands*

From behind the bar, I have a clear view of the entrance. The lunch shift is almost over. One hour and freedom is mine. I wipe the countertop again and entertain myself with my habitual game. *Red wine*, I think, as an elderly man and his wife shuffle in. *And a bottle of sparkling water, lemon, no ice.* The host traces a finger down the reservations list and ushers them to a corner table.

'Red wine and a large bottle of sparkling please, Seb. Ice and lemon,' says Siphiwe, sliding his tray along my bar. (I like to think of it as *my* bar, this piece of oak that separates me from everyone else.) When Siphiwe has left with the drinks, I duck behind the counter. Quick shot of vodka. I was close enough.

The host's heels are impossibly high, her expression vacant as she stares through the glass doors onto the street, hands clasped behind her back. She's Debbie, or Deborah. She's new. I wonder what she's thinking about. Her shift ends at the same time as mine.

A clutch of forty-something women with varying shades of dyed blonde hair arrives. One of them is tied to a giant inflatable champagne bottle. There is much shrieking as they decide how to seat themselves around the table. *Bottle of Prosecco*, I think, and *two bottles of white – Chardonnay, not Sauvignon … One bottle of still, one bottle of sparkling.*

'What did they order? I say, my fingers twitching.

'Gin and tonics all round. Oh, and one bottle of still, one bottle of sparkling.'

I feel a draft on my cheek as the door swings open. I double-take. It's her. Pale denim flares and a white cheesecloth shirt with billowy sleeves. Her thick blonde hair is tangled in the strap of the leather bag slung across her body. The look on her face belies the cool Seventies vibe she's trying to project.

Tortoiseshell sunglasses balance precariously on her head. As Deb leads her to a four-seater she pitches forward, like she's wearing someone else's shoes. *Decaf cappuccino*, I think, or *vodka, lime and soda*. Too close to call.

She gazes around the room but doesn't seem to see me watching her. I cut lemons, twist a gin bottle in my hands. She pulls something from her bag; it's a grey block of … Oh! She has a cellphone – *fancy*. I had no idea. She looks at it, puts it back in her bag. Runs her fingers through her hair, straightens the charm on her necklace.

'Do we have ginger beer, Seb?' says Siphiwe. 'Or only ginger ale?'

I pour her a ginger beer and consider my options. My replacement will be here any minute. I flick a cloth over my shoulder. She drums her thumb and index fingers on the table, straightens the menu.

'Franky?' I blurt. She lifts her head from the menu at the sound of my voice.

'Yes?' Her eyes are intense. Green instead of blue.

'I'm Sebastian!' I say, placing the ginger beer in front of her.

'Oh! Charley's Sebastian?' she says, eyebrows raised.

'The one and only!' I point at my gold name tag.

'You … work here?'

'Yeah, it's part-time. I'm doing my drama degree – but you probably knew that already, right?'

She stiffens, gives me a false smile. 'How did you know that I … I'm me?'

'Charley has a picture of you two in her room. You're like twins!'

'Oh, no … we're …' she says, rearranging her knife and fork, so they sit exactly parallel. 'She's taller and … I …'

'Yeah, but, you know, pretty similar. It's so great to meet you! I feel like we should hug or something.'

She pushes back her chair and there's an awkward embrace. She smells of artificial watermelon.

'Charley said you were having a party this weekend,' she says, still standing, arms folded.

'I was going to come. She wanted me to meet you first … so she …'

'Yeah, it's going to be kif. You should definitely come! Are you … waiting for someone?'

'I … Oh, yeah, I was waiting for someone; she … he … *they* didn't show up, so I guess I'm going to call my dad to pick me up.' She fumbles in her bag, retrieves the grey block.

'You don't have a car?' She has a phone; surely she should have a car. She's nineteen – same age as Charley.

'I've … just failed my licence. I have to wait three weeks before I can take it again, so … I'm a nervous driver.' She laughs and the laughter relaxes her features.

'My shift's over soon. I can totally take you home,' I say. 'I have my bike. You're cool with that, right?'

'Oh, yeah … My dad would be … no,' She's warming to me, I can tell. I'm no longer the crazy stranger. I'm her best friend's new boyfriend – what could possibly go wrong?

Outside in the parking lot, she shifts from foot to foot. I hand her my spare helmet and offer her more reassurance. 'I'm a safe driver, like *crazy* safe. Plus – I'm going to meet Charley, after. She'll be so pumped I met you!'

'Are you?'

'Pumped I met you? Sure.'

'No, are you going to meet Charley?'

'Yeah, at her mom's place. Why?'

Her eyes become a darker shade of green. She looks confused. She hesitates, then climbs behind me. Her body is rigid and doesn't press tightly to mine like Charley's would. 'Hold on tight!' I say. My Vespa roars to life. Her hands clamp my sides like salad forks, tentative but firm. As I manoeuvre through cars I call back to her, try to strike up conversation, but she concentrates on the road, as though controlling my driving with her mind. Every now and then she says, 'Uh-huh.'

The insides of her thighs push against the outside of mine as I pick up speed.

We pull up outside the house she directs me to. It's her mom and dad's house in Constantia. Enormous. Huge gates, those lollipop trees, the works. She hops off the Vespa, stumbling on her wedges, presses the gate buzzer. I idle the bike, feeling the engine roar through my legs. She hands me back the helmet, face pale. As the gate opens I see Charley, in the gravel driveway, leaning against a stone fountain.

'Well, look what we have here,' she says, arms folded, a curious smile on her face. She's wearing an almost identical outfit to Franky, only instead of flares she's wearing cut-off shorts, exposing her long, tanned legs.

'Hey, you!' I say. I park the bike, remove my helmet and kiss her on the lips. She smells familiar, like lemon sweets.

'Hey, Frank,' says Charley. 'Enjoy the ride?'

'You stood me up,' says Franky.

'Well, you met him anyway, didn't you?'

'This was your … *plan?*' says Franky. 'Why would you do that?' Her voice is wobbly, tears forming.

'Ag, first meetings are so awkward, don't you think? Besides, it was … a test.'

'Did we pass?' I say, throwing my arm around Franky, giving her what I take to be a brotherly cuddle.

'You did,' says Charley, looking directly at Franky. 'You, on the other hand …'

Franky's tears finally run down her cheeks. She wipes them away with the back of her hand, pushes past us towards her parents' house.

'Frank! Frankfurter! I was only kidding!' shouts Charley. 'It was just a joke! Franky! I love you! You know that!'

The front door slams and Charley says, 'Oh, well. Win some, lose some. She'll be fine.'

# SEVEN YEARS AGO

## Sebastian

*Skiathos, Greece*

The walls appear to be as thin as the over-laundered sheets folded at the bottom of our bed. I shouldn't eavesdrop but what else can I do? It's my wedding day. It's not like I have anywhere else to be. Their voices are muffled. A few words drift through the open doors of the balcony. I can't see them but I know Charley is wearing too much make-up and right now it's running down her face. Franky must be close, an arm around her shoulders.

'He hates me,' says Charley.

'No, he doesn't,' says Franky, a laugh rounding the words.

'Okay, well then, I hate me.'

Here we go again. The self-loathing dance. I need to get her to quit that shrink. I swear she's putting ideas in her head.

'I just want everything to be perfect.'

'Of course you do.'

'It's my day … I mean, it's his day too, but you know what I mean …'

Half an hour ago I watched Charley from the balcony of our hotel. She was on the beach attaching stone weights to the thirty-seater tablecloth. The table sits at the water's edge. A gentle Mediterranean breeze lifted the corners of the starched linen cloth. This wouldn't do for Charley. I went down to help her and she lost it, said I wasn't supposed to see her on the day, it's bad luck. I laughed. She did not. I shook my head and walked away. Now I'm here, wrapped in a towel, listening to my wife and her best friend analyse our relationship.

'It's like I can't stop myself,' says Charley. 'I just need everything to be the way I want it to be. I can't stop bossing him around, and I feel like one day … he's going to crack and tell me what he really thinks and then … and then …'

'He loves you – everything about you – the weird stuff and the good stuff.'

'Do you think?' She's sniffing. Franky is turning this around. She's on my side. She's always been on my side.

'Weddings are stressful,' she says. I imagine her stroking Charley's hair. Wiping the mascara from under her eyes with her thumb. 'They bring out the worst in people.'

'That's just it!' she says, her voice rising. 'I feel at my worst. I'm supposed to feel light and easy and in love, and I feel anxious and stressed and tired and I want to not feel like that. I want to feel calm and cool, like he does and I … I just can't. What's wrong with me?'

'Deep breaths, okay? I'll be right there by your side. You are the cleverest, most beautiful, most perfect bride ever. I, on the other hand, look like a marshmallow in this dress.'

'Frank.'

'No, I'm serious. I'm jealous. In a good way. You get your perfect dress off its hanger, I'll sort the tablecloth. Okay?'

'Frank, will you always be there?'

'Of course I will.'

'I love you.'

'I love you, too. Now stop blubbering and let's get this show on the road.'

Later, Charley glides across the sand towards me, new make-up softened by the setting sun. I look only at her, but I feel Franky's gaze penetrate my periphery. She is watching me, willing me to have the appropriate expression on my face. I only hope I can live up to both of their expectations.

# TEN YEARS AGO

## Sebastian

*Main Road, Constantia*

Have you ever been to the funeral of someone you've never met?

So far, it's pretty life-affirming. I wouldn't say I'm *enjoying* it per se, but I'm finding it soothing. All these people crammed into this church to say their final goodbyes to a guy I probably wouldn't be able to pick out in a line-up. I find myself wondering if there will be any strangers at my funeral. I'd want to be liked, even when I've snuffed it.

Charley and I are sitting in the middle pews. I crane my neck to see if I can catch a glimpse of Franky. She and her mom are seated in the first pew. Their blonde heads tilt towards each other like pieces of something broken.

I can't remember the last time I was inside a church. All this *Yea, though I walk through the valley of the shadow of death* stuff reminds me of school assemblies and the thought induces a yawn. I never could understand the difference between a rod and a staff and what possible comfort they could offer anyone.

This place is packed. I mean, standing room only. If you tune into the whispering, it's clear the guy Franky's dad was operating on is here too. Behind me I hear a woman say, 'One of the attendants *took the wheel,* and … well, I guess you'd have to think of it as some sort of miracle. I know I would, if it was me.' Franky and her mom probably don't see it like that. Heart attack while performing heart surgery: what are the chances?

The prayer has ended and the priest has started some sort of sermon. I can tell it's going to be a long one, so I let my mind wander down the aisles, across the backs of people's heads, three-quarter angles of their sagging faces. What is it that's so comforting about stained glass? As churches go, this one's pretty low-key on the Jesus motifs. A pigeon flies above our heads and out the open doors. Now, if that had been a dove ... wouldn't that be something?

My parents are alive and well, thanks for asking. Even three of my grandparents are still alive. Grandpa Phil died when I was too young to remember him. I've never known death – except for that one gerbil, Mr Scruffit. Oh, and my sister's cat. Other than that, at the ripe old age of thirty-two, no one close to me has died. Thank God, or whatever.

I guess one day my parents and my grandparents will die, and I should probably wrap my head around that.

My dad had a car dealership, my mom was his top saleswoman, until she became his wife. They're technically both retired now and they live on a golf estate in Hermanus. My sisters are both doctors, and they both married doctors, so you can imagine how my dad felt when I announced I wanted to be an actor. When I brought Charley home, my parents were visibly relieved she was not a *Charlie* – if you know what I mean. They'd never admit to that, though. They are even more relieved Charley has convinced me to try my hand at directing. We have our first job this weekend. Softswell toilet paper. Franky's the copywriter; she secured us the gig. I'm nervous, but Charley believes in us, so I guess it's sort of like I'm *playing the part* of a director for now, and if all goes well, I may actually be one. Right now, I'm playing the part of a mourner. And ... *background action!* I inhale through my nose and try to hook my mind to a sad thought.

Charley is crying. Not ugly crying, more tearful sniffing. I wonder if she's thinking about Franky's dad or her own dad. Charley's dad topped himself. Pretty bleak story. Charley's younger brother drowned in a swimming pool while her dad was focused on three-year-old Charley. Two years later he went for a hike up Lion's Head and never came back. They said he fell, but Charley sees it differently with adult eyes. She's had a lot of therapy.

On the drive over here, she told me that when she and Franky were little, she was jealous Franky had a dad and she didn't. She said she spent so much time at Franky's house in Constantia, Dr Allen felt like a father to her too. He worked a lot, but when he was there on weekends, he used to take them for ice creams and he was the only one who ever let them have three scoops. They never finished them, but he said that taught them something. He was that sort of guy, she said. He was reliable and straight-laced but still cool. It was Franky's mom who made all the rules. I've met Mrs Allen a few times over the years, but I'd be lying if I said I know her. She's a mom, you know – they all kind of have the same vibe, like my mom. Same sort of hairstyle, same taste in white linen shirts and white wine.

The priest's voice echoes around the room and there's a dignified calm in the audience (congregation?). Then a shift in the atmosphere as the priest calls Franky up to say a few words. Charley gives me a tearful smile, squeezes my hand, and I give her a wink. She narrows her eyes at me. I pat her leg once and she softens at my touch, resumes clutching the programme.

Someone coughs. Franky stands at the podium, unfolds a piece of paper. Even from this distance I can see her hands are shaking. 'My dad was …' she begins. She freezes, like a gargoyle. 'My dad was …' Her voice wobbles. She takes a deep breath. People look down at their feet. There's another cough. It's painful, and even though it's meant to be, it's too much. I feel tears at the back of my eyes in sympathy, a tightening in my throat. The sharp *clip clip clip* of heels on stone breaks the silence. Charley has left her seat next to me and is walking briskly towards the podium. She puts her arm around Franky, cupping her hand around her shoulder. In her calm, clear voice, Charley reads Franky's words.

'My dad was … a really good public speaker.' There's a titter in the audience, not quite a laugh. She continues. 'He was a great conversationalist. He could speak to anyone, and he always seemed to know the right thing to say in any given situation.' Charley nods at Franky, who gives her a half-smile. Franky takes a deep breath, and with Charley by her side, she takes over the reading.

'He was loved by so many, not just by my mom and I … or is it me and my mom? He was such a stickler for grammar and spelling, I can hear him saying now, *Grammar counts!*' The audience laughs with Franky this time, giving her the fuel she needs to continue. Charley is rubbing her back now, gentle circles. 'He saved so many lives, and meant so much to so many that now it's hard to find the words …' She stumbles again and Charley takes over, squeezing her tightly to her side.

'I will forever be grateful for the childhood I had, the memories I will keep with me always, and the knowledge that somehow – in some small way – some of my dad lives on inside us all.'

I resist the urge to clap. Charley and Franky hug. The priest takes to the podium. The hug intensifies. It's hard to tell who will let go first.

# NOW

## Sebastian

*Llandudno*

Her funeral isn't what I expected it to be. Did I expect a funeral, ever? My perspective has been limited to the television shows I have seen, black-clad mourners in wide-brimmed hats and bee-keeper veils dabbing their faces with neatly folded tissues.

I am the guest of honour at a cocktail party. I've always been told to imagine your audience naked, but as I took to the podium to recite the waffle I wrote last night, I found it more helpful to imagine them all dead – slumped over in various states of repose. Only then could I summon the courage to speak. My biceps are bruised from all the sincerity I have had to endure for the last few hours.

Billed as a 'celebration' and devoid of any religious undertones (because she had no beliefs, or at least hadn't had time to decide what her beliefs were) the tone is somehow confused, *too* celebratory. Wine flows as do the tears, but there's laughter too and smiling, which I can't stomach. Katie seems oddly excited that there are so many people in our house.

'Daddy, can Sarah sleep over?' I don't know who Sarah is. The woman I take to be Sarah's mother is looking at me, biting her lip so hard I fear she might draw blood.

'Another time, Katie,' she says. 'Your daddy needs you now …'

Do I? Do I need them right now – or would I rather someone sweep them away and carry them off to a place where their mother isn't dead and their father isn't losing his grip on reality? I spot Leo outside with a neighbour's son – completely oblivious, playing tag on the lawn as though this is just another day in their unfolding childhoods, which of course it is.

I keep expecting to see her. Where is she? Why am I at this party at our house without her? The anti-shock medication is making me delusional instead of calm. I have tied my hair in a short ponytail, scraping it away from my face. I feel silly, exposed – but my mother told me this is an appropriate look for a widower. I don't recognise myself. I am looking for my own reflection, something in someone else's face that will somehow explain the events of the past five days.

Franky. Only her face makes sense to me, like when you wake from a strange dream and forget the contours of your own bedroom, are suddenly suspicious of your surroundings until they fall into place. She is my landmark. Now I feel like I am bobbing on a sea of people and she is my life raft. She gives me a look as if trying to communicate something. I stare back at her dumbly. She always seemed so much younger than Charley, despite being the same age. The last few days have aged her. Her hair is more dishevelled than usual and she is paler than I have ever seen her. She's been with me all morning, setting out the candles, rearranging the flowers, cleaning glasses while I lay in the guest bedroom staring at the ceiling, attempting to solve the Rubik's Cube my life has become.

'Hey,' whispers Franky. 'I've been looking for you everywhere. Stay next to me, I'll keep the weirdos away.' She hooks her arm in mine and I let myself be dragged outside. We are links in a short chain. She wears a single silver bangle – Charley gave it to her. It makes my knotted leather cuffs look childish in comparison. She leads me into the garden and we find a spot behind one of the tropical ferns, near the pool. This reminds me: who will pay the gardener? Where is the gardener? Another mundane thought for me to push into the abyss.

'Come on,' says Franky. 'Life's short … apparently.' Her hands are shaking. Is she cold? Or is she taking pills like I am? Mine are slowing me down; hers appear to be speeding her up. I stuff my hands into the pockets of my jacket, waiting for her to say something meaningful. I remember how philosophical she gets when she's drinking. But this time she says nothing, and the glass of wine in her hands is suspiciously full.

'Where's Nick?'

'He's here.' Cryptic.

'Fuck this,' I say.

'Yeah, fuck this a lot,' she agrees.

'Are we hiding from something?' I look at her sideways.

It's not like her to be so silent, so lacking in conversation. I need her to lift me above the ocean of despair I'm swimming in, but it's as though she is bobbing along with me, waiting for someone else to rescue us both. I consider throwing myself into the icy depths of the pool, waking myself from this nightmare. Instead, I try to start a conversation. It feels like lighting a match in the rain. 'I don't know what's going on. I'm … confused and … I feel scared. It's probably obvious, but I just … can't quite …. understand anything.'

'You're not drunk enough yet,' she says, handing me her glass, which I now realise was meant for me all along. I tip the wine back, drink the whole lot like it's grape juice. I become aware of how thirsty I am. I should go inside and get a glass of water, but I know there will be at least ten ghosts from the past I will need to encounter before I get to the kitchen. I am drifting, hoping Franky will tell me what to do next. I can hear my mother-in-law, Deidre, calling my name. She is wandering around the garden like a woman who's lost her dog in a park. She arrived from Johannesburg on Sunday. Her botoxed face rendered the emotion of losing her daughter insincere, which hurt me deeply. I retreat deeper into the bushes next to Franky.

'It's going to be okay,' she says now, holding my sweaty hand in her cold one.

'No, it's not,' I say, squeezing, feeling the small bones of her hand in mine.

'You're probably right.' She drops my hand and takes the empty glass from me.

She is not herself today; then again, neither am I. I can't quite grasp what it is I need her to do for me, but it's not this. She feels distant. I feel like I am in a fishbowl; no one can hear me banging on the glass.

'Sebastian,' she says now. 'I need to tell you something.'

'I hope it's a joke!' I say, forcing a laugh. She swallows.

'That night … you know, when Charley …'

My eyes find Nick in the garden talking to Deidre, hugging her, letting her smear her make-up on his blue shirt. He looks up; his eyes lock with Franky's before she looks away.

'What? Franky. What?'

'I was waiting … for the right time … Nick and I … We're having a baby.'

She folds her arms across her chest and there is no sound as she starts to cry.

# NOW

## Sebastian

*Hout Bay*

I have decided denial is the way forward. This is a test. One module after the other until I feel better. Christmas was a write-off. New Year a non-event. These things are perhaps obvious, but children – so seemingly accepting of death – are unable to fathom that Father Christmas did not put on quite the show he did in previous years.

Charley was the artisan when it came to all things parenting. She bought the presents long in advance, hid them in some unknowable place. Of *course* I hadn't read the notes the kids had written to Father Christmas, slid through the mouth of the starved and mostly ornamental red postbox in Hout Bay, never to be seen again. I had absolutely no idea what they had asked for, no idea where these magical gifts might be stashed – and, more worryingly, I didn't care.

'Panda!' said my four-year-old, Leo. 'Where's the Panda?!' I was at a loss. Were the hundreds of gifts my parents had cobbled together and wrapped in silver and green paper not enough?

'Were we bad?' said Katie. 'Was Father Christmas cross with us?'

'No, baby,' I tried, 'Father Christmas was just extra busy this year, and he sent me a text to say you can get all the things you asked for on your birthday, okay?' Katie was sceptical, her brown eyes narrowing. 'I changed my mind,' she said. 'I don't want a Barbie that can bend any more, I want Mommy back!'

'So do I, love,' I said, almost adding *She'll be back … She's just … you know, otherwise engaged.* So, here we are at *Denial* and it feels good. I am like Leo, with his 'blankie'. *Denial* is a soft, blue corner of a blanket – spongy fibres, lined with satin. I will clutch it, feeling the fabric between my thumb and my index finger until the fear and despair subside. *Maybe* this is all a construct of my imagination. *Maybe* I shall wake from this dream, lesson learnt.

Charley is attentive and kind, warm and funny. She adores me, makes me feel masculine even when I feel childish and needy. It's the way she looks at me, even as I age – like I am golden; I'm shocked when I look in the mirror each morning and realise I am not. I often find myself recalling our first meeting, rewinding a film I'd like to rewatch even though I know the ending.

Purple Haze, the university cafeteria. Charley was in her first year of fine art at Hiddingh campus, before she switched to business. I was a third-year drama major. I wore a lot of tie-dye back then, a fork fashioned into a bracelet. I smoked weed and drank boxed wine. I felt misunderstood, until I met Charley.

The art faculty had put out a call to drama students for life drawing. I guess they assumed drama students had a talent for sitting still for long periods of time, which couldn't be further from the truth. Anyway, I thought I'd give it a go – for the cash. I know what you're thinking, and no, I wasn't required to get my kit off. All I had to do was sit there – my raw unedited self, while Charley drew her opinion of me in charcoal. She talked a lot, which was unexpected. It was hard for me to talk because I tend to use my hands – and if I did, I'd forget where they were before. I was rendered incapable of contributing to the conversation, like I was her shrink, or she my dental hygienist. There was a strange pleasure in this, a worthy sacrifice, delayed gratification.

She showed me the drawings five weeks later. I was suitably impressed and definitely in love with her by then. I felt she knew me in a way no one else did, knew me through my skin.

Purple Haze was our meeting spot, mornings and afternoons after class.

Three years later, we were pretty serious. I was making money as a barman and pretending to make money as an actor: a few commercials here and there, couple of lines in a movie, third guy from the left. Charley was now studying business. She wanted money, she said, and art wasn't going to get her there. (What wasn't said, but may have been inferred, was I wasn't going to get her there either.) I can't remember when Charley cooked up the production company idea, but it was definitely her idea. By that stage the disillusion of acting had kicked in and I thought, 'Why not?' Advertising agencies were hungry for the opinions of the young and misunderstood. It seemed experience was less important than self-belief, and Charley had us covered in that respect.

Our first commercial was for toilet paper. We followed a year later with one for Swiss cheese, then mayonnaise, a bank, a cellphone company, until we realised we had an actual business. Over the space of twenty years we bought a Greek wedding, trips to Paris, Rome and Los Angeles, Katie and Leo materialised, and finally, before my fortieth, we bought the glass house in Llandudno. Now I am forty-two, I have six awards for pointless commercials, and I'm a widower.

Was I the best husband I could possibly be? Did I tell her I loved her enough? Did I take her for granted? Well, if it turned out this was the case, I could change. I have learnt my lesson and now she can come back. I believe this is called *Bargaining*. Good, I'm moving through the 'five stages' more swiftly than I thought I would.

Franky has insisted I see her and Charley's psychologist. I'm trying hard to give her the impression I am fine, but she isn't buying it. I believe studying psychology only gives you an acute ability to see through people – probably the same thing you learn if you study drama. I can play her at her own game. The challenge of this gives me a reason to get out of bed.

The psychologist practises from her home in Hout Bay. A domestic worker greets me wordlessly at the front door. She knows why I am here. To her, I am another privileged white person looking for meaning while she cleans the carpets and empties the bins I will no doubt throw my tear- and snot-stained tissues into. I am ushered into a comfortable-looking room that resembles a lounge. Store-bought abstract art hangs on the walls and scatter cushions are embroidered with the words *Relax*, *Now* and *Breathe*. I inwardly roll my eyes.

On the floor is a selection of children's toys: doll's houses and babies in baskets. My own children are no closer to coming to terms with their mother's death than I am. 'But where is she?' is Katie's constant question.

'In the sky?' I offer, but she's not convinced. I cannot explain the ways of the universe any more than she can. This is almost like discovering that you can't do the maths your six-year-old has been assigned. As I wait for the psychologist's appearance, I imagine scenarios where kids might need to use the toys to explain certain emotions or unthinkable crimes committed against them. I wonder what tools I would use to describe my own emotional state. Perhaps I could rip all of the dolls' arms and legs off and see how she interprets that. I have one clear question in the forefront of my mind today: *When will this end so I can carry on as normal?*

My thoughts are disturbed by the psychologist's sudden appearance. She is rushed, a bit flustered, and then instantly calm as she takes a seat and fixes me with sparkly eyes. She has a thin fringe and practical shoes, a floaty skirt and a fleecy jumper – part hippie, part nursing sister. I believe her name is Wendy.

'Hello, Sebastian,' she says, consulting her notes. 'How are you feeling today?'

My mouth says, 'I feel tired, Wendy … and … call me Seb.'

Truthfully I feel like a wall has built up around me, keeping all my emotions inside, and one small thing could break the wall and everything will come pouring out – but, crucially, I'm not ready. The more people ask me how I am, the more bricks I add to the wall. I am unbreakable.

'Tired and ...?' she asks, an English teacher looking for more adjectives. My mind starts a random search for synonyms of 'tired' (*worn out, exhausted, fatigued, weary, sleepy, drowsy, sapped, spent, drained, jet-lagged* ...).

'Jet-lagged,' I say. 'I feel jet-lagged.' Let's see what she does with that.

'Sleep is the body's way of processing trauma. It's natural to feel sleepy as your body needs to absorb the shock it's been put through and find a way to heal.'

'What if I don't want to heal?' I say.

'Why wouldn't you want to heal?'

'Because it's ...' I search for the right word, '... disrespectful.'

'Disrespectful how?'

This is like that game Katie tries to play with me where you lose if you say 'yes' or 'no'; you have to keep asking questions until the other person cracks. I give it a try.

'Do you think it's disrespectful?'

'In what way?' she counters.

'To heal, to move on ... Do you think it's disrespectful?'

'Who are you trying not to disrespect?'

'Her, obviously.'

'But she's not here, is she, Sebastian?' she says gently.

*Or is she?* I think to myself, imagining music and a crash zoom as the camera moves to my face to reveal my wild eyes. Instead I look at my feet, inspecting my sneakers, which I shall probably never clean again. What's the point? She is silent. Waiting for me to speak. I can play that game. The clock ticks noisily and I will it to move faster.

'Only you can decide how you want to feel in this moment.'

I feel anger bubble inside me. A white-hot rage threatens to spill onto this nice oatmeal-coloured carpet I'm staring at, but I resist. *Keep it small,* I think. She cocks her head and looks at me as if evaluating if I really *have* gone off the rails. Perhaps I should go with this, say something completely left field like 'I like cherries', and see if she follows me down that rabbit hole.

'Sebastian, Seb ... you are not the first and, sadly, you won't be the last man on earth to lose their partner. People do move through this, and people do heal. Healing doesn't mean you erase everything before the "injury". You will always have the scars.'

I keep staring at the floor and try to focus on my breathing, which has become unnaturally shallow. If I squint just enough, I can see my own eyelashes – small black smudges overlapping my vision.

She is silent, waiting for some sign that I have bought in. I'm too clever for this, I think. I let out a sigh of resignation, and the silence continues. It is a game of who blinks first and it won't be me.

After a few more attempts, she says, 'I think we've reached the end of our session,' and relief floods my arteries. Now I can go back to *Denial,* as I had planned to this morning.

Outside the door to her home office is a wooden bench. I imagine this is her outdoor waiting room, where patients unwittingly strain their ears to hear if the patient before them shows signs of being worse off than themselves. Today the bench is occupied by a dark-haired woman who studiously avoids eye contact. *What did she hear?* I think, and then, *Who cares?*

While driving, I think back to our last conversation, in the Uber, on the way home that night.

*'You think she'll be okay?'*

*'Of course she will.'*

*'I love you.'*

*'I know you do.'*

We were discussing our daughter's lack of interest in her schoolwork, the teacher's concern. We were trying to be good parents – not too pushy, not too overbearing; the right amount of concerned, in a modern way. We were people who listened their kids, not people who told them what to do. We wanted the best for Katie. Now it was just me. Now I wanted the best for her, and through no fault of my own, Katie would not have the best. She was now irrevocably tainted. There goes the girl who lost her mother … *Shame*, they'd all say. *That's why she takes no interest in her schoolwork.* If only they knew.

Sleep is all I crave. Beautiful, never-ending sleep. If I could only keep sleeping for a few days, I know I would wake up refreshed and everything would be as it was. Right now this all feels like too much hard work. When I get home, my mind whirs into action as I physically force myself to remember where Leo and Katie are and when they will be home, before I allow myself to drop through the escape hatch – deep, unending sleep.

I am woken by the sound of the doorbell – so loud in my dream that I feel myself scrambling to the surface, opening the door to my real life as if gasping for air, remembering The Awful Truth. *Deny, deny, deny.* I stumble down the stairs; I am still fully clothed. Did I forget to pick up the kids? It's possible. Charley usually reminds me.

As I get to the door I see two ominous shapes behind the frosted glass. I remember opening this same door to those two same shapes, a week ago … or was it a month ago?

'Good afternoon, Mr Hastings,' says the taller of the two policemen.

'Hi,' I say, hugging myself. 'Can I help you?'

'Uh, we were wondering if you might have a moment to speak with us.'

The other one chimes in, 'We've had some information come to light about your wife's death.'

'Oh,' I say, feeling every hair on my body rise out if its follicle. 'What kind of information?'

'Could we come inside?' says the shorter officer.

'All right then,' I say, mentally evaluating the current state of my living room. Our domestic worker, Clara, has been and gone so there should be no telltale signs of neglect. 'Wait,' I hesitate, once again feeling like a character in a film. 'Do I need a lawyer?'

# NOW

## Sebastian

*Llandudno*

The cops didn't stay long. It was an awkward conversation, but it pushed me into what I understand to be The Next Stage. The larger one consulted his notes frequently, the smaller one hooked his fingers inside his belt loops and looked around the room – too curious for my liking. I didn't ask them to sit down. I wanted the information standing up.

At that point, I was already in possession of a number of facts. I knew my wife's car had hit an oak tree at speed. The 200-year-old specimen might be cut down by the council: death row. My wife and our still new Porsche Cayenne were a write-off. What caused Charley to hit the tree was the subject of an investigation. There was alcohol in her bloodstream. She shouldn't have been driving; that much was clear. Where she had been going *before* hitting the tree was also a complete mystery, one I did not dare contemplate. She was driving away from us. This is the most significant fact.

The initial theory was that she fell asleep. This progressed to a possible heart attack, or perhaps an aneurysm. She was healthy; she'd mostly stopped smoking since she fell pregnant with Katie, except for the occasional late-night joint – to help her sleep, she said. The autopsy revealed internal bleeding in her beautiful skull. Her death was caused by the impact of the crash.

Suicide was not unheard of in these types of situations, I was told. I know Charley had experienced bouts of depression, especially in the first year after Katie was born, but she was never medicated. She drank red wine and her feelings mellowed. We laughed a lot when she drank. I drank too – always more than her. I was the type who needed to finish the bottle. I would never classify myself as a drunk, but I liked drinking. I figured as long as I wasn't tempted to drink at breakfast, I was still safe. There were starving and depressed people on this African continent of ours. We should not waste the elixir while we had it.

Charley wanted things. She needed a horizon. She had plans. She wanted us all to be our best possible selves. She worked hard. She wasn't a quitter – no, that was my domain. She was a thinker, always thinking, solving, remembering. She was always in charge.

Yesterday the police showed up with their new and, it would seem, final theory. The accident reconstruction specialist said the tyre tracks indicated Charley had undoubtedly swerved to avoid something. A partially decomposed body of a baboon was found near the scene. The larger cop relayed this information in his thick Afrikaans accent.

When he finished I made what I took to be a reasonable statement. 'If the baboon was dead, then what makes you think she swerved to avoid it? Either she killed it, or someone else did.' The smaller one's body language told me he was anxious to leave. His radio gargled and bleeped. He said something incomprehensible into the mouthpiece.

'Also …' I was on a roll now, suddenly remembering a long-forgotten word from high-school biology. 'Aren't baboons … diurnal?'

'We just thought you might want to know,' was the larger one's reply.

I am surprised I *did* want to know. I wanted to know the size of the baboon and which troop it might have come from. I wanted to know every detail. I asked them if they had pictures they could show me. I wanted to know if they knew the age of the baboon. Was it young? Was it male or female? They shifted their feet and said they didn't know. Missing animals weren't part of their jurisdiction. I could call SANParks for that information and they hastily scribbled the number for me on the back of a receipt. The pen didn't work. It took them several attempts, holding the receipt against the wall, the lid sticking childishly out of the larger one's mouth.

It's clear that the case, as far as they are concerned, is now closed. She was entirely responsible for the accident. It was unfortunate, but *these things happen*. It didn't matter where she was going or why – not to them, anyway. It was a dark road, she'd been drinking, there was no one else to blame and nothing more to be done except collect the insurance and move on.

And so, today, I am doing just that. I'm told it will be a while before the insurance finds its way into my bank account, but I must prepare all the same. Dirty money, I think, which I will not know what to do with. If only I could get a refund. 'I'm sorry, I'd prefer my wife back,' I joked with my mother-in-law, who did not laugh. She has offered her services in handling the insurance, the paperwork, the details that I cannot, and will not yet, face.

Despite her penchant for plastic surgery, Deirdre is no fool. She places high value on looking her best at all times. Today she is wearing a black suit and a thin cashmere scarf draped around her neck. I am in jeans and a hoodie that bears the remnants of last night's takeout. She should be lucky I made an effort to get out of my tracksuit pants. She has invited herself and a 'friend' to our home to discuss the best course of action to take with respect to the insurance money – which, I'm told, is significant. Charley was not the breadwinner as such, but she was the one who knew where we kept the bread. Our company was profitable, as far as I knew; we had lots of expenses, camera insurance, staff costs, rentals, our mortgage. Charley was organised and meticulous about these things. She took pride in showing me rainbow-coloured spreadsheets detailing production-line items, the ways in which we could make and save money. I nodded and made noises of approval, not unlike the noises I make when looking at a piece of art my four-year-old son has done. Now I regret not paying more attention. The whole experience is decidedly emasculating – another maths test I'm not prepared for.

'I'd say you have three, maybe four years. But we need to err on the side of caution.'

The man speaking is what I would call burly. He looks more like a farmer than a financial advisor. I press my fingers together in what I hope resembles a listening pose and not a praying one.

My mother-in-law speaks for me. 'Right, well, that is sobering, isn't it, Sebastian?' I feel bile in my throat. Time is a cruel trick.

'The market isn't great at the moment,' adds the farmer. 'I would say pay off the house if it suits you, and perhaps put some into a fund for your children's education. We need to establish what your monthly expenses are so we can decide what you would like to draw for the time being. Of course you will work again, but it's best you use this time to … you know, not worry about your finances.'

It only now dawns on me: aside from a new wife, a new mother to my children, I would also be in the market for a new producer. I balance my chin on top of my fingers, my thumbs pushing against my sternum. The farmer is raising his eyebrows, a nervous smile on his face.

'You've been so kind to us, Derek. Thank you for taking the time.' *She's flirting with him. She's actually flirting with him!* 'Sebastian and I will look at all the options and get back to you with the final go-ahead as soon as we've discussed it with the rest of the family.'

I haven't the energy to fight with anyone about anything. I have no idea what my monthly expenses are. I never did discover the password to her laptop. Everything was frozen once the death certificate was issued. That bloody death certificate. Certified copies of it lay strewn around the house like Wanted posters. The phone company needed one, the bank needed one, the undertaker needed one, even the school needed one. Almost all of our accounts were in her name and now needed to be changed to mine. What I would do with those accounts was a problem to be solved another day.

'Glass of wine?' says my mother-in-law once her associate has left. Deirdre runs a boutique and fancies herself as a self-made woman. 'Maxwell left me nothing,' she once told me, as if this was the start to a longer story. Maxwell Hanekom, Charley's dad, was only thirty-eight when he went up Lion's Head and never came back – one year younger than Charley, I note. The phrase *family history of suicide* tiptoes across my mind like an unwanted black cat.

Deirdre tells me she relied on family handouts for years until she started her own business with an ex-boyfriend, a man I'm convinced she was seeing while she and her late husband were still mourning the death of their young son, but who is, as far as I know, no longer in the picture.

'Darling, I know it's hard,' she is saying now, squeezing my biceps with manicured red nails. 'We all lost her.' Her eyes liquify. She is adamant the tears stay obediently inside the pink frame of her eyelids. She's a woman who has known heartache. She's experienced at death. Experience (and Botox) has hardened her. I'm a novice. She pours me a glass of red wine and delicately sniffs back her emotion. After only a few sips of wine I feel the familiar weightlessness take hold. *Perhaps I will decide to become a drunk?* I think to myself, not for the first time.

'Now,' says Deidre, or Dee, as she insists people call her, and which I won't. 'What's the latest on the investigation? Tell me everything.'

I sigh. I am bored of discussing the facts with friends and family who are hungry for information – like guests at a party snatching hors d'oeuvres from a plate: *I really shouldn't,* they say before devouring another new fact. The most pressing question continues to be, 'So, Sebastian, where was Charley actually going that late at night?' It's as if everyone else knows the answer, but no one wants to tell me – for fear of hurting my feelings. As if anything could be worse than what I feel right now.

'I'm not buying the baboon theory,' I tell Deidre, the wine loosening my muscles, giving my mind an excuse to wander laterally. 'It had to be a car coming in the other direction she swerved to avoid.' There were no cameras to prove my theory, other than the one on Constantia Nek circle, but I had a strong feeling this was true. Someone, not a baboon, had caused my wife's death. Someone had taken her from me, from my mother-in-law, from our children. Now, all I needed to do was find them. Finally … here comes *Anger*, my old friend and confidant.

The wine fuels my rage, Grand Marnier on a flambé Crêpe Suzette. It's almost enjoyable, this feeling. My mother-in-law shifts in her seat, offers platitudes about moving on as best we can, for the sake of the children. It's not that she doesn't entertain the possibility that my theory is true, but she isn't ready to go down the slippery slope of blame. She's still fixing and doing and organising and drawing straight lines around everything – which is what Charley herself might be doing were she in this predicament.

But, true to my own personality, I am colouring outside the lines, pushing aside the spreadsheet and the predictions and looking for something more. I am sniffing the air for clues. As I finally close the door behind Deirdre and pour myself another glass, I decide I will now apply all of my energy to finding my wife's killer and making sure justice prevails. I will do this for me. I will do this for her. I will do this regardless.

'Daddy?' The sound of Katie's voice as she looks up from her tablet jolts me. I have actual children I am meant to look after. I must now be mother *and* father and I am qualified for neither. I throw back the glass of wine and shove another frozen pizza in the oven – which, I am almost certain, I will burn.

# NOW

## Adam

### *Gardens*

'He's hired a private detective.' Nick isn't looking at me when he says this. His eyeline shifts around the coffee shop, as if he suspects someone could be listening in. We are surrounded by pairs of housewives shrink-wrapped in exercise gear, congregating after the school run. One always talks and gesticulates, the other nods sagely over (I'm guessing here) an almond-milk cappuccino. Nick has already finished his black coffee. I sink my teeth into a croissant and feel momentarily comforted.

'That's ... weird,' I say.

Nick is revisiting Franky's implausible theory my accident on Constantia Nek road could be connected to Charley's. Same night. Same stretch of road. What are the chances? We were on opposite sides, almost four kilometres apart. Who would seriously draw the conclusion she swerved to avoid me at some point? Maybe, I swerved to avoid *her.* I mean – while we're going there.

'Adam, we're going to have to get a lawyer. I hate to say it, but I think Franky's right. This could get messy. I'm only looking out for you here, bud. You need to take this seriously.'

'I am taking this seriously!' I say. But, truth be told, I am not. There must have been hundreds of cars on the road that night. In what possible universe could I have had something to do with Charley's accident? From what I can gather, the accidents were in different suburbs, for Christ's sake. Charley was heading from Llandudno in the direction of Constantia. I was coming from town, through Constantia, towards Hout Bay – although granted it's all still pretty sketchy.

'You're going to need to remember.' Nick looks at me squarely now. He's chastising me. I am the younger friend, the sidekick, the fat bastard. He's the leader and he is telling rather than asking me to comply. I am annoyed with this line of questioning and consider if there's time for another croissant.

'I told you ...,' I say, reminding myself as I remind him, 'I stopped drinking at that club we went to. I felt like I was sober. I got in my car, and then I woke up at your place. I know it sounds crazy, but that's what happened. Are we going to have this conversation forever?'

'You still don't remember getting out of the car? You don't remember Franky's mom's house, lying in the driveway, washing your hands, commenting on the soap?'

'The soap? Seriously, what the fuck, man? Where are you going with this?'

'I just feel like you're ... I don't know, faking it.'

'Faking it!? Nick, what happened to you being on my side?'

'I am on your side. That's the fucking point. Things ... could get weird.'

This is already weird, I think. Nick was the one who told me not to worry, not to panic, not to blow things out of proportion the way he knew I was capable of. It's a trait Franky and I share – and one that makes us ever more indebted to Nick and his level-headedness. When Nick panics, like he appears to be doing now, I find myself sliding into malaise. Fight, flight, freeze – and let's not forget playing dead. That is how I feel now, inexplicably tired. I am a sloth. Nick is jittery, like a bird pecking at crumbs. He must be testing me. That's the only reasonable explanation – or something has spooked him. He fiddles with the salt and pepper cellars on the table before he speaks.

'You were out of it, fair enough, but we spoke. You were in a good vibe. I've been out of it before, but I've never had a proper blackout. That kind of shit only happens in movies. In real life you always remember something.'

I squeeze my brain to consider this. Am I making this up? Do I remember any more than I think I remember? I have tried and failed to search the storage cupboard of my mind for answers; every time I come up completely blank. I feel as if I'm reaching for something on a high shelf before realising there's nothing on that shelf. My efforts are wasted. I am Winnie-the-Pooh looking for honey that isn't there. The more I look, the more *not there* the honey is. I summon the waiter and order another croissant, with honey.

Nick leans forward, his steady tone concealing the slightest hiss of annoyance. 'Sebastian told Franky the investigator has found a way to gain access to the camera on Constantia Nek circle. There's a chance he might look into other reported accidents on the road that night, start digging things up. When it was only the normal cops involved I was sure we'd be fine ... but these guys ... these guys ... get *paid* to solve things.'

A sudden image of my car flips into view in my mind – upside down in tangled vegetation on the side of the road, early-morning dew still on the grass. Nick showed the tow-truck where to pull over, handling all the details, while I looked on in abject horror. I had absolutely no clue how my car had found itself in that position. I have never been *that* drunk before.

'So you swerved to avoid something?' the overweight policeman asked me, his pencil poised for my statement. I noticed the spelling mistakes he was making, *swurved* being one of them, my surname another. *Berelowitz* isn't an easy one, I'll give him that.

'Yes,' I said, remembering what Nick had told me to say in the car. 'It was an animal, I think; I saw its eyes reflected in my headlights and then I don't remember what happened next.'

The truth is I don't remember any of it. Not an animal, not the flipping over, not one single thing involving my car or my journey home. But the rest of my evening, the bit that happened *before* I climbed into my car – that is fresh and clear in my mind. That's the part I told, and continue to tell, Nick – in detail, as if the more explicit I am on the prologue, the less he will need on the *inciting incident.*

I remember that afternoon, gathering myself in the privacy of my Audi (silver, black leather interior, souped-up sound system, in case you're interested). Maria was angry with me again, for the usual reasons.

'You make my skin crawl!' was the last thing she said before I slammed the door. I savoured the cold wind on my skin after the heat of our argument. She doesn't find me attractive any more, she said. She has a new psychologist friend, a grandmother from playgroup. This woman espouses the idea of complete honesty at all times, in order to rid relationships of any and all lies and deceit. She calls it a 'communication sandwich'. First you are meant to give the person you wish to be honest with a compliment. Then you tell them some unpalatable truth, followed by another compliment. Maria is from Spain and it's clear she misunderstood the sandwich metaphor and has made her own tapas of truths which she flings at me when I am not performing in a way she sees as husbandly.

Arguing with Maria has always been complicated, especially when she rants in Spanish, which I choose not to understand. In the old days, our arguments always ended with sex, her smooth, honey-coloured legs intertwining with my sallow hairier ones.

Those days are clearly behind us now. She refuses to sleep with me, choosing instead to sleep in a bed with one of our children. She's spoilt for choice as there are three of them. She no longer makes excuses; she tells it like it is. I am hurt, and I have no idea how to dress up my hurt and in which part of my body to store it in.

That afternoon, before I went to golf, I remember scratching my inner elbow, small spots of eczema erupting beneath my fingernails. I drew blood. She said she didn't want to go to the anniversary dinner. She was feeling unwell and couldn't face people or talking. I said I wanted her to be with me; she could meet us at the restaurant. I walked over to her and gently put my fingers on her shoulders, massaging her back. She shook me off.

I said, 'What?'

She said, 'Don't talk to me like that!'

I said, 'I'm trying to make you feel better.'

'You want to get drunk with your friends. You don't need me there for that.'

'Fuck you,' I said under my breath, not looking her in the eye.

'Oh really?' she said, in the voice she uses to mock the English language for its inability to express real emotion.

'Is it so bad to want to have some fun sometimes? To want to go out and be with my wife, to laugh, to have a drink, to … to … be happy?'

'Oh, please! You're not happy, you're depressed!' The Ss came out like there were six of them in the word. I was silent. Our arguments are the same subject on repeat, hardly any details change; even the setting is familiar.

'I don't want to talk about it any more,' I said.

'That's convenient for you. Selfish!'

'I'm selfish?' I said, throwing out half a laugh, a bark. 'It's selfish for a husband to want to have fun with his wife?!'

'You make my skin crawl!' she said and stormed into the other room.

As I banged the front door behind me, golf clubs rattling, I heard our youngest, Diego, start to cry. I smiled secretly to myself, knowing that cry was not for me. I was not programmed to answer that call. That was her problem to deal with. I love my children, and I love my wife, but that afternoon I wanted freedom from the weight of all that love.

The drive from our house in Hout Bay to the golf course in Westlake was three tracks long: 'Boys Don't Cry', 'A Forest', 'Let's Go to Bed'. Thank God for The Cure's *Greatest Hits.* We made up a four-ball with some guys from the office. Nick had the best score. I hit a ninety. I was pretty impressed with myself. All in all, I felt good. I felt like I deserved a celebration.

After the game Nick and I rushed to get to the restaurant. We showered at the club, then drove in convoy to town. As we parked I saw Maria pulling up in her vw. My heart felt like it might burst from my chest. Maybe she did still love me, after all.

But from the moment we sat down, it was clear she hadn't forgiven me for whatever sin I'd committed this time. Either way, I was determined to prove her wrong. I would have one beer. Maybe two.

When Charley suggested dancing afterwards, I hesitated. What was a club without a drink? But if Maria was with me, I would make a point of showing her just how resistant I could be. I held her hand on the way in. She wriggled free and said she had to go home to relieve the babysitter. I almost left with her, changed my mind when I saw her marching towards her car. She was still angry and I hadn't the energy for more arguments.

Susie Winchester was a surprise. I've never seen her outside the office. I'd been dancing with Franky and Charley when I saw her standing at the bar. When she clocked me, she leaned in for an awkward double kiss. She's at least half my age. She's good at answering phones and bringing people water and coffee and saying things like, 'Make yourself comfortable; Mr Berelowitz will be with you shortly.' Which always makes me feel more important than I am.

'This is Shane,' she sang, introducing me to a man who leant purposefully against the bar. I could only deduce that he was a boyfriend, although he could have been a relative. He's not the kind of guy I expected her to be with. He was short, wide-shouldered, a little overweight – like me – but unlike me, he hadn't adjusted his wardrobe to his new reality. He wore a too-tight leather jacket. I imagined Susie Winchester, with her blunt fringe and trendy wardrobe, to prefer the more tattooed variety, like Sebastian – lean, mysterious, perhaps even bearded. This guy was clean-shaven, late thirties.

'Hey, Shane,' I said, offering my hand.

'What did you say your name was?' he said, shouting louder than necessary above the music and the rumble of the crowd. I suspect he was not charmed to be meeting any man his new girlfriend shared an office with.

'I'm Adam,' I said. 'I work with Susie.'

'I know,' he said flatly. 'Can I get you a drink?'

I hesitated. 'I'm having a gin and tonic,' quipped Susie.

'I'll have the same,' I said, before saying, 'Actually, you know what, I'm just going to get a Coke.'

Shane stuck his head back in the scrum of the bar. Susie leaned in, and in a whispered tone she said, 'Shane's a lawyer. We met on Tinder. This is our second date. He's totally into me. I haven't made my mind up yet. What do you think?'

'Wow,' I said, 'he's … it's, yeah.'

Shane extracted himself from the bar, holding our drinks above his head.

'Shane's driving tonight,' she giggled, 'in case you're wondering! This is my third.'

'What kind of law do you practise?' I asked, becoming 'interested' the way Nick always suggested I should be – a Dale Carnegie trick I had yet to master.

'Criminal,' he shouted.

I wracked my brain for something funny to say but came up short. We stood in awkward silence. The crowd noises rose and fell around us.

'Adam's working on an app to help people buy medication,' said Susie.

'Sounds dubious,' said Shane, cracking a half-smile.

I sipped my Coke, forcing myself not to gulp it down. I am always thirsty these days, and I always need to pee. After another three excruciating minutes (enough time to have earned the price of the drink, right?) I managed to extract myself from the non-conversation I had tangled myself in before finding myself safely back on the dance floor with Franky. Charley and Seb offered me a ride in their Uber. I think they knew, as well as I did, I wouldn't accept.

The men's bathroom was decorated with black-and-white pictures of jazz legends from Fifties Sophiatown. I checked my phone: 10:40. It was late enough; I should go. My Coke was now officially gone, ice crunched between my back teeth. Maybe one more beer for the road – my desire to drink now slightly more powerful than my desire to prove my wife wrong.

As I emerged from my trip to the men's room, I saw Susie stumbling towards the entrance with Shane in tow. He held her arm, keeping her upright as she walked precariously in red-soled black heels. She had a black leather bag in one hand, a half-drunk globe of gin and tonic in the other. 'Bye, boys!' she shouted to no one in particular.

I raised my hand in her direction and, as though confusing me for a passing waiter, she handed me her drink, pursing her lips in a stylised air kiss, lipstick long gone. A sprig of rosemary, a peel of orange and a stick of cinnamon floated on the surface of the drink like debris in a river. I shook my head and downed the dregs of her glass.

Then I found a waiter who was brandishing a plate of what looked like asparagus wrapped in bacon. I wrestled the tray out of his hands and ate the lot before retrieving my keys and walking towards my car. I can remember the relief of the interior, the shutting out of sound and air, and then the slow, careful and familiar drive home, 'The Walk', 'The Love Cats' and then, somehow, there is nothing. I woke up on Nick's purple sofa with Nick telling me we needed to go to the police station.

At first Nick found my bafflement funny, thought I was putting it on. His irritation has increased with each week that passes. He told me the plan and I went along with it, called Maria and explained I was sorry, even though I wasn't and still had no idea what everyone was getting so hyped about. It all seemed like a good story to tell at some future social engagement, until later than morning, when Nick took the call from Franky and we found out about Charley.

Charley, Franky's beautiful, funny best friend – a woman I have fantasised about on more than one occasion – dead. Impossibly dead. And now, this strange suggestion that somehow my actions may have caused her death. It's not possible; I would have remembered something. The only logical explanation is that I fell asleep and swerved off the road, down the incline – or she fell asleep and I swerved to avoid her. I remind myself Charley's accident was in Constantia, mine was in Hout Bay; she was on the other side of the road, heading in the opposite direction. Where was she going? That's the big question everyone wants answers to. Unlike Charley, I was quite clearly on my way home.

At least Maria believes me. This small vote of confidence has cleared my eczema and put a spring in my step. I expected only anger. When Nick dropped me in front of the house, he hovered and I shooed him away. I didn't need Nick to solve all my problems. The hug she gave me was the closest to intimacy we've experienced since our youngest was born. It took my breath away.

'I do love you,' she said then, like she'd just decided this, ten years in. 'I want us to work harder.'

'Maria,' I said, terrified of breaking the delicate and rare atmosphere between us, 'last night, Charley … she had an accident too – on the same road … I …'

As the details of what I knew spilled out of me, I let slip that there was a suggestion the two accidents might be linked. Nick had told me to avoid all references to this, but my wife had opened a door to me for the first time in months, and I couldn't help but walk through it.

Her face became a mask during our conversation, but she held onto my hand, rubbing it with her thumb – a gesture usually reserved only for our children or her sculptures.

'We'll get through this,' she promised, tears in her eyes. 'I'm quite sure none of this had anything to do with you.' The relief of her trust, the sensation of her touch, her motherly confidence in me: something broke and I found myself in rare floods of tears. Boys *do* cry, as it happens. She hugged me for a long time, rocked me in her arms like I was her fourth child.

'I love you. I love you,' I said into her shoulder, my voice muffled and hoarse.

Of course I didn't tell Nick any of this, only that she had forgiven me, understood why I needed to let off steam. Three kids was hard. Money was tight. I was not who I thought I would be at forty-one.

'Do you remember telling us that you met a lawyer?'

'Yes! Well, I don't remember telling you, only that I met one,' I say to Nick, happy I can finally concur with at least one thing he is saying.

'Well, you need to call him. Seriously, I'll go with you when you meet him – we need to make sure you're covered if the investigator makes any kind of connection between your accident and Charley's. They were on the same road, around the same time, four kilometres apart, but still.' He demonstrates these last points by shifting the salt and pepper cellars around in an approximation of my car and Charley's. 'They might say your accident proves you were on the road at the same time and she could have swerved to avoid you.'

'Or I swerved to avoid her,' I say meeting his eyes. He holds my stare but doesn't respond.

'There is no connection, Nick. There is no connection,' I say this with certainty, wiping the croissant crumbs aggressively from my shirt. But the way Nick looks at me when I glance up makes me doubt myself all over again.

# NOW

## Adam

*Gardens*

When I find her in the office kitchen, Susie Winchester is pouring an unbelievable amount of xylitol into a chipped coffee mug that proudly displays the company logo – *SoftW.co.za*

'How about I buy you a proper coffee,' I say, giving her what I hope is a platonic wink. She furrows her brow. Her eyes fall to my wedding ring, which once wobbled on my finger but now sits tight as a gastric band.

I laugh nervously. 'I wanted to ask you about your boyfriend.' I realise I'm making even more of a hash of things. 'How's it going between you two?'

'Berelowitz, I don't have a boyfriend,' she says, still looking at me quizzically, sipping her coffee, her eyebrows raised above the line of her fringe.

'What happened to Shane?'

She wrinkles her nose, shakes her head, inhales. 'Didn't you see my post?'

Susie Winchester is the girl who believes firmly in the power of social media. Her relationship with the digital documentation of her life has taken on religious significance. She believes every person in this office, given the nature of our work, should share her particular obsession. She's also under the illusion that because we follow each other, I must see every single one of her posts.

'I rarely check my Insta,' I say, hearing how old I sound. Do people say *Insta*, or is it *The Gram*?

'I think maybe you will need to buy me that coffee after all,' she says, pouring the brown sludge in her cup down the drain. Claire from Accounts agrees to cover for her while Susie and I make a dash in the rain for the same coffee shop where only this morning Nick told me I needed to find a lawyer.

As we slide into one of the red leather booths, Susie says conversationally, 'He raped me.'

'What?!' I cough, checking to see that no one else is tuning in to our conversation.

'Well, I'm almost sure he did,' she clarifies, pursing her lips. It's this gesture that makes me notice for the first time the unnatural curve of her lips, a slight swelling, like she's been stung by a bee. I remind myself to breathe.

'I posted about it the night after it happened.' She searches my eyes, checking for signs I knew this already, signs I am playing dumb.

'I … I … Oh God, Susie, that's horrific.'

She raises her eyes to the ceiling. Tears gather on the lower rims of her eyelids, only falling when she closes her eyes. 'He has made his account private, and the police are dragging their heels; not enough evidence etcetera.'

Her sentences run into one another with no audible breaks, no pause for breath, and, aside from the tears, there is almost zero emotion. I am stunned by her revelation, and also blindsided by its possible implications. *My God*, I think, but I say, 'So, you … have a lawyer?'

'Yes,' she says. 'She found me, actually, after the post. Prudence Ngoma. She's so good. She's going to nail him. I know she is.' Her neck has turned red and blotchy like it's been painted with a sponge. She lifts her hand to her throat as if to disguise her reaction or help the words escape. I'm afraid to ask any further details, but she offers them up without prompting. She speaks to the table, her head bowed her eyes fixed, talking to herself. 'I don't remember anything. All I remember is him picking me up, taking me to Vintage Rose and …' She looks directly at me, eyes wide. 'Oh! I saw you, hey? Then it's kind of blurry.' She returns her gaze to the table. 'I think I must have been smashed. Prudence recons he spiked my drink. She says it's super common, and him being a lawyer and everything, he would know all about it. There's a chance he only took me back to my place. That's what his lawyers will say. No conclusive evidence I was raped, 'cause, like, he probably used a condom, and so, yeah, but Prudence is on it, says she just needs to determine how he scored the drugs – link him to it, because that's a crime on its own – but he may have had a friend, a doctor or a dentist.'

Dentist. As she says this, I think of my late father and my eyes involuntarily water. I feel words forming in my mouth but they seem to come out in the wrong order.

'Susie, I'm so fucking sorry this happened to you.'

She grabs my wrist, seeing the emotion in my eyes. More tears spill from hers and she bites her lip. I shake my head, hoping to put a full stop on her retelling of the story. I'm suddenly unsure of what to do with my hands – I feel as if I should hug her, pat her back at least, but could this be misconstrued? I'm clearly in enough trouble as it is. Her grip is fierce on my sleeve.

'Listen, Susie, do you think you might be able to give me your lawyer's details?'

She looks at me the same way she looked at me in the kitchen, suddenly distrustful. Her hand returns to her lap. I suppose I can't blame the woman for feeling uncomfortable around men. I feel completely out of my depth with this conversation. I am appalled by everything she has said and have no clear way to express it.

'Sure,' she says, not ready to switch focus from her unpacking of events. 'I'll tag you. So, like, anyway, Prudence says we have a strong case. She said I'm, like, helping other people too 'cause with people like him, it's never just the once …'

I nod sagely while she flaps her hands, pausing only to sip my cappuccino.

# NOW

## Adam

*Cape Town* CBD

Prudence Ngoma is Amazonian. She stalks across the office towards us, head slightly bowed as though avoiding the ceiling. She has sharp feline features and a long ponytail that twists against her dark green suit like a tail. When my wife was a model, I knew many specimens like her. Tall and intimidating. These attributes combined with her subtly unisex perfume are overpowering and, quite frankly, scary.

Nick sticks out his hand and introduces himself first, then gestures to me. I become aware of her firm grip, my clammy and too pale and hairy hand in her dark manicured one, and feel smaller, fatter and clumsier than I normally do.

'Gentleman, right this way.'

Once ensconced in her corner office, Prudence listens patiently as Nick relays the story. Her eyes narrow every now and then, hands clasped in front of her on the glass desk. And then she repeats the story back to us in lawyer-speak.

'So, Adam, as I understand it, you were involved in a single-vehicle accident on Constantia Nek road, which you assume was the result of you unknowingly imbibing a substance intended for one of your colleagues. You have no knowledge of the incident and its implications. You have since come to understand further circumstances, including the tragic death of a woman you were acquainted with, which took place on the same stretch of road, and you are now concerned your actions, while under the influence of this substance that you did not knowingly imbibe, may have contributed to her death and you are looking to defend yourself from such criminal accusation should the need arise.'

'Exactly,' I say, using my voice for the first time since we sat down.

'Right,' she says, unclasping her hands.

'First, let me be clear: my services are R3500 per hour and this rate is charged for in-person communication and for phone or Zoom calls. Anything over half an hour is charged at the same rate; under half an hour will be negotiated. Do you wish to proceed under these terms?'

'Yes,' says Nick, taking the lead. We have already discussed his desire to help foot the bill. He felt he might be complicit. He had something to lose; not as much as I did, let it be noted.

Nick would defend me, at any cost. He's proved this time and time again throughout our twenty-three-year friendship. He taught me how to drive, gave me tips on how to impress women, guided me when it came to part-time jobs, what to study. I grew up with only a sister. Nick was a big brother, even though he was only six months older than me. Nick was practical, he was dependable, he was handsome in the most classical sense and people generally found this reassuring. No harm would befall you when Nick was in the room.

There has been only one time in the tapestry of our friendship when I have come to his aid. I was the hero, the one on the white horse, and I reminded him of it shortly after I told him about Susie Winchester's revelation.

Nick is nodding at Prudence. She is speaking a language I cannot understand. Lots of *henceforth* and *notwithstanding* and Latin phrases I've heard before but which hold no meaning.

'There's no evidence,' she says now. 'As far as I can see, there is not a shred of evidence linking your accident to the potential crime you speak of. They need to prove you were involved, beyond a reasonable doubt. At this point we don't need to prove you weren't.'

While I understand her logic, I am suddenly nervous, out of my depth. I feel as if I am opening a door to a world of courtrooms and subpoenas and other hard-to-spell words I've only ever heard mentioned in films.

'That said …'

I don't like her tone.

'… as I am already working on a case against the man who may have ultimately been responsible for this accident, there may be a claim to be made there.'

'Oh, no!' I say, too loudly, not wanting to involve myself in the awfulness of Susie and Shane's situation. Prudence's fingers tap the straps of her gold watch.

'All the same, fill this in.' She slides a document across the table. 'I'll need access to your phone records, both of you, and the case number you obtained when you took the police to the scene. Also copies of your ID documents, the car registration … Adam, how sure are you that someone can corroborate that Shane Fergan bought you a drink, or that you drank from Susie's half-full glass?'

'I … I'm sure someone … must have seen us; Franky maybe?' I look at Nick. His eyes reveal nothing.

'Good. Well, you give it a think and if anything sticks, you'll need to make contact with that person and provide me with their details. Gentleman, it's been a pleasure.'

In the glass lift Nick gives me a paternal pat – ironic considering I'm the only father between us. 'It'll be fine. We're going to deal with this. One step at a time.' As the doors open, releasing us onto the ground floor, I find myself unexpectedly praying he's right.

# TWENTY YEARS AGO

## Adam

*Kenilworth*

Nick's blue Beetle struggles up the curb.

'This can't be it,' I say, leaning forward to get a better view of the squat suburban house through Nick's corroded window frame.

'It is. Dr Barrow's cool. You'll see.'

Something doesn't feel right. I stifle a yawn. Anxiety makes me tired. If anyone should be anxious right now, it's Nick. Nick presses the doorbell. It plays a tune. The security gate pops open with an electronic clank. The man I take to be Dr Barrow appears from a doorway behind a reception desk. The desk is unmanned but for a purring ginger cat. Dr Barrow is tall, mid-seventies, half-moon glasses balanced on the end of a nose that's a different colour to the rest of his face. He clutches a pink card.

'Ah, Mr Williams! Welcome back.'

Nick steps forward, shakes the dentist's hand. The reception clearly doubles as this man's lounge. I turn to the battered couch, ready to open a page of one of the curled magazines on the coffee table, when Dr Barrow says, 'Please, won't you join us?'

He ushers us into a small room, cordial, as if he's about to seat us at a restaurant.

'I'm Adam,' I say with what I hope is an equally friendly smile. My hands are behind my back for fear of contaminating the room.

'Aren't you … a Berelowitz?'

I'm momentarily thrown. 'Yes, I …'

'How *is* your father?' he says, directing Nick into the reclining chair.

'Uh, I'm afraid he … passed away.'

'Oh, I am sorry,' he says, 'Such a great orthodontist – extremely well respected. And you? Didn't you ever think about following in his footsteps?' He slips on a fresh pair of latex gloves and pokes around inside Nick's now open mouth.

'No, I'm … a waiter,' I say. Nick's chair reclines further. He shoots me what could be an open-mouthed attempt at a smile. His face is bathed in a greenish florescent glow.

'Hospitality! Now there's a career! I had a niece in hospitality, ended up in Bahrain. Great salaries over there, you know …'

I nod as Dr Barrow continues to extol the virtues of working in the Middle East. Almost absent-mindedly, he places a plastic mask over Nick's face.

'… I've always been of the belief that you should let your children go overseas for opportunities; don't let them sit around because you want the company or you're waiting for grandchildren …' He pauses, interrupting his own ramble. He looks directly at me over his glasses and speaks in a low tone. 'Now, Adam. He's going to look like Nick, he may even sound like Nick, but let me assure you – *Nick* has left the building …' He smiles and winks, a magician about to saw his assistant in half.

Nick looks me straight in the eye, and for the first time ever I see genuine fear. I squeeze his forearm in response. The gesture makes me feel as though I am channelling my father.

The dentist lifts a large metal clamp and pulls at Nick's wisdom teeth as though extracting a particularly overgrown weed in the garden. The sight of blood confirms this is not something I am imagining. Nick howls in agony – a low, guttural sound, animal-like. He arches his back and fights to sit up. Dr Barrow calmly but firmly holds his torso against the chair.

'Is this normal?' I say, trying to keep the shock out of my voice.

'Yes, perfectly normal. It looks worse than it is. Trust me.' And then he says, 'Help me hold him down, won't you. I assure you he won't remember a *thing*.'

After five excruciating minutes, it's all over. The teeth, impossibly large and pre-historic, are dropped unceremoniously into a metal kidney dish. Dr Barrow removes his gloves and Nick mumbles incoherently.

'Can we see the cat again?' he says, spittle and blood escaping from the side of his mouth. The dentist ushers us into a small, sun-filled room off the surgery. The room overlooks a bean-shaped swimming pool lined with slasto. Nick collapses into a beige easy chair. The ginger cat is purring in a patch of sun. I sit awkwardly on the chair's arm. Nick yawns with abandon and leans back to trigger the chair's recline mechanism.

'Here, kitty, kitty,' he says, clicking his fingers and making kissing sounds before turning to me. 'It wasn't that bad, hey?' he says dreamily. 'Really quick.' I do not contradict him.

On the way home, while I negotiate the unfamiliar gears of his car, I ask Nick if he wants anything from the grocery store.

'Strawberry milk.' They are the only words he says on the journey home. I pull into our parking space outside our flat, sneak a look in his direction. His head is leaning against the window. He stares at nothing, mouth ajar. He seems unable to remember how to undo his seatbelt. After a bit of fiddling I manage to get it untangled. He laughs uncontrollably, leaning into me, as I steer him towards our front door.

'I'm so tired,' he says. 'But it wasn't that bad … It really wasn't, hey?' Again, I am tempted to contradict him, but sense now is not the time.

Once in his bedroom, I pull off his sneakers and arrange the dark blue covers around his shape, tucking him in. I leave the plastic bottle of luminous strawberry milk on the bedside table with a single, paper-wrapped straw. I look at his already sleeping face, loose lips, head heavy on the pillow. I give him one final pat and leave the room.

Later that evening, he is groggy as he emerges into our shared living room.

'What's with the strawberry milk?' he says, rubbing sleep out of his eye.

'It's what you asked for,' I say. 'Remember?'

'What?!' he laughs. 'How long have you known me for?' He gives me a playful flick on the back of my head with his fingers. 'I hate strawberry-flavoured anything!'

'It's what you asked for,' I protest with a nervous laugh.

'Gross,' he says, throwing the full bottle in the kitchen bin. He yawns into his next sentence. 'Wow, that was so weird!'

'It was,' I agree, not entirely sure if I want to get into it.

He is searching in the fridge, the light unnatural in the room. 'Still, way less scary than I thought it would be. Piece of cake,' he says. 'Didn't feel a thing.'

'Mm,' I say, keeping my eyes on the TV.

# NOW

## Adam

*Hout Bay*

'You killed no one,' says Maria, head shaking. 'Not you ... you're the nice guy ... the funny guy.' As if these qualities could protect me at a time like this.

I could never have imagined Maria being on my side in such circumstances. This was her opportunity to dig the knife in, to call me out for the drunk I almost was – but so far she has stood by my side, unflappable. I so appreciate her dogged irrationality right now.

'You should see my friend Wendy, Luca's grandmother, from playgroup? You should see her ...' she says, laying a fragrant omelette in front of me. This is not the first time she's made this suggestion, or an omelette such as this to accompany it.

'Oh my God, Maria, please tell me you didn't mention any of this to her!' I say, my appetite wavering.

'Of course not!' she says, wiping her hands on her apron. She sighs and raises her arm to massage the hardened flesh between her shoulder and her neck. I want to touch her, to rub away her tension, but I know she will pull away from me if I try. 'You need to see someone. You need to get happy again. And maybe ... this is the time to do it – while you feel so much ... emotion.' She rolls her shoulders, cricks her neck.

I can feel the potential for this to slide into an argument, so I make conscious efforts to lower my tone. 'I think ... Nick said, we do need to be careful who we tell ... We need to ride it out, but also be prepared for a fight – if it comes to it.'

'*Psycho-logists* aren't allowed to talk to the police, unless someone is in danger, and no one is in danger – this is done. We must all get beyond.'

I am in awe of Maria's dispassionate attitude. Perhaps this is the way everyone should be in the face of death. We all have to die; the only mystery is how. Grandmotherly Wendy seems the perfect tonic. But suddenly I'm afraid of myself – afraid I can't be trusted not to say too much; plus she probably costs a fortune.

At night, my mind is fertile. During the day people comment that I am *chilled, easy-going, zen* even, but they don't know the real me, the me that comes out at three in the morning when I can't sleep and have only the swirling fireworks on the backs of my eyelids for company.

I killed someone. I might have killed someone. I actually might have killed her. I knew her. She was a person, with kids, and I killed her. And like Nick demanding the strawberry milk he didn't even want or like, I may have done these things, no matter how strange and illogical they might seem. These ideas took a while to surface; they were kept at bay by my own disbelief – if I couldn't remember it, then it couldn't possibly have happened. If a tree falls and all that. But slowly, as more details are sprinkled over the ideas, crystallising them into some immovable form of truth, the panic has found me and my pulse beats a steady rhythm to it. Yes, there may have been more in Susie Winchester's glass than gin and tonic, but that doesn't take away from the fact that my car and I could in fact have been the murder weapon. Mr Berelowitz, on Constantia Nek Road, with the silver Audi. Even if I am never discovered, I will have to live with this … *idea* I cannot un-know. I killed someone. I *might* have killed someone. It *is* possible. God, imagine if Sebastian caught wind of any of this: I would be a dead man.

I don't remember the first time I met him – it must have been early on in Nick and Franky's relationship – a birthday party, New Year's, or maybe it was one of those awkward dinners where new lovers introduce each other to their circles, secretly evaluating each other through the friends they chose and the family they couldn't.

Sebastian was smooth, in every sense of the word. He was childlike, creative. Tangled shoulder-length hair, a fresh tattoo every few months to bore us with. *The beehive represents the place in the body where we store our spirituality,* he once said, stroking the hexagons on his forearm. *So, not just good luck, then?* I'd countered. He'd laughed and slapped my shoulder. To him I was nothing more than an audience member, part of a focus group. *What does Average Adam think of my commercial, my tattoos, my wife?*

He was a former actor, he had money, and this last fact was the thing that made me most uneasy. I was fascinated by him: he looked almost homeless sometimes, channelling Johnny Depp, all the old shirts and leather bangles. Yet I knew he lived in that glass house in Llandudno, the venue for his fortieth which we'd all dutifully attended, like extras in one of his commercials. He was a classic rebel but he had an almost feminine air to him. I remember him glazing over when Nick and I spoke about the rugby or the cricket. He had a hyper, distracted energy to him. Nick told me he'd had a drug problem but had quit when he met Charley. I'm not so sure. Charley was gorgeous – the kind of woman you would change yourself for. She wasn't as beautiful as my wife, of course, but more attractive than Franky. Franky was cute, Charley was hot.

And now she was dead.

What would prison feel like? Would I go to prison, or would Shane? Would we appeal? Would it be manslaughter? An image of a side of beef hung up to mature slides across my conveyor belt of thoughts. I am alone in bed – Maria has been called by one of our children in the small hours, and is most likely asleep in one of their beds. Pink sky filters through the blinds in our bedroom. *Yes*, I think, as I start to fall asleep. *Maybe I will call Wendy after all.*

# NOW

## Adam

*Hout Bay*

I miss my father. The feeling of missing him is physical, hollow, a hunger. My insides fold into themselves. I can see him now, scratching his inner elbow, his brow furrowed. 'Bide your time, son,' he used to say. 'You've everything going for you. Do what makes you happy; the rest will follow.'

He'd been sick for only a year. I had tried to hold onto a clear happy memory of him as I watched him being lowered into the ground. People threw soil on the surface of the pine coffin in noisy clumps, the uneven *thump, thump* of it an assault on my senses. Dull faces turned towards me like dead sunflowers, gestured for me to lift the spade, make my own contribution to the Jewish burial act. I couldn't perform the rituals that added yet more finality. I didn't want to light candles or say prayers or sit shiva or whatever we were expected to do. I was seventeen. I ate the canapés my aunt had prepared. I drank the Kiddush wine like a shot during the prayers and then I smoked myself into oblivion. My mother was not impressed. I didn't give a shit.

That year of high school was a write-off. I had absolutely no idea what I wanted to do, except maybe be a musician, which was stupid. Even I knew that. As I stumbled through my life, biding my time in one job and then the next, I found myself asking, 'Is this what you meant, Dad?' But he never answered me. There were no signs.

When my children were born I looked for his face in theirs, but I saw only my mother and Maria – the women whose expectations I always seemed to fall short of. Nobody quite believed in me the way my father had done, although Nick came pretty close.

I was never a massive hit with the girls – that was Nick's area. Any action I managed was always purely because the girl in question was hoping to leapfrog over me to him. My first girlfriend was Molly. She had red hair, straight and thin, like the rest of her.

We held hands on the way to and from school, but she let go once we were inside the gates. Shortly before our end-of-year exams she fell pregnant, which came as quite the surprise, seeing as we hadn't had sex yet. Divine conception crossed my mind before Nick took me aside and clarified what he knew about Molly and her 'other guys'. This news was crushing. We'd only been together three months and I was so sure we were both virgins. I went with Molly to the clinic, held her hand and even let her mother slap me across the face so Molly could feel better. I apologised like I always do and two months later we broke up. I was still a virgin.

After that, Nick gave me tips on girls, mostly on how not to seem too eager. Nick always maintained his distance – just enough to keep every girl's attention. They hung on everything he didn't say. They looked at him in a way no one has ever looked at me. Molly had laughed at my jokes. She'd said she didn't find Nick attractive *at all,* something about not liking guys who were 'boringly handsome'. I'd swelled at her words, but her words were just that – they came to nothing. In the end I lost my virginity to a drunk Carley Sumners after the matric dance. She said she wanted to get it over with; I agreed. I never saw her again. The act itself did not live up to my expectations.

Heather was Nick's first proper girlfriend. She was everything her name conjures: ethereal, delicate, beautiful, something you want to run your fingers across. They were together for the last year of high school and three years after. Her parents were wealthy – stupid wealthy. Her dad owned a private bank, her mom was the CEO of an auction house that regularly sold art for six figures. After school Heather's dad offered to pay for Nick to study engineering. God knows his own mom and dad weren't in a position to pay; he didn't know where either of them were half the time. Nick has always looked after himself.

He almost made it to his third year of university before Heather caught on. She thought it was just the one girl. I knew the number was well over ten. Nick told me it was his way of not feeling trapped. He felt as if he'd been bought. He loved Heather, I think, although he never spoke in those terms. Her dad withdrew his financial support. There was a lot of shouting.

After that Nick took a job in a bar, interned at an engineering firm, managed to secure a student loan. He paid Heather's father back with interest over the next five years. He flip-flopped from one girl to the next, sampling one after the other.

I had naively hoped I could follow in his wake, but once Maria fell pregnant the die was cast.

These are the thoughts that occupy my mind as I contemplate what exactly I will and won't tell Wendy at our appointment this afternoon. I have been driving Maria's vw Golf since the accident. Insurance is umming and ahhing about whether to make good on our agreement. Usually I would push, but I'm reluctant this time. What if the insurance starts sniffing around like the private investigator? They've already asked me to send them the medical bill I would have received during my fictitious trip to the hospital. I'm holding off until I can think straight. The last thing I need right now is more attention.

Wendy's house is on a private estate on a hill in Hout Bay. It's not far from my house, so the drive seems unnecessary, but no one walks anywhere in Cape Town – a fact I still have to explain to Maria. The house is double-storey, white with grey shutters. It matches all the houses around it. Lavender grows on either side of the cobbled walkway that leads to her front door. A domestic worker greets me, a tiny baby strapped to her back with a purple blanket.

'Hello!' I say, cheerful, as if trying to not give away my condition. She says nothing, leads me into a room off the hallway. As I take a seat on the couch, I wonder: will Wendy ask me about Maria? What does she already know about me? What has Maria said? I need to stay on message if I'm to get anything at all for the R1000 I am prepared to pay, just this once. Maria thinks I am here to fix my depression – relieve the guilt of maybe having accidentally killed my best friend's wife's best friend. What I really want to know is *how can I get my wife to love me?*

I met Maria when she was eighteen; I was thirty-one. As the years went by, our ages converged, my waistline expanded and I woke up one morning feeling like a useless child, unworthy, unlovable, unsuccessful. Will I admit all of this? Or will she know it all already? Wendy arrives in a haze of sandalwood. She has the non-judgemental face of a kindly woman who bakes cakes in her spare time. I feel secure. She gives me a warm smile, followed by a sigh.

'Adam! How are you doing today?'

In normal circumstances I would say, *Fine, thank you, and you?* But today I'm keen to get my money's worth.

'I've been feeling a bit down lately. A friend of mine recently died and my wife thinks I'm depressed.'

'I'm sorry about your friend. Do you think you're depressed?'

'Yes.'

'What gives you that impression?'

'I'm tired all the time and I feel sort of sad, and my wife doesn't want to sleep with me.'

'Oh, that must be difficult. Do you want to sleep with your wife?'

I hesitate. Do I? 'I do … but she doesn't find me attractive any more and I feel kind of useless.'

'Useless how?'

'In every sense of the word.'

'This friend of yours, who died – did you feel this way before they died, or only after?'

'Before. I think I was depressed and now I feel more … anxious.'

'Describe what anxious feels like.'

'My heart beats fast sometimes. My thoughts run away with me. My palms sweat and it feels like there's a boulder on my chest; like, breathing is hard.' I wedge my hands between my knees.

She scribbles in a notebook. Could this information actually be useful? Surely she's only humouring me. She knows what anxiety feels like.

'When do you get this feeling?'

'Mostly at night … but sometimes in the day … when I'm thinking.'

'What are you thinking about when you get these feelings?'

'I think I might have killed someone.'

There is a long silence before she says, 'I see.' She writes a single word in her notebook – underlines it several times, or maybe she's crossing it out.

'Let's start at the beginning, shall we?'

And so I do. I tell her absolutely everything that has happened to me over the last few weeks, months, years. The accident, the not knowing, the plan, the funeral, Susie Winchester, the strawberry milk. I don't pause for breath. She nods and occasionally writes. I feel there will never be enough time for me to say everything I need to say. She listens, *really* listens, saying nothing, every so often giving a nod to keep me going, and then it's over.

'Well, Adam, I think that there's a lot to unpack there. Should we meet same time next week?'

It's like a favourite series ending when you know there is no next season. I am short-changed. But at the same time, there is the sense I have expunged something awful, popped an emotional pimple. Maybe this is what I needed after all. She stands, smooths her floral skirt and raises her arm in a gesture that says, *Off you go, then …* I move into the hall and out the front door. Outside I walk slap-bang into Sebastian coming up the lavender-lined path.

'Adam!'

'Sebastian! Hey, man … How are you … doing?!' I grab his bicep, hoping for sincerity, my mind screaming *Fuck!*

'You come here?' he says.

I try to make light of this: 'Yeah, you know – Maria … she suggested … I haven't been sleeping so you know … women!' A high-pitched laugh. I'm digging myself a hole. Any mention of Maria seems to highlight the absence of Charley. The squeeze on his bicep becomes a slap, too much force. 'Good luck!' I say pointlessly as I rush towards my car. Sebastian takes a seat on a wooden bench positioned outside the door and watches me drive away.

# NOW

## Franky

*Ocean View Drive, Green Point*

'I love you,' he says.

He holds my hip with one hand, the side of my face with the other. He lifts his head and searches my eyes. I imagine he is looking for my response in the depths of my pupils. I prefer to close my eyes – to feel the solidity of him, the surety of this one thing. But I keep them open so he feels the connection. 'I love you too,' I whisper. His half-beard sandpapers my skin and I feel both comforted and exposed. Together and alone.

Sex while pregnant has a charge, an urgency not unlike those first times. I'm not sure if this is a result of the hormones coursing through my system or our shared experience – the death of Charley somehow making us feel more alive.

He kisses me on my forehead, my mouth, the back of my neck, telling me he loves me, he'll always love me. While I am charmed by these displays there is also a faint, innate suspicion. *Never trust a man who buys you flowers out of the blue* is what my mother always says.

Nick and I haven't argued since that night. It's hard to recall everything that's happened in between. These last three months are tear-stained, alcohol-soaked pages of a calendar, the contents unreadable through the emotional spillage. There's no denying one awful fact: Charley's death has positively affected my relationship. Nick and I now know first-hand what can happen. We know, in a way we didn't before, that each kiss, each goodbye, each conversation could be our last.

I'd never seen Nick properly cry until the moment I told him Charley had died. His shoulders shook, his eyes dampened and then his anger was volcanic.

'Jesus! Fuck!' he said, over and over again.

I was still playing the part of the messenger. My emotion was suspended: it hung like a makeshift washing line somewhere between Seb's Confusion and Nick's Anger. Crying usually had a calming effect, a sedative that unbuttoned my sinuses and softened my muscles, but it didn't work this time. My tears came in fits and starts, small weather systems outside of my control, offering little comfort or release.

Perhaps, back then I was still in shock, not quite believing the surreality of the preceding twenty-four hours. And so, instead, I tried to focus all my emotion on calming what was then *the grape*. 'It's okay,' I murmured when I was alone in the bathroom, listening to Nick relay the story to Adam. 'Everything *will* be okay.' It became a chant.

When the sun set on that strange Saturday, Adam, Nick and I had managed to convince each other (if not ourselves) there was absolutely no chance Charley's death could have been a result of Adam's actions. Adam insisted he couldn't remember anything. They were both accidents and one had nothing to do with the other.

The question that still haunts us all is, *Where had Charley been going that night?* All we know is that she was driving away from home, away from her family, towards Constantia. Adam was driving towards his family, in the direction of Hout Bay.

Seb has no answers, and pressing him on this still feels inappropriate. He said he woke up thinking she was next to him, and then slowly realised she wasn't. He scanned the room, half asleep, thinking she might be in the bathroom, or with the children, or having a midnight spliff outside on the patio. He convinced himself it was one of these things and he went back to sleep. An image of Oscar Pistorius pops into my head unbidden when I think of this. I remembered how Charley and I had talked about the Valentine's Day murder for hours. *How could he not have known it was his wife in the bathroom and not a burglar?* she'd said to me, hands in the air in exaggerated disbelief.

'You mean he didn't get up and look for her?' said Nick when I told him the details of Seb's confession.

'Maria sleeps with the kids most nights,' said Adam. 'I never know where she is. I don't even think about it any more.' I felt a pang for Adam when he said this, appalled I could feel any sympathy for a man who may have inadvertently killed my best friend. No matter how I tried, I couldn't feel genuine anger towards Adam. The only accurate way I could describe my emotion would be 'deeply and desperately sad'. This doesn't seem like enough.

In the weeks that followed the funeral, we saw less and less of Adam and Maria, and I went over the story again and again with Nick until he squinted into the middle distance when the subject arose. As far as Nick and Adam were concerned, we had reached a conclusion. They had a lawyer lined up and were ready to act should the need arise. They had prepared answers should any fingers come pointing in their direction, and they were quietly confident that everyone was innocent and time would fix this.

I changed my mind as often as I changed maternity clothes. Of course I didn't want Adam or Nick to face any kind of questioning about that night, least of all myself or my mother, but I've always had a propensity for compulsive honesty. I like to externalise. It's the gift and curse of being a writer: I need to articulate how I feel. Few thoughts stay trapped in the confines of my mind. Maybe I should tell Seb, clear the air. Maybe he won't draw any conclusions, agree the accidents can't be linked. I think of how his eyes had lit up when he told me about the private investigator, how he'd seemed alive for the first time since Charley's death. He seemed almost invigorated by the possibility that he could pin the blame on someone other than Charley. *No*, I think, *I must keep my mouth shut.* 'What will it achieve?' says a hologram of Nick in my mind, blue eyes pleading.

I visit Seb at least twice a week, call him most days. I find it hard to be around Leo and Katie. I feel certain they will see pity leaking through my eyeballs when I look in their direction. Their subtly changing faces make me imagine all the celebrations their mother will miss – where they will feel her absence like a presence. My attempts at normality will fall flat, echo in the room like an ill-timed, lone clap. I can't comply with the performance of it all. So, I choose times when I know they're at school, or at friends' houses. Seb is the one I need to comfort. Seb is the one who needs to remind me what Charley meant to me, to anchor me in the present so I can carry some small part of his loss, in order to feel my own.

At first Nick was understanding about the frequency of my visits and calls, but then he seemed jealous. 'He's looking for a replacement,' he said over dinner one night. We'd been watching a romantic comedy and at first I thought he was talking about the characters in the film.

'He's just … lonely,' I said. 'He wants to be around someone who knew her as well as he did. He's looking for someone to reflect his pain.' I am aware now, as I was then, that I was spouting stoicisms I hadn't fully connected with. I wouldn't characterise my feelings as denial; it was more *What would Charley do?* and I knew she'd say, *Get on with it, moron.* And so I was.

I've been talking to my psychologist about all of this. Wendy is helpful, to a point, but expensive, and the expense makes me anxious for her to fix me expediently. I think of all the other things I could buy with the R1000 she charges per hour: the baby clothes, the scatter cushions, the bottle of perfume – something new to define the next chapter of my life. All these things seem infinitely more desirable than unburdening myself to a stranger. But I've always taken my mental health seriously. This situation feels like it calls for a proper head-shrinking – preventative medicine, lest I find myself in the grip of post-natal depression, or pre-natal depression, which I'm told is also a thing.

Today she is watching me carefully with her green eyes, a small smile falling shy of a smirk. 'How are we today, Francine?'

'I'm … okay,' I say almost believing it. This morning's sex has given me a lift, and I am determined to hold on to the feeling for the rest of the day. 'Well … I've been thinking about hypotheticals, about how Charley died and what caused her death and if there's anything I could have done to stop it, or if I can make it better for Seb somehow by telling him things …'

I am careful when I have these conversations. I know all about the doctor-patient confidentiality argument, but I'm still hesitant. I hardly know this woman. What if she has a brother or a friend *in the force* who might find this information useful? I tread lightly around the subject, hoping for some insight, for some way to assuage the last remnants of my guilt.

'Boundaries.' She uses the word often. 'You need to establish boundaries.' I picture chalk lines drawn on a tar road, the shape of a body.

'Of course you feel a connection with her and with her husband, but it is not your job to make him feel better. Quite the contrary – this is a road he can only walk alone.'

'But, what if …' I say, twisting a tissue in my fingers, 'what if I knew something about how she died, some piece of information that would be helpful to the investigation, but I don't want to bring it up … because it might cause more hurt and …'

'And …?'

'And … more pain for more people, not just Seb.' I am talking in riddles and she sees through it.

'You could not have stopped what happened to her. You need to accept this before you move on.'

'Yes, but … I don't know where Charley was that night. None of us do … and that's the part that's so … so confusing. The not knowing … like, we can't

Google it … There's no way of *ever* knowing why she was driving around that late at night.'

She nods, offering no theories of her own. This is not the first time I've brought this up. Every time I do, I hope she'll make a suggestion as to where Charley might have gone. She was her client, for God's sake! Surely Wendy, of all people, would have some opinion, some insight that could release us all from our misery? I hate the one-sidedness off this. I would pay double to hear Wendy give me her real opinion, not the one she's trained to give.

Seb has told me repeatedly what he knows. They came home in the Uber after ten. He paid the babysitter – the younger sister of the Malawian woman who works for them during the day. They peeled off their damp, smoke-infused clothes and stumbled into bed. Charley fell asleep before he did. He woke up at around midnight and she wasn't there. She literally had … *gone*. The next time he woke was to the sound of the police at his door.

'Nick says …' I say, hyper-aware of making my husband sound dictatorial or dominant in any way. Her eyes narrow at the mention of his name.

'Nick is pragmatic about these things,' I continue. 'He says you can sit around all day crying – what does that achieve?'

'That's a bit cold,' she says, shifting in her seat.

'It's not,' I say. 'Death is part of life, isn't it? He's trying to keep me sane.'

'Grief is part of life. Death is the end of life.' Her eyes close and then open again, as if for dramatic effect. 'To feel grief you must experience it fully. You cannot second-guess or analyse your emotions. You cannot change the way you feel; you can only change what you do with the feeling – how you act.' She pauses. 'How are you feeling about the pregnancy?'

'Fine,' I say without properly considering the question.

'Are you afraid the baby is picking up on all this turmoil in the outside world?'

This is the closest she's come to esoteric. I have been thinking this, but for her to confirm this as a possibility is making me see her in a new and unflattering light.

'No, I … It's weird. It's like the baby is being controlled by something else,' I say. 'You know when you tell yourself to breathe deeply and then you do, and then you wonder why you don't have to tell yourself to breathe at all, because you just do? I feel like the pregnancy is like … breathing: it just happens. Some other force is manipulating and facilitating growth, not me, and I feel like … like I should be doing more, on all fronts.'

'Francine, I think you need to give yourself a break.' I sense the full stop at the end of our session. 'You are chastising yourself. It is noble that you want to help

Sebastian through this, and believe me, your attention is appreciated, but you have your own family and your own child to think of now. You must make yourself the priority.'

I nod, wondering if she knows how much I wish that were an actual possibility.

# TEN YEARS AGO

## Franky

*Sillery Avenue, Constantia*

It's called Oasis, the cubes piled high on my mother's kitchen table – dark green, damp, floral foam. I have it under my fingernails. I know this will be a smell and texture my body will recall when I look back on this day.

There are so many flowers addressed to my mother, their artificial arrangements at odds with the rambling English garden outside the kitchen window. Paper ribbons in every shade are curled around baskets and vases. Someone, somewhere, has profited from my father's death.

I want to be useful, so this afternoon, while my mother sleeps, I have taken it upon myself to pull apart every single arrangement and rearrange the flowers in a manner more fitting my mother's taste. A manner that doesn't say *death.* She loves flowers, but only when they're in the ground, or wrapped in newspaper.

First, I set aside the obviously tacky stuff: carnations, chrysanthemums, gladioli, lilies and proteas. Nothing says kitsch quite like a protea. I wonder if people in other countries feel a similar aversion to their own national flowers. I keep the white roses, a few sprigs of eucalyptus. I tiptoe into the garden and cut long swathes of lavender. The stalks perfume my fingers. I tear off a black refuse bag, throw the mountain of green foam into it. I know the Oasis is expensive, an essential tool in flower-arranging, but there's a strange pleasure in the casting aside, a refusal to accept what has been given.

Next, I throw away the cards. My mother won't mind. On the contrary, she'll thank me. The *I'm So Sorry, Deepest Condolences, You're In Our Prayers* are now smeared with the Oasis, dropping like dried leaves in the bag. I throw the discarded blooms onto the compost heap.

I play classical music, pour myself a glass of white wine. I find a crystal vase, two jugs made of thin grey pottery and a large terracotta olive-oil jar my mother and I fought over at an antique store last summer. I rearrange the few remaining stalks in haphazard bunches.

While I do this, I decide my mother's grief is heavier than mine. It should be.

Only now do I see how alike my father and I were. It was never something commented on, but in his absence, his traits seem to magnify in me. It is less than forty-eight hours since that phone call – I can already feel myself adopting his mannerisms, his way of speaking, of framing my chin between my thumb and two fingers when I am deep in thought. Instead of mourning him, I am becoming him. I will fill the space he has left. I will assume the shape of him. By doing this I will alleviate some measure of the pain I can only imagine my mother feels. Losing a partner, while perhaps inevitable, is not a rite of passage like losing a father. I want to feel it so she doesn't have to. This is illogical, I know that too, but nothing about this situation feels worthy of rational thought. I finish arranging the flowers and place two of the vases on the table in the dining room. I take the bag of wet rubbish to the outside bin, push it down forcibly with my fists.

The next morning I wake to find my mother painting the ceiling in the lounge.

'Morning, darling!' she says, her face splattered with white flecks. It's in her hair, on her fingers and all over the fabric of her khaki boiler suit. I'm afraid to ask why she's chosen this moment to renovate.

'Cup of tea?' I offer.

She climbs down the ladder. Sits her paintbrush on the highest rung.

'Darling, thank you for the flowers. What a wonderful job you did.'

I beam at her praise before she adds, 'You know you don't need to stay here with me. You need to get back to your life. Although … I have had an idea.' There's a childlike excitement in the twitch of her fingers. I'm afraid to ruin her mood by saying too much, so I take a seat on the dust-covered couch.

'Even though this is a shock,' she says, joining me, 'your father was nothing if not prepared.' I nod, feeling the sting behind my eyes as she says *your father*. 'He has left me everything, of course, but he has made a provision for you in his will – and I want you to take that money and put down a deposit on a flat.'

'Oh, Mom, that's … I'm not sure I'm ready.'

'Oh, please, what are you waiting for? You're working, you have money to service a bond, and I can always help too. I can even help you renovate, make it special for you.'

'It's just I was waiting …'

'Waiting for what? You're twenty-nine, my darling. It's time you stepped on the property ladder, and if something good can come from your father's death … I want it to be this.' Her eyes shine.

'I'd always imagined I would buy a place with …'

'With a boy? Oh, sweetheart, you need to get on with your own life. Don't sit around waiting for Mr Right to walk through that door. He'll come when he's good and ready. Right now, you need to take this gift and run with it.' She picks up a selection of discarded newsprint lying on the floor, mostly covered in paint. 'I found these this morning; lots of places to look at. I think we should start the process, together.'

This is her project and seeing it through will keep her sane. How could I possibly refuse? She climbs back up the ladder. 'I'm just going to finish this corner, and then let's get in the car and go. Looking will be good for both of us.' As she says this, she makes large bold strokes with the brush, the paint splattering fine spray across her face. 'We can even go for lunch afterwards.' She stops to look at me. 'Let's make a day of it!'

Back in my childhood bedroom, I contemplate my mother's current state of mind. The room has long been cleared of the detritus of my teenager years. My mother renovated this room the week I left home, two days after my nineteenth birthday. The wooden ceiling has been painted white, and the room has been finished with tasteful shades of green. Gold-mounted prints of foliage and plants adorn the walls. 'The Garden Suite' she calls it, and it's mostly reserved for my parents' friends who visit from overseas. I had planned to stay for a few weeks, keep my mother company while we both came to terms with my father's unplanned absence. Over time, I've learnt that my mother is anything but conventional. Why should she be any different in this situation? Far be it for her to wallow, as I would. No, my mother is a person of action and I am being carried in her wake.

My mother manoeuvres her Merc into the space between two parked cars. Sunday in the centre of town is bright and quiet. The world is still spinning despite the fact that our axis has shifted. My rented studio flat isn't far from here, but the thought of returning to its cavernous, too-hot or too-cold space fills me with dread. So far, we have seen a two-bedroom flat and a studio loft, and we're about to take a look at a duplex set against the mountain.

'Not much character,' says my mother in relation to the flat. 'I liked the studio myself, but it's your choice, obviously.' She climbs out of the car, clutching her handbag. As I'm about to interject, I feel something pulling on my shoulder. My bag feels heavy. My bag is being pulled and my arm lifts involuntarily so the thief can finish his act without resistance. I squeeze my eyes shut. The pavement liquifies to wet cement.

I open my eyes and see my mother running up the steep city street in her luminous yellow flip-flops, shouting, 'Come back here, you fucking bastard!'

'Mom!' I yell, still unable to move anything but my tongue. 'Leave him! He could have a knife!' My mother's profanity catches the attention of every passer-by. The thief is cut off by the driver of a white truck. I watch the scene play out in miniature from my perspective at the bottom of the hill. The truck driver leaps from his car and tackles the man to the ground. My mother retrieves the bag and shakes hands with the driver, who has pinned the man to ground with his foot and his elbow. She marches back towards me, triumphant. She hands me back my bag and says, 'Right, shall we go for lunch, then?'

# FIVE YEARS AGO

## Franky

*Constantiaberg Hospital*

The room is too bright and I am alone. Fake wood floor polished to a shine. Fear and static root me to the plastic of the chair. I am trapped in my body; it shakes and snaps without my instruction. My left arm stiffens, wrists pulsing. Numbers on the monitor flash with urgency, even though the nurse has long since left the room.

I'm too young to have a heart attack. Men have heart attacks. My dad had a heart attack. I'm a woman, a child in my mind, because I still take comfort from my mother. *My mother!* I must say goodbye. But the shaking makes it hard to hold the phone, type a garbled message – *Goodbye*? *Thanks*? *I love you*? All too little too late, already said, already recorded. *Oh, there it is!* Stab of pain in my left breast, a dark and sharp thing. *Nick.* I should message Nick first so he knows he comes first. Imagine them at my funeral checking their phones to see the irrefutable truth.

Later, a nurse dressed like a cleaner (maybe she *is* a cleaner) shuffles in with instructions for me to follow her. I stumble out of the room, holding the wall for support. She pays me no obvious attention. I am shown a spotlit bed.

'I don't want to die,' I say to a new nurse who is wheeling a contraption towards me.

'It's my wedding day,' I say, and she laughs. She *laughs*.

'Not today. You're not going to die today.'

The shaking, so much shaking. *Whose body is this?* I need to talk – to tell her again to help me – but I cannot speak, cannot form words. My jaw has petrified, or maybe it's my throat, but the rest of me is moving violently. The nurse is connecting me to the machine. She has propped up the bed to help me breath.

The room is for children. A monkey holding a banana that has been inexpertly painted on the wall. I fixate on the monkey and its banana in an attempt to hold on to what little sanity I have left.

A woman, too old to be a nurse, too thin, sticks her head around the corner and looks down her nose at me, a teacher who has just noticed I am outside of school without my blazer.

'You need a paper bag,' she says.

'I need …' I manage through clenched teeth. She hands me a bag, white and made from hard cardboard, too thick, I think, and there's a hole. This is farcical. I am strapped to a machine that probably costs more than my car, but this discarded paper bag is expected to save me from death. Really? The monkey looks on, shadowed eyes smiling, banana poised, never to be eaten.

I do what I'm told because I'm terrified these are my last moments – until I imagine myself in another hospital bed, one with a window, shafts of light falling across the bottom of the bed.

*You had a heart attack,* I hear a fictitious doctor say. *It's a miracle you are still here. There will be changes you'll need to make, but you're here …*

People have heart attacks and they do survive. The bag is expanding, contracting, expanding, contracting – small puffs escaping through the hole. My body is still now and the nurse returns to me from behind a curtain, not a trace of concern in her features. The machine spits out a series of jagged lines that hold no meaning, a fax from the future. *I could live*, I think, but my body does not yet concur.

The paper of the bag crackles. Maybe they only gave me the bag to give me something to do – make the helpless less helpless. More help. I need more help. I am angry and grateful in equal measure; I have fallen for their trick. They are weary, these nurses, slow and considered. No rush, no fear. I hear the doctor in the room next door, a muffled instruction. A nurse, or maybe a doctor, with a tight ponytail is just visible through a glass partition in the RhinoBoard wall. 'Your husband will be here to fetch you soon,' she says, but not to me, to someone else, someone else who has just touched the face of death, just woken from the dream of their life. Oh, to be *fetched,* scooped up, and carried away.

The doctor is here and he is impossibly young: tall, curly-haired, orange mask and cap, a whiff of the children's entertainer about him. His arms are folded, which I think is rude. Then, almost simultaneously, I think, this is a good sign – I am judging him, no longer trapped in my familiar mental loop. My brain is now capable of other tricks.

'What seems to be the problem?' he says.

I tell him about the pain in my arm and the lack of breath and the pressure on my chest. My jaw has loosened, just enough, my head is lolling on one side, the expanded bag holding its shape on my lap. I can see the reflection of my green dress on the TV screen above. Do people watch TV in the ER? Or is that a monitor connected to another expensive machine?

'I'm going to give you something,' he says.

He disappears behind the curtain like a puppet. I stare at the mustard-coloured fabric and wait for the next performer to appear. It's the nurse, the one I had asked to save me. She hands me a plastic cup with two tiny white pills and tells me to put them under my tongue. They look and taste like artificial sweetener. Could this be another diversion? They dissolve immediately and so does the feeling in my feet. I'm still breathless and in pain, but no longer trying to stop the pain and the breathlessness; it's there and I am here and the monkey watches on regardless.

'Nice veins.'

I avert my eyes from the nurse and her needle. My new wedding ring sparkles in the strip lighting.

Ag, no!' she says. I feel pain I don't care about and watch a perfect circle of red materialise on the white sheets. *Finally!* Some outward evidence of my distress. There is it – my blood, as real as anything, staining everything it comes into contact with. She tries the other hand, fiddles with the drip.

'What is that?' I say, noticing my jaw has returned to its usually mobility.

'Painkiller,' she says. 'You're going to be skipping out of here. You'll feel amazing!'

'Thank you …?' I say, reading the name on her badge as she leans over me. 'Thank you, Helen, thank you for saving me.'

She shakes her head and leaves the room, pushing the machine like a shopping trolley.

The doctor reappears, tells me the tests they took are all normal. He has a friend who has OCD. I'm not sure how this relates to me and then he says, 'Lots of people have this. Life's short. Try and enjoy it.'

And then he's gone.

I don't remember leaving. I remember paying, handing someone my credit card, papers being handed back to me, my signature scrawled on some of them, lots of words and numbers and logos, receipts. I don't remember who drove me home, or what happened next. All I know is, the next day I woke up – not a resurrection or a revelation, but rather a continuation. I woke up. I'm still here, and I'm not sure why.

Nick strokes my hair and tells me everything will be okay. My mother calls and tells me to pull myself towards myself. *Talk to yourself,* she says. *What should I say?* I ask. She sighs heavily. She's angry. Angry with me for not being stronger, angry with Nick for not being able to fix me once and for all. They are angry with each other and all I want is for someone else to take the wheel.

# NOW

## Franky

*Bree Street, Cape Town* CBD

My baby is the size of a *mealie*. It has facial features, so I'm told. I picture an effigy made from sacking and a dried ear of corn: a tiny voodoo doll with crosses for eyes and a single stitched line for a mouth. It's been just over three months since Charley passed away, and while the swelling of my belly is a sure sign there is life inside me, there is no such physical delineation that a life was lost – no missing limb or keloid scar. All I can attribute to the absence of Charley is the burning sensation at the base of my throat. Most days, I marvel at the act of swallowing. Why don't we choke on our food? This slippery slope our meals must travel, never damaged by a spiky crisp or a fistful of plastic-coated vitamins.

Some days, forgetting is luxury. *You should think about her more,* I think, although I'm not sure what the thinking will achieve. There are not enough reminders. Charley wasn't part of the fabric of my day-to-day life the way she was when we were in high school. There was no empty desk, empty chair or empty side of the bed for me to contemplate.

Grief has to happen. I know this. Grief needs to be *done*, like the washing, or sweeping the floor. Seb wants to escape the truth because the truth is too heavy to hold. Numb fingers can't touch the edges of anything. Numb feet can't feel the ground beneath them. And so I find myself vicariously feeling his feelings on his behalf. I imagine Nick snatched from me, no preamble. I imagine the pain and it feels real, it feels present – because it is, for Seb. The worst has finally happened. I trace all the edges with my tingling fingers. My nerve endings fire. If grief is a sickness, I want to let it consume me, so it can be over.

Only now I can't be consumed, not this time. There is another person in this sequence, a person half formed, taking on this grief with me, and I can't let this tiny vessel carry something so large and abstract. I resist, and in the resistance lies the return of my anxiety.

When Charley was pregnant she told me she felt earthy. *Ripe* was the word she used. I feel more like the foetus is a parasite, living off the food I eat, the emotions I process, taking and taking until there is almost nothing of me left. I am still surprised at how little involvement I have in the creature's metamorphosis. I imagine it has a mind of its own, a will of its own. I am a carrier, like one carries a virus. And yet I still speak to it; I still do my best to offer a nurturing voice, no matter how pointless this act might be. It comforts me, this thing inside me. I assumed I would comfort it, but no, this tiny scarecrow, made of straw, whoever he or she will be, is comforting me, giving me more reasons to keep moving forward.

The feelings pile up like rocks in a wheelbarrow, waiting to be moved from one place to another. We thought about naming the baby Charlotte or Charlie, depending on whether it's a girl or a boy. But it feels too close, too soon, insincere, expected. It feels a lot of things that don't feel right. 'Perhaps a second name?' Nick suggested and I nodded, although I know I will avoid all reference to Charley when it comes to our baby's name. I don't want my *mealie* to be named after someone who died before their time: this seems like a terribly bad omen to bestow upon a child.

The gynaecologist says I should keep exercising. This will be good for me mentally and physically, good for the *mealie* too. He recommends walking. During my lunch-hour, I find myself walking past the place where Charley and I had our last proper conversation. The restaurant's slate floors and dark panelled walls hold the smell of expired wine and wood polish. During the day, the space has none of the glamour we felt that night. This is not the right place to contemplate losing her. *Ashes to ashes* is the cliché that comes to my mind as I watch a woman brush the floor, empty the dustpan onto the street.

I walk past another familiar pavement café and remember one particular afternoon, years ago, when my blood ran cold at the sight of Charley. Dark rings, dark roots, dark mood. She'd been decidedly withdrawn after Katie was born, cold and snappy in our phone conversations. I'd heard about post-natal depression but, as Nick and I were still new, parenthood had seemed like something very far away.

We met for lunch at this trendy café near my office – my choice. I remember it had a French-sounding name, red-and-white tablecloths, chairs that left marks on your legs when you stood up. Charley and I hadn't seen quite as much of each other as I'd thought we would after the birth. I felt she needed space, but I was worried she'd read this as disinterest, so I had asked her to lunch. She'd seemed relieved to have an excuse to get out of the house. Once we'd ordered drinks, I said, 'Are you going back to work?'

'I'm not sure,' she said, a vacant expression on her face. 'I miss it. I do. I just can't imagine anyone else looking after my child. It seems weird – like getting someone to sleep with your husband.' I laughed then, a hearty laugh, and remembered how much I had missed this. I missed us. Katie lay asleep in her buggy, eyes closed, dreaming the dreams of a person who has so little information to draw on. I imagined her dreams could only have been swirls of colour and snatches of sound.

'I have something to show you,' Charley said then, eyes alight. 'Promise you won't be mad.' She pulled up the sleeve of her sweater and I saw a large bandage on her wrist. She looked at me expectantly, a watery smile.

'What the hell, Charley?!' I said, my voice a loud whisper. She laughed, a silent laugh, so as not to wake the baby. She peeled back the bandage and there on her wrist was a dark twisting line, rimmed with red.

'What …' I started, before she interjected.

'It's my dad's signature. I found it on one of his old passport documents.'

'Oh God, that's so … wow,' I said, unsure of the appropriate response. Charley and I had always been on the same page when it came to tattoos. Tattoos were not *our* thing. That was Seb's domain.

'I've been thinking about my dad a lot,' she said then, neat tears forming on her sallow cheeks. 'And here …' She lifted her thick blonde hair up on her left side to reveal another bandage behind her ear, this one much smaller than the one on her wrist. My heart beat faster, my fingers clutched the sides of the table. A strange mix of emotions passed through me – disgust, intrigue, sadness, betrayal – and then, curiosity.

She lifted the bandage and tilted her head up towards the light. There, on the pale smooth skin behind her ear was a tiny skull, its contours glowing angry red.

'It's a memento mori,' she said, thumbing it gently before pressing the bandage back in place. 'Dedicated to my little brother … and my dad.'

'Remember you must die,' I whispered, recalling one of our many late-night adolescent existential conversations. 'Jesus, Char … that's … Fuck. I'm speechless.'

She smiled, proud of herself, proud that she'd shocked me, daring me to comment.

'I love it,' I said, reaching for the hand that wasn't bandaged. 'It's … they're … beautiful.'

'Thanks.' She flicked her hair back into place. 'Shall we order?'

Every so often, as I continue my walk through the city, I catch a glimpse of myself in a window, the strange new shape of me. Strangers often ask, 'How far along are you?' which sometimes feels like, 'So, how long ago did you consummate this child? How *was* the sex that night, by the way?' Just this morning a rotund man with a white beard shared the lift with me on my way up to the agency. I nodded and smiled, as seemed appropriate, almost anticipating the 'So how far …' when he eyed my belly and said, 'That there is a burden you carry for the rest of your life.' As if choreographed, the doors slid open. He left me alone in that mirrored box to contemplate his grim pronouncement. It was then that I realised: keeping this baby alive was my priority, not only for the requisite twelve weeks and subsequent six months, but always.

# NOW

## Franky

*Bree Street, Cape Town* CBD

'How's that mock-up coming along?'

Gabby is opposite me, staring at the screen of her computer. She doesn't shift her eyeline as she says, 'Meh, you know … plugging away.'

I'm fairly certain she's updating her Tinder profile rather than working on the project we've been assigned. I could get up and confirm this, but I am so remarkably tired that even the thought of moving exhausts me. Instead, I mentally calculate the days left until the chimeric maternity leave. Ten more weeks.

I return my attention to the plastic container on the desk. Its contents: a clear gel I must name and describe. A hint of suntan lotion, piña colada, a promise of warmth, an afternoon with a book spread across your chest – half finished, a holiday, an escape. My senses seem to have heightened in the last few weeks, but my ideas continue to hover in the realm of cliché.

'Did you have a Peaches 'N Cream Barbie when you were younger?' I say, picking up the container to smell its contents again.

'I wasn't into Barbies,' says Gabby. 'I was more … emo. Although we didn't call it that back then, did we? What did we call it?'

'Goth?' I offer.

'Yes!' says Gabby, looking at me for the first time. This is how our conversations have gone for the last three years since we've been a creative team. Dissecting the meanings of words and cultural references, unpacking morphic resonance theory. Anything to distract ourselves from the ticking clock, the deadline and the actual words I am meant to be spinning into advertising gold. Around us, the hum of phones and photocopiers, someone laughing too loudly. I roll my eyes at

Gabby, hoping for camaraderie, but Gabby is back to her screen and its contents.

'Fuck, what does this fucking shampoo actually smell like?' I say to the room at large. The swearing tastes youthful on my tongue like a creme-soda lollipop.

'Didn't you say peaches?' a voice pipes up from the printer next to Gabby.

The owner of the voice looks at me expectantly. She's someone in finance. Her name escapes me. 'Go with peaches. Everyone likes the smell of peaches.'

'Yeah, but it's been done,' I say.

'Everything's been done,' says Gabby, yawning without covering her mouth. Her hair has recently been dyed an unnatural shade of maroon. 'I'm so over this,' she says: her catchphrase.

Advertising was like this – agonising over details while making sweeping generalisations about what makes people 'tick'. It was impossible not to impose a bit of your own taste into everything. Hours and hours spent waiting for the elusive and, quite often, illusive great idea. *Blood on the walls*, my advertising lecturer used to say; *there must be blood on the walls for you to know you have a good idea.* In other words, a copywriter (me) was meant to argue with my Art Director (Gabby) about a concept. We needed to passionately debate the scent of the shampoo before deciding its name, its packaging and its subsequent advertising campaign. This plastic pot of nameless, colourless gloop needed an identity, a reason for being, and Gabby and I needed to declare it. Only at this moment in time, with my baby moving from *mealie* to *melon*, my inability to permit myself to sufficiently grieve my dead friend, and Gabby fixated on a possible future love match, there is little chance of a light-bulb moment.

'*Holiday*? Why don't we just call it Holiday? It smells like a holiday,' I say.

Girl From Finance looks up from the printer. Her silence says everything.

'That's a shit idea,' says Gabby. 'Now I have Madonna in my head. Thanks for that.'

What about *Lotion*?' This from twenty-something Gavin who has just walked into the office eating a foul-smelling sandwich. I close my eyes and hope when I open them again either he will be gone, or the time on my laptop will read five o'clock.

Gabby throws a ball of paper at Gavin's head; he ducks. They look at each other for a moment – Gavin grinning and chewing, Gabby smirking.

'Lotion?' I say.

'Yeah, just call it Lotion. It's a good word, right? *Lotion* – says what it is on the tin. *Have you tried that shampoo … Lotion?*'

'Yes, but it isn't lotion – it's shampoo,' I say.

'No, it's *hair lotion.* Lotion for your hair …' He taps his nose twice and points at me.

Gavin clearly doesn't know what conditioner is. There's no point debating this with him. Gavin is widely regarded as the agency's most creative creative. He has a Cannes Lion as a doorstop in his office – advertising's answer to a Palme d'Or.

I always thought moving to a smaller agency would be more *me*, help me get noticed, do the kind of work I would be proud of, but it's been more of the same: more unremarkable marketing junk mail. Gabby and I are the oldest people in the office. We've been passed up for Creative Director at least three times. It's clear that unless we start our own agency (something I don't have the appetite or the wherewithal for right now), it's just a matter of time before we are both retrenched and replaced with someone younger and cheaper.

The hands of the wall clock make the requisite turns, delivering me the freedom I crave. I am finally pressing the button for the lift – no further in my naming of The Shampoo, but confident the idea will come to me while I am driving, in the shower or about to fall asleep.

# TWENTY-THREE YEARS AGO

## Franky

*Rondebosch*

Our voices echo off the tiles in the girls' bathroom.

'Hand me that, will you,' she says. I pass her the plastic bottle. She tips it upside down, squeezes the honey into her mouth, swallows. '*So* good.'

'You know most people our age are smoking cigarettes in bathrooms?' I say, taking back the bottle and emptying the last of its golden contents into my mouth. She laughs. I love it when I make her laugh.

'Yeah, but we're different, you and me. We're performers!' And then, as the honey works its magic on her vocal cords, she sings the opening bars of 'Matchmaker, Matchmaker'.

I regard myself in the mirror. A trainee make-up artist has attempted to make me, a sixteen-year-old girl from Cape Town, into Golde, Russian mother of seven. She has used brown eyeliner to make deep crevices around my mouth, three straight lines across my forehead, crow's feet at the sides of my eyes. Talcum powder dusts my hair, mostly hidden by a brown headscarf.

'I wonder if I will actually look like this when I'm sixty,' I say, smudging the eyeliner with a dampened finger. I wanted to look less like Golde and more like Charley's character, Tzeitel. The fact that Charley is playing one of my daughters in this high-school production of *Fiddler on the Roof* is an endless source of hilarity for us both. Secretly, I would have preferred to have been cast as one of the daughters – especially considering the majority of the cast in this production are boys.

There's a rap on the door. 'Five minutes, girls!' booms Mr Brown's voice.

'You nervous?' says Charley, holding both my hands in hers. Her hands are sweaty and warm.

'A little,' I say. We jump up and down with excitement before Charley breaks away.

'Must go to the loo. Last time.'

'Who's coming to watch tonight?' My voice carries over the door of the bathroom stall. Charley's voice floats back over the stream of her urine. 'No one. My mom's coming on the last night. She's bringing some guy. You?'

'My mom and dad are watching tonight. My gran, maybe my aunt, and then my cousins are coming tomorrow. I think my mom said she'll come every night if she can. Hey! Wanna come for a sleepover after?'

'Definitely,' says Charley, flushing, opening the door. She looks beautiful in her fake eyelashes and wide printed skirt. Her hair is swept off her face, the scarf on her head more Grace Kelly than mine.

'I'll call my mom at intermission.'

Charley is impulsive, confident and shy all at the same time. She's lived through so much already: her little brother's death, her dad's disappearance. My life is so boring in comparison. Charley's life has jeopardy, adventure, ups and downs – like a good book. My life so far is predictable, safe, contained. I make up for it by worrying about everything I can – anticipating the stroke of bad luck that will soon find me. Charley tells me I'm a *moron* often. She also calls me *Frankfurter* and it feels like love.

'Okay, Frankfurter … let's do this! Where's that frigging broomstick?'

Opening night is a success. I sing the duet 'Do You Love Me?' with my co-star David Morrison, who has the same number of wrinkles inexpertly etched on his face. Then later, he and I belt out 'Sunrise, Sunset'. We'd been asked to sing it with wobbly voices – a nod to our characters' advanced age – but we can't help belting it out. My father sits in the front row and smiles. His face and the reflections in his spectacles are the only things I focus on as I sing 'Sunrise, Sunset' to the sea of shadowed faces. I have no idea what I am actually singing about, but I find fake emotion in the shape of the words. In this moment, I feel heard.

After the show, my mom gives Charley and me a bunch of red roses each. I can tell she's hastily split one bunch into two when she heard Charley would be sleeping over. Back at my house, we spend at least half an hour taking off our make-up and giggling. My mom makes us cups of hot chocolate with tiny marshmallows floating on top and agrees to let us pull my double mattress outside into the garden so we can experience the thrill of sleeping under the stars.

'Technically we always sleep under the stars, don't we? Even when it's daylight!'

I say, once we're settled under my down duvet. 'It's the absence of a roof and a sun that we refer to when we say *under the stars.*' I feel philosophical tonight.

'So true,' says Charley. 'We're so small and insignificant, aren't we, when you look up at all that.' I look briefly at her moonlit profile, her straight nose in relief.

I turn on my side, hands in the prayer position, under my cheek. 'Do you think we're ever going to get boyfriends?' This is a question we spend a lot of time discussing. There is never any real conclusion. Of late, I've become worried Charley is keeping something from me.

'I kissed Tom at Allie's party,' she says, still looking up at the stars.

'Why didn't you tell me?' I sit up. I'm hurt. There's also a pulse of anger.

'I dunno. It just felt wrong. Like, I was bragging or something. Who do you think your first kiss is going to be? Jesse?' She's deliberately changing the subject. I picture the boy she's referring to. Tonight he played the trombone in the school band, his cheeks puffing comically with each blow. The jury is out on his sexuality, but I like his face.

'Maybe,' I say, wanting to be mysterious and cryptic like Charley can be. My natural personality takes over. 'I just feel like … like it's all so forced, you know? Like I just want to be an adult and have all this weird, awkward time behind me. Like, do you think it's cool to let a guy know he's your first kiss – or do you act like you've been kissing guys for ages?'

'Mm, good question. I think the second thing.'

I can sense my mom switching off the lights in the main house behind us, making the stars suddenly seem brighter. I search for a shooting star, eager for a sign.

'But, like, you don't want to seem, like, slutty or anything …' I say. 'At the same time I don't want to seem like a total pleb. Know what I mean? What was your strategy with Tom?'

'I didn't really … it just, he just did it.'

'Do you think you'll sleep with him?'

'Like *sleep* sleep, or have sex?'

'Both …'

'I'm not sure yet …'

'Hey, Charley?'

'Mm?'

'What do you think happens when we die?'

Charley's soft snore is the only reply.

# SEVEN YEARS AGO

## Franky

*Skiathos, Greece*

'I'm Charley. This is Franky,' she says, giving me a shove.

'Hey,' he says.

*This is it,* I think. *This is what love at first sight feels like.* For someone in advertising I should probably know better. Such signals are usually a trick of the light. There's the warm Greek air, the sunset framing his face, the promise of an endless night with no responsibilities tomorrow. My bridesmaid duties are over. I'm free in every sense of the word. I have no doubt every woman in this bar could have similar feelings about this particular man in this particular setting with this particular drink soaking their nervous system. Nevertheless, I indulge in the fantasy. *This is it.* I think. *I am thirty-two and Prince Charming has finally arrived.* Another Capetonian in Greece: what are the chances?!

'I'm Nick.' His hand is dry and warm. He holds mine for a beat longer than necessary. 'This is my girlfriend, Tatianna.' She wipes a hand dampened by her cocktail on her dress before offering it to me.

'Hello!'

This is not the first time I've found myself in this situation.

When I was in college, more often than I care to admit *I* was the other woman. This is how the story went: I'd meet someone, we'd kiss, maybe more, hang out, and a few weeks later I'd see the person I now thought was my burgeoning boyfriend *out with someone else.* He'd give me a meaningful look and introduce me to his actual girlfriend, and I would nod and shake hands or hug, compliment something she was wearing. These encounters always made me feel dirty, illicit and stupid. Was I incapable of determining a real boyfriend from one who was already taken? Charley and Sebastian – to whom

I always exaggerated the anecdote – blamed the boy in question for leading me on, but secretly, I always knew it was me who was at fault. Was I not girlfriend material? In my desperation not to get hurt, was I playing it a little *too* cool?

'So nice to meet you,' I say to the woman with the drink. 'I love your necklace!'

'Thanks!' she says. She sounds foreign. Her hair is like Charley's, thick and full. She's wearing a thin cotton dress over a luminous bikini. Charley has her attention, in the throes of a story I've heard many times before.

'So, you lot have been doing the wedding thing?' says Nick. 'Till death do you part,' he smiles, looking only at me.

'Oh, I wasn't the bride,' I say, feeling my cheeks redden against my sunburnt skin. 'That's Charley.' I look over his shoulder to see Charley reaching the climax of her anecdote, the punchline moments away. They both run their fingers through their blonde hair as she talks. One of them is mimicking the other.

'And you. Are you … on honeymoon?' I say, fact-finding. He laughs from deep inside himself.

'No, we're not married. She's just a fling,' he says.

I'm taken aback, not sure if he's being serious or doing that thing couples who've been together for a long time do, joke about divorce and breaking up only because it couldn't be further from the truth. I laugh awkwardly and hope my reaction covers both possibilities.

'So, what do you do in Cape Town, Franky?' he says, his beer paused below his lips.

'I'm a copywriter. Advertising?' I add, hoping I don't need to explain the intricacies of what I'm finding to be an increasingly unrewarding career.

'So you're good with words.' He tilts his head to the side.

'I can be,' I say. I straighten my shoulders. *Is this flirting?* I've been wrong so many times before.

'And you're … Wait, let me guess …' I say.

'I'm a structural engineer,' he offers. 'Boring, I know.'

'You're good with … stability,' I say.

'I can be.' He smiles and I find myself wanting to cry.

The next morning, a text from an unknown number: *See you back in Cape Town?*

'What do you think that means?' I ask Charley. We're in the queue to board the plane. The airport is hot and dusty.

'Let it be recorded …' she says, '*I* gave him your number.'

'He has a girlfriend!' I say. *Not that that's ever stopped you before* hangs in the air between us. Charley raises her eyebrows at me, links her arm with Seb's.

There is no one to help me heave my bag onto the conveyor belt. Seb and Charley are whispering in each other's ears, kissing each other on the nose, oblivious.

'You're overweight,' says the Greek ground-staff member in front of me.

*How very dare you,* I think. I haul the bag off the conveyor belt and wheel it to the corner of the room. I lean against the cool of the wall, seat myself on the smooth floor tiles. The zip of my bag surrenders as I open it. Rifling through its contents, I think, *What can I leave behind?* Everything's so heavy. I need to feel lighter. I pause my repacking and retrieve my phone.

*Not if I see you first,* I reply.

# NOW

## Franky

*Newlands*

My mother's car has died and resuscitation seems unlikely. It's almost as old as I am. We're in an unremarkable parking lot watching a team of high-vis-clad parking attendants attempt to push the Merc off the road and into a more suitable resting place. The men shout instructions at each other in French. *DRC*, I think. 'Merci beaucoup!' I shout. My mother's eyes are misted.

'Well, that's that then,' she says, handing me the now worthless keys.

The tow-truck driver arrives, grunts in our direction and begins the slow process of winching the car onto his truck. The clunk and grind of the machinery remind me of a coffin being lowered into the ground in reverse.

'I picked you up from ballet in that car,' sniffs my mother. 'All those school discos.'

'That rave in the warehouse where you fetched me and Charley at four in the morning and we left glitter all over the seats,' I offer. It seems fitting we give this car a send-off, a eulogy of sorts. I wrap my arm around my mother's small shoulders as we watch the Merc's final ascent onto the flatbed. Windscreen wipers like sad eyebrows. One headlight flickers on and off, as though offering us its own tearful goodbye.

My mother sighs, 'Oh, well. I suppose I always knew this day would come.'

'Don't worry, Mom. You know Nick's into cars. He'll find you a new one. He'll get it sorted.'

'Oh please! A new car? You must be joking! I have a better idea … How about you give me your car, and Nick can help you buy a new one? I'll pay you, of course.'

My mother and I are not car people. Cars are functional, mostly hazardous, and in no way reflect our personalities or our tastes. And yet, this car, this burgundy relic from the Eighties with its mournful front lights, feels so connected to us, like a faithful pet. Dependable. A one-way relationship, doomed to a short life. The car and the dog know nothing of mortality, the brevity of their allotted time on earth. Wouldn't that be a blessing?

'How will you be paying?' says the tow-truck driver between puffs on his cigarette. 'This thing insured?' Thing. There it is: just a thing.

'My daughter will pay on the internet,' says my mother, raising her chin and flicking her fringe.

Nick insists on a brand-new car. I protest, but he says it will be best for the baby. He's excited. I find myself pretending to be interested so as not to offend him. What I want is for him to choose the car and hand it to me. What I'd like is to not have a car at all. I'd prefer to be driven everywhere if possible. I'm most often terrified behind the wheel. The thought of strapping a small child to the inside of this machine and joining a stream of traffic makes my muscles seize. I'm quite certain I will need to be accompanied on all journeys involving me and our child.

Luckily, I'm reaching the point where I will technically no longer be allowed to drive. 'Just sit in it,' says Nick, his eyes shining. 'Smooth, right? Can you feel the suspension?' I nod and smile in the places I think he wants me to, my mind wandering always to my pregnancy, to Charley. Will the baby come out all right? Will I come out all right? Will we all still be here in a day, a week, a year?

# NOW

## Franky

*Claremont*

'How are you doing?'

'My wife died. How are you?'

The dark humour is wearing thin. I have ulterior motives for calling Seb. One is to ascertain that the private investigator has not yet made any connections between Adam's accident and Charley's.

*It won't bring her back,* my mother is fond of saying. She hugs me tightly when we have these conversations, tells me things like Charley's with my father, they're having a laugh up in Heaven. I smile and sniff and shake my head. The tears become a laugh, and I breathe in and thank the universe I am alive. This latest call with Seb is short and stilted. He's distracted, says he'll call me back.

I park my new car and count my breaths, scanning the footwell for a discarded paper bag. There is none. The phone call with Seb was meant to be my distraction. Now I must go and face my own moment of truth.

'Are you sure you don't want to know the sex?' The sonographer is petite. A henna tattoo unfurls like a tiny creeper on her cold hands.

'Absolutely,' I say, assuming the position. 'I just want to know it's healthy and that I'm doing all the right things.' She rubs blue gel across my expanding belly. I consciously widen my nostrils to accept the air-conditioned air.

Nick arrives flustered. 'Sorry I'm late. Did I miss anything?' He takes a seat on an uncomfortable-looking chair, holds my hand and watches the black screen to my left, as though he doesn't want to miss the start of a film.

When the screen flickers to life, Nick squeezes my hand, never taking his eyes off the scan. I'm disappointed. I can see the slightest outline of a profile, etched in white, possibly a leg – it looks like every other scan of a baby I've ever seen. I feel desperately homogeneous and deeply disconnected, but I make the appropriate noises for Nick's sake.

The baby is healthy, we are told. This after the sonographer showed us a hastily scribbled graph that illustrated a cliff edge in women over thirty-five: the likelihood of problems for both mother and child. I can tell she is practised at drawing this diagram upside down. I'm thirty-nine but I'll be fine, she assures us when she sees the look of dread on my face. I can't help but imagine Charley going through all of this, twice no less. Had she told me about these experiences in any detail? Had I listened with half an ear, not taking anything in that had no direct bearing on my life at the time? I'm longing to talk to her, to ask her questions, to get her insights. The tears that come are for Charley, but Nick and the sonographer will assume they are for the *melon* on the monitor.

The baby's tiny heartbeat can be heard through speakers. A thick and roaring sound; too fast, I think, before verbalising as much.

'No, it's completely normal,' says the sonographer with a well-rehearsed smile. 'It's no heartbeat we want to avoid!'

I think now of Gabby, of her in this situation hearing no heartbeat and feeling what she must have felt. The tears come faster now, although I am silent and Nick and the sonographer are absorbed by the screen. I think of Gabby's devotion to not-talking-about-it. When it became clear she and her boyfriend had broken up, I felt certain she would look for another job, a clean slate. But, quite the contrary, she threw herself into her work – and her social media presence.

After the scan, Nick takes me for lunch at the café opposite the clinic. He holds my hand on the table, only shifting it when the waitress asks if she can remove our menus.

'I like the name Dylan,' he says.

'And if it's a girl?'

'Dylan can be a girl's name too,' he says. 'Like Franky, or Charley.'

'Very clever,' I say.

He holds my gaze. 'I love you, Franky.'

'I love you too.'

The phone buzzes on the table, Seb's name on the screen. Nick rolls his eyes. I consider not answering the phone – I want to stay in this bubble with this man and this *melon* that may one day answer to the name Dylan – but I feel the burn as my oesophagus constricts, pull back my chair and answer the phone.

'They've found something,' says Seb, without preamble.

‘Found what?’ My pulse quickens as I pace the clinic parking lot.

‘The private investigator, he’s found something. Can you come here? Today? Like, maybe now? My mom has the kids and the investigator thinks it could be useful to talk to you.’

‘To me?!’ I say, my voice rising, my hand instinctively on my belly – protective. I must stay calm, I think, imagining the baby as a misshapen sea sponge, absorbing the cortisol in my system. Nick is standing up, he’s sucking on a mint, waving at me, pointing at his car – oblivious. ‘Okay, Seb, let me chat to Nick. We’ll be over as soon as we can.’

There’s silence on the line. I can tell he’s trying to figure out a way to convince me that Nick doesn’t need to be there for our conversation. After a beat, I say, ‘Seb?’ and he says, ‘Just get here soon, okay?’

# NOW

## Franky

*Llandudno*

I remind myself that in thrillers, the suspect can only be one of the characters already established. In life, killers are random strangers, indoctrinated terrorists, abused victims looking to abuse the first person to cross their path. Right place, wrong time.

'So, he didn't give you any clue as to what the investigator found?'

'None,' I say. 'Should we call Adam? Maria?'

'No, I'll handle it, okay? Please, love, leave the talking to me. Whatever happens, leave the talking to me.' He knows my tendency to externalise. My philosophy is: if it's out in the open, it can be aired and made good. The only way I have been able to keep this secret so long is that I've managed to convince myself of Adam's innocence, especially once we found out about the Rohypnol or GHB, or whatever drug Adam might have been exposed to thanks to Susie Winchester and her Tinder date. The big bad monster *might* be some lawyer named Shane, who has since vanished from Instagram, and, seemingly, the country.

Try as I might, I don't hold this Shane character responsible for Charley's death either, but the idea that he *could* be responsible is much easier to swallow than the possibility that Nick's best friend murdered my best friend, or that Charley took her own life. No, these thoughts are not to be indulged.

'Let's not jump to any conclusions,' says Nick, holding my hand. He's driving faster than usual. My car remains underground, beneath the doctors' suites – no doubt racking up an eye-watering parking ticket. Nick wants to get to Seb's and get this over with. I am hoping for traffic so we have time to discuss an actual game plan. So far, the plan is for me to stay silent, which Seb will spot, because silence is not something I'm known for.

As we reach the intersection before Charley's road, or rather Seb's road, I find myself wondering what the PI will look like. Will he be wearing a trench coat and a thick, soup-stained, polyester tie? Will he own a pair of binoculars? I shake my head, dislodging the random thoughts filling my brain to suppress the other thought, which is *Fuck! We're going to get done for this! We're all going to jail! Jesus! Fuck! Fuck! I will have a baby in jail!*

Seb answers the door. His shoulder-length hair is still wet, face pink and fragrant as I lean in for a one-cheeked kiss and a half hug. Nick gives him a hug too, a confident slap on the back, and we're inside the oversized front door, inside the glass box.

'Can I get you guys something to drink?' he says, walking through to the expansive kitchen; views of the ocean stretch out beyond. A man is seated at the kitchen counter. He's wearing a bullet-proof vest and combat boots. A walkie-talkie sits on the counter. He has a strong handshake and smells vaguely of cigarettes and a deodorant a younger version of himself might wear.

'I'm Jan,' he says with an Afrikaans accent, moving to shake Nick's hand in turn. I hope our clammy hands don't give us away.

'Jan works part-time for Llandudno Armed Response, part-time as a PI,' offers Seb.

'Right!' I say too loudly.

'How far along are you?' ventures Jan.

'Oh, I'm six months today,' I say, terrified of blurting something Tourettes-like during the small talk. The surface of the kitchen counter is marble, veined. I trace a vein with my index finger.

Seb slides a glass of water in front of me. I'm trying to decide if this is a good or bad omen. What does he know? Is he looking at me differently? I can't look at him, so I continue my fascination with the countertop. Jan is flicking through a fat black folder of plastic sleeves, diagrams, photographs, scribbled notes, receipts. I wonder if the evidence he is about to present is some sort of fingerprint, Nick's or mine, or Adam's – something linking us to the scene. *We weren't there.* I remind myself. *We weren't there.*

Jan has found what he's looking for. It's a photograph. Nick's hand is on my back, consoling me as if I'm a child. I'm confident the emotion he and I display is consistent with losing a friend, and not guilt or complicity.

'Here we go,' says Jan, pulling a glossy picture from the folder, placing it on the marble countertop. The picture shows Charley's silver Porsche Cayenne, concertinaed against the torso of the oak tree. The light of the camera's flash bounces off the metal of the car. I find myself looking for Charley in the image, and I'm disappointed and relieved in equal measure when there's no obvious evidence of her.

Jan points to the corner of the image, slides another photograph over the first. There's a silent understanding that this is a zoomed-in image. *Zoom in and enhance,* I think, remembering every crime thriller I've ever watched.

Seb has his hands in the pockets of his jeans and is rocking slightly back and forth, soothing himself. I try not to look at him. *No eye contact,* I think. Nick's hand has stopped moving on my back.

'What you can see here,' says Jan, 'is a footprint.'

Nick breaks the silence. 'The photographer's footprint?'

'No, the cops all wear the same shoes. This is not consistent with anyone who was at the scene. And the footprints are facing away from the car.'

*Charley's footprints,* I think. She was a size seven, sometimes eight. We could never share shoes. I had my mother's small feet.

Seb can no longer contain himself. 'Someone was in the car with Charley that night. Someone fled the scene of her accident. Someone was in the passenger seat.' He is almost triumphant with the accusation.

'Fleeing a scene,' says Jan, 'is illegal.'

I nod, lift the glass to my mouth and drink.

Nick says, 'So, Charley had a passenger in the car with her that night?'

'That's what these images seem to indicate.'

'But couldn't they be the prints of someone who came to see the accident, a neighbour or passer-by?' says Nick. He squeezes my shoulder and I feel his relief and confusion flood my veins.

'No, then you would see prints in both directions. These only move away from the scene. We've applied through the courts for access to the car so we can get prints – try and find a match, establish who this passenger may have been.'

'A hijacking?' says Nick, looking from Jan to Seb.

'It's possible.' says Jan. 'But the security camera from the driveway shows the deceased leaving alone.' *The deceased.* My mind rejects the words as a descriptor for my friend.

'What's more likely,' says Seb, through clenched teeth, 'is that some fucking dickhead she knew left my wife to die in her car.'

'What size are the prints?' I ask.

Nick squeezes harder on my shoulder.

'Size eight,' says Jan, pressing play on a recording device I hadn't noticed before. Nick's hand is clamped on my shoulder, the heat of it boring into my muscles.

'Can you confirm where you were that night?' asks Jan.

'We were at Vintage Rose,' I say, making my voice even. 'It's a club in town.'

'We came home around midnight,' says Nick. 'We only heard about Charley the next morning.' The recording device seems to pulse on the marble surface, its small red light laser-like in my periphery.

'I need you to tell us what you know,' says Seb, catching my eye.

'I …'

'How would Frank know more than you, Seb?' says Nick, keeping his tone slightly too conversational, in my opinion.

'She must have been seeing someone,' says Seb, looking out towards the sea, hands still wedged in his pockets. He turns his head slowly, looks me straight in the eye. I am now one with the marble counter.

'You were her best friend, Frank. You must have known who she was seeing. There's no point keeping it a secret any more. I know … there was someone and I'm trusting *you* to tell me who it was.'

# NOW

## Sebastian

*Constantia Nek*

Franky's eyes darted around the room. She touched her ears, her nose, the sides of her wrist. Nick was unblinking, faux concerned, his Adam's apple bouncing. I've studied this shit – I know what bad actors look like.

Jan excused himself after it became clear Franky wasn't going to say anything in front of Nick. I knew she knew. *She's always known!* That's why she's been acting weird. It has nothing to do with pregnancy hormones or some tidal wave of grief. She has something to hide, and I'm onto her.

So today I am meeting her in private. I need to control the anger that has swept through me like a veld fire, threatening every part of my sanity in its wake. I can feel my personality crumble under the weight of my new knowledge. My wife – my first and only real love – must have been seeing someone behind my back.

Did I know this on some level? Did this thought enter my mind at some point when I pondered where she could have been that night? No, it did not. There was nothing – ever – to suggest her unfaithfulness. I was a fool. There is a hard, glowing lump of anger burning, just for Charley. She did this. She left us, one way or another. Her actions brought us here. Fuck her.

I've had my chances. The casting couch works both ways. You wouldn't believe how many women approached me when they found out I was some sort of gatekeeper for their careers. Me, a lowly commercials director, who made ads for toilet paper and washing powder starring animals and children. I'm the guy who has yet to make the noir film for which I will forever be lauded. Let's be honest – at this rate, I'll never make a film. I'd hoped it would premiere at Sundance – even though the film itself is just a few scribbled pages in the purple notebook Charley bought me last Christmas. Writing makes my fingers hurt; I prefer to type. She should have known that. If she really loved me, she would have known that.

I'm meeting Franky on the mountain. We're going for a hike. This is strategic: I am removing the need for eye contact in an attempt to get to the truth. Walking loosens people up metaphorically and physically. I have no idea if she's told Nick about our meeting or not. Needless to say, if he shows up, I'll make my excuses and leave.

Don't get me wrong, Nick and I get on. He's not a *bad* guy, but he's … for want of a better word, boring. Franky and Charley work in advertising; even Nick's best friend Adam has a job that involves some sort of design. His wife's a sculptor … but engineering? There's no room for creativity there. When we're out to dinner, the six of us, Nick drones on about his projects while my ears try to tune in to what the girls are saying. I've always been more comfortable in the presence of women. I can't talk sport – especially not golf. I'm not interested in the stock market, and although I do know how to change a tyre, I'm not the type of guy who would volunteer his services if he saw a stranger in need on the side of the road. Nick is. Nick's the guy who's practically *searching* for people on the side of the road to rescue.

I turn off Constantia Nek circle. This is the first time I'm forced to use the valley road where Charley's accident happened. Usually, I go the other way around the mountain.

Thankfully, the circle is a good three kilometres away from the spot. I will avoid that for now. I have enough to deal with.

It's warm, unseasonably so; it should be cooler, but summer is holding on, defiant. There is not a breath of wind. Everything feels suspended and lit from within. A man in a yellow hi-vis vest navigates cars to makeshift parking spaces, invisibly demarcated on the pine-needled ground. With enthusiastic hand gestures he instructs drivers how to negotiate rocks and exposed tree roots. He makes eye contact and nods – a silent contract. He will protect our cars from theft and he expects to be paid handsomely upon our return. I see him direct Franky and her new car over a root. The vw wobbles before coming to a stop. Small scratches on her front bumper remind me she's a less-than-competent driver.

Her belly touches my torso as we hug awkwardly. She smells of sunscreen. She's wearing black leggings and a grey sports vest that strains under the pull of her expanding midriff. The rest of her body is still slim, still the same old Franky, but for her breasts, which I studiously ignore.

Once we've dispensed with the pleasantries, she says, 'I told Nick I was meeting a friend. It's been a while since I've been up here.' She puffs as we begin the sharp incline to the contour path. Her hair is pulled back. Fine pieces soon escape. She attempts to blow them away before deciding to take down her ponytail and retie it again – a nervous tic. She needs to keep her hands moving.

Green metal signs explain details of the mountain routes; letters set in a sharp white font form words and warnings. Tourists are studying them, giving themselves away. I wonder how Franky and I look to them – another expectant couple, out for some exercise, testing the sound of baby names, planning the future of our unborn child. We could not possibly be about to discuss my real wife's infidelity or the gory circumstances of her death.

'How are the kids?'

I'm instantly annoyed by the way she says this. I am done with the small talk. I play along until we are on the less populated path around the mountain. She is moving faster than Charley would have when she was six months pregnant. She seems just as anxious to get to the straight path as I am.

'Shade or sun?' she says, as we reach a fork.

'Shade.' I point to the downward track. There are fewer people here than there are moving up the mountain on the sunny side. For a while, it's just our footsteps and our breath and the crunch of other people's footsteps, the occasional kid whining, *Daddy, it's too far, I'm too tired.* And then, as the groups of hikers thin out, she says, 'Okay!'

It's the start of a sentence or an affirmation of something, but she doesn't continue. I decide to start with something simple, even though I'm desperate to begin my interrogation.

'Jan says he's pulled a list.'

'List?'

'Of accidents from that night, on the same road. Can you believe there were three accidents around the same time as Charley's?'

'Oh,' she says.

'Yah, it's taken him so bloody long because he had to get a court order together, and two of the accidents were actually in Hout Bay – and it seems the Hout Bay police don't spend much time cross referencing with Constantia police, which is technically known as Diep River police, which makes things even more complicated; I mean, they're right next to each other for Christ's sake, the road goes through both suburbs, you'd think … Frank, are you okay?'

I've only just become aware that Franky has stopped. I've continued walking, thinking she was next to me. I turn back and see her leaning against a tree, one hand on her belly. She's breathing audibly through her nose. I take advantage of her apparent vulnerability.

'Was she seeing someone?' I say.

'Seb,' she says, like she almost doesn't have breath for the rest of the sentence, 'I *honestly* don't know.'

'Bullshit.' My heartbeat is fast and angry. 'You know!'

She starts to walk again, stumbles over a tangled root. The ground becomes mud as we approach a small waterfall. A pink-cheeked couple wearing matching bandannas drink from cupped hands. Their Labrador (also bandanna-ed) pants furiously. Once we're out of earshot, Franky says, 'Seb, Charley and I talked about a lot of stuff, but I swear to you, she never mentioned another guy. I wish I could give you more …'

'But you won't.'

'There isn't anything more, Sebastian!'

This is not how I saw this conversation going. When she uses my full name I feel like she morphs into my mom or one of my sisters.

'All she used to say to me is, you were the best thing that ever happened to her. You could be … challenging sometimes, when it came to work …'

I watch my sneakers tread the orange soil. I can feel her gaze on the side of my face like a heat lamp 'She loved you, Seb. *Only* you. You have to know that.'

'What about exes?' I say. 'The guy she dated before me … the one with the white-blond hair.'

'Rowan?' she laughs. 'God, Sebastian that was, like, twenty years ago. He's a nobody – a random guy she dated for five minutes. Before you, there were … a handful of guys, and they were all meaningless, you know that. You were her … everything.'

I can hear emotion scrape the last word of her sentence. I'm done with supplication.

'We only slept together on weekends,' I say.

'So?' she says, looking towards the horizon. 'Isn't that what most couples are like?'

'She was always tired, moaning about call times and pretending to be asleep. I thought she was just lazy, but now I know there was someone else.'

'Seb, do you hear yourself? She was tired! She worked a lot. You put pressure on her!'

'Pressure! How?'

'Pressure, with work. She told me you always wanted everything to be perfect and sometimes you were a hard taskmaster.'

'Me? She *wanted* to do all the work.'

'She did, but she … she thought you expected it of her, that you'd somehow lose respect for her if she couldn't pull off what you wanted. She was a fixer, so if something went wrong, she felt compelled to fix it for you.'

She is breathless now. I recognise the truth in what she's saying and my heart burns.

I stop. She walks a few paces ahead. I walk faster to catch up. The trees seem to rise up from below us. A bird of prey circles above. No other hikers are in sight now. An ominous green sign to our left says, *DON'T hike/cycle/run ALONE. Stay in a group!* There have been stabbings up here, literal daylight robbery. The usual suspects are teens, high on something other than the altitude. Once their victim is incapacitated by their crude weapon of choice, they make off with a single cellphone or a crumpled hundred-rand note (no doubt earmarked for an after-hike coffee or two). Their victims are left to bleed until another hiker finds them and calls the police.

My breath feels hot. Franky stops, hands on hips. The sun is blazing now, all hint of shade left behind. She is sweating. I am too.

'Seb, I …' she starts. 'I do know … something. But I …'

I lunge towards her. She tastes of salt and peppermint. She stands dead still, not moving, not kissing me back. She is not Charley and there is a small and strange shape wedged between us – three people in this tryst. She pulls away and wipes her mouth with the back of her hand; in her eyes there is pity, mixed with fear.

Here, on this mountain, I have reached a new low. My wife is not coming back. I will probably never find out what happened to her or what she was thinking that night. I will never speak to her again, or hold her, or laugh at something with her, or look at her over the heads of our children. I will never lie next to her and tickle her back, listen to her moan with pleasure. 'It's better than sex,' she'd say, half insult, half compliment. I will never hear her voice on the end of a phone, asking me to pick up takeaways on the way home from the edit suite. I will never look up to find her staring at me while I scamp out a story board, chewing on my pencil, imagining my secret world. She will never look up at me, or sideways at me, or straight at me again. She is gone. This is the giant full stop. It is so obvious but still so incomprehensible: death is *The End*.

Franky turns, walks back in the other direction. I try to catch up, reaching for her shoulder. She shakes me off. We fall into step. I concentrate on the ground beneath my feet. The couple with the Labrador pass us; they smile in recognition. Their expression changes as they clock Franky's face – her angry tears.

'Frank, please,' I say. 'I'm sorry. I didn't mean that. I didn't mean to freak you out. I was just testing … I just feel confused and you *know* me. You *know* me – maybe not as well as she did, but you *know* me.'

Franky stops and whips around to face me. 'Yes, Seb, I know you. I know you will never, ever let this go. I know you want blood. You want revenge. You want someone to pay for what happened to her – to *you*. You can't fathom that something like this could happen to *you*. Well, guess what? This kind of shit happens all the time! My dad died of a heart attack. Charley's dad topped himself. Adam's dad *and* Nick's dad both died of fucking cancer. Gabby's unborn baby died, because … because who knows why?! Shit fucking happens, Seb – and there is nothing you or I can do to undo it.'

'Who's Gabby?' I say.

She sighs, starts walking again. 'Never mind. The point I'm making is: Charley was a fatalist. She wasn't religious, but she had a fucking memento mori tattooed behind her ear. She understood the concept *We must all die*. Does it really matter how or why, or under what circumstances? What does it matter, Seb? Please … what does it matter?'

She's properly crying now, and as I spy a group of (possibly German) tourists walking towards us, I try my luck and pull her in for a hug. I feel her tears and mucus wet my T-shirt. She's hiccupping, breathing unevenly like a child in distress. I breathe into her hair and hold her as I would Katie if she'd skinned her knee. The German tourists give me a sympathetic wave. I give them what I hope resembles a 'pregnant women, hey?' shrug. Their luminous trainers crunch the path, incoherent conversation floats through the air.

'I'm sorry, Seb,' she says to my shoulder, her voice muffled. 'I'm really, really sorry. There's nothing I can tell you that's going to make you happy right now.'

'I know,' I say to her scalp, and the realisation hits me like a brick to the head.

*Depression,* I think. I didn't want to invite you back in, but it looks like you're making yourself at home anyway.

# NOW

## Sebastian

*Llandudno*

Joy is here Monday to Friday mornings to look after Leo and get Katie ready for school. Technically I could do this myself now, but the routine, while both calming and maddening, forces me to at least pretend to be productive.

Mid-mornings are the worst. I've made it out of bed; now what? I'm in my study – the room earmarked to enhance my creative process. There are sprawling views of our expansive lawn and the ocean beyond. The grass is almost knee-high and the pool is green. Sunlight sparkles on the sea. Tiny black dots I know to be surfers slide across the undersides of waves as they break. A hoover hums. Clara is here to clean. I should be grateful, but today her scrubbing and scraping and opening and closing of doors feels particularly annoying.

Joy has been here since 7 a.m., letting herself in with her own key so I don't have to suffer the pleasantries.

I am avoiding my children. This fact hovers in my consciousness. I've never considered myself an especially competent parent, but Charley's death has set me back even further. I am not trained to help them through this. Charley's mom insisted they see a play therapist once a week. *What about me?* I wanted to shout. *Could a play therapist help me?* Anything's preferable to Wendy and her pop psychology. I feel detached, unhinged, out of order. Charley, if she were here, would be appalled by my lack of parental interaction. This act of defiance is my last attempt at attention seeking – as though if I am a terrible enough parent, Charley will be forced to come back from the grave and help me. I need you, Charley – I need *you*, not them. *They'll be fine*, I tell her ghost. Their pain will be delayed. Years from now they'll blame everything on their mother's absence. I will never be able to plug that hole.

When we worked together on that first toilet-paper commercial, I remember the agency's chief strategist handing me a folder of research about child development. It was some form of post-rationalisation for using cute kids in the commercial. The research showed that a child's adorableness is a survival strategy. Their chubby cheeks, smooth skin, toothless grins, even their natural powdery scent trigger human caregiving behaviours. And what could be more caring than three-ply toilet paper? I'm confident Katie's blonde curls and Leo's button nose will trigger someone to appropriately care for them. To get the comfort and solace *I* crave, I will need to access some other primal pheromone – or dig deeper into my pockets.

Life is a farce. There is no colour, no flavour. I am sentenced to live the day before she died over and over again. My mind is eroded with each recollection so I am sure I am adding or omitting something that will, one day, wake me at midnight – like the night I lost her.

One minute she was sleeping next to me, then something woke her – something that didn't wake me. As far as I know, the kids slept through this too. For reasons I must now spend the rest of my life searching for, she climbed into her car and drove away from the sanctuary of our Glass Castle. Somewhere on that journey she picked someone up and crashed into a tree – another mystery I am compelled to solve. Her death was caused by injuries sustained in the crash, several wounds to the head, shards of glass embedded in her brilliant mind; her face was almost untouched. I imagine her sleeping peacefully on the airbag, because it's easier than imagining anything else. And now I know, when all of this happened ... someone was next to her. Someone watched this scene play out before they ran. All I know for sure is this: they ran because they had something to hide.

I haven't worked in five months. There is no creativity, no reason to be grateful. I'd been so excited about the Mercedes commercial and now I can't muster enthusiasm for anything. All of our planning came to nothing. The job was cancelled, insurance kicked in. Another production company took the gig. Everyone lost money. I lost that, *and* my wife.

I marvel that people can get up and *do stuff* every day. They keep going, day after day after day, living their pointless lives, spending pointless money on pointless things. Cleaning houses and riding waves to nowhere until it's time to leave this world for the next.

I remember when we made an offer on this house. It was just after we'd shot our twentieth commercial together – Marybelle Cheese. A strange family had sat in our soon-to-be kitchen – a pretend family: twenty-six-year-old black male model, thirty-year-old white childless ballet dancer and two children who looked like they might be the product of this fictional union. They laughed and bit into cheese (spitting it out discreetly when the cameras weren't rolling), until I told them we had everything we needed, and then they were gone – back to their real lives, away from the lie.

The house had charmed us, its shape, its limpidity (Charley's word). It said everything she wanted to say about herself. It was cool and wild, but also dazzling and sharp. It was the ultimate symbol of success. Of course we were paying it off, so we'd have to make many more commercials before we were mortgage-free – but in all other respects we were living the dream. And now, I was living a nightmare.

Downstairs, Joy is making Leo laugh. I'm grateful for that sound, if slightly jealous that I don't have the capacity to elicit the same response from him any more. I used to be the dad who made the funny voices, but today – most days – I struggle to find humour in anything.

Franky called last night. I didn't answer. I'm too ashamed. My face flushes when I think of it. I'm shocked and embarrassed, and afraid, too, that she'll tell Nick, and he won't wipe my strange attempt at connection away like she did. He'll act. Nick is a man of action.

The fog of depression is all around me. There's still a hint of residual anger, not for the person or thing or God who took Charley away, but for Charley herself. She left me. This is still true, no matter which way you look at it.

Someone once told me: Erich Fromm, the German philosopher who first declared that love is a decision, was married three times – clear evidence that we are not bound by our choices. We choose something, and then inevitably that thing is taken off the menu. We are forced to choose again. I don't want to choose. I don't want another wife, another mother for my children, another producer. I want Charley back. And then, it comes to me …

'Remember!' I say out loud.

'Did you call me?' shouts Joy. I run down the stairs like a child on Christmas morning. 'The gardener! His name is Remember!'

She looks at me quizzically. 'The Zimbabwean?' she says, cocking a painted-on eyebrow.

'Yes!' I scroll through my phone and find his number under *Remember,* a leaf emoji. Why hadn't I thought to search for that?

*The number you have dialled does not exist.*

'Fuck!' I say.

'Goes quack!' says Leo, triumphant.

The guilt I usually feel in these moments is not there. There is only a strange and sudden desire for action. I open the sliding door from the kitchen and head to the bottom of the garden. The grass is still wet and I can feel my tracksuit pants slick against my knees. I pull open the door of the shed – a room I have never been in – and I see it: the lawnmower, slightly rusted and archaic-looking. I retrieve my phone from my pocket and google *How to start a lawnmower.* After a few fumbled attempts, I hear the roar and my angry heart pounds with the thrill of it. I slide my phone into my pocket and I push.

The next three hours of my life are spent in the pure pursuit of taming the garden whose fictionalised renderings I once agonised over. The smells of cut grass, sea air and petrol fill my nostrils. Everything reminds me of the days I used to ride a Vespa, Charley clinging to me like a barnacle. I'd felt so in control, so supported. I feel the weakness of my muscles as I push and push and push. Up the incline, down the incline. I am only vaguely aware of Clara hanging out washing, Leo shouting, *'What you doing, Daddy?!'* over the thrum of the engine.

There is another euphoric memory there too. The sound of a distant lawnmower reminds me of summer, of studying for my final exams in my parents' old house in Newlands. It's the sound of hard work that will end in a sense of accomplishment, a long holiday, a promise.

After the grass I tackle the pool. I unearth the blue-and-white pool-cleaning implements, feeling my skin stretch against my muscles as I work. It's a cold day, but I am sweating. Dead leaves are fished out of the filter and thrown into the bushes. I rake up the grass clippings in green plastic bags, carry them to the front of the house for someone else to take away. This is the most activity I have done in three months – aside from my ill-fated hike up Constantia Nek. My lungs feel tight and alive.

'Good job!' giggles Clara, now sipping a mug of tea and watching me as if I'm a street performer.

'Thank you!' I shout back, surprised that I'm genuinely taken with her praise. Inside I make myself a sandwich, pour a glass of water and think about taking a shower. Joy has made some sort of vanilla cake. Its smell radiates like one of the scented candles Charley was so fond of lighting.

I watch as Leo climbs onto a kitchen-counter stool. I plant a sweaty kiss on his head, hoping it will convey the depth of my love into his developing mind. He shakes me off.

'It's Joy's birthday today, Daddy! She's twenty-seven!' He holds up a selection of fingers to approximate the number.

'Very old!' Joy laughs.

'Oh, my word, Joy,' I say, 'I had no idea! Happy birthday!' I wish I knew the Malawian phrase. 'You shouldn't be working on your birthday …'

'I always work on my birthday!' she says, with another one of her trademark laughs.

'Well, I insist you go home early today, then,' I say.

'It's okay, I'm babysitting tonight anyway.'

'Oh, really?' I say, draining my glass.

'Yes, for Miss Charley's friend, Miss Maria.'

I resist the urge to explain that Charley was never *friends* with Maria – 'acquaintances' would be a more accurate term. 'I didn't know you did work for other families.' My face reddens at my own arrogance. I had no idea Joy wasn't exclusively ours.

'No, it's only now and then,' she says. 'The last time was …' she stops herself, turns to lift Leo from his precarious position on the stool. When she looks up at me, her eyes are wet. Leo's tiny hand appears luminous on her dark cheek.

'Last time was the night before your wife …' She trails off, not wanting to finish the sentence.

'Joy,' I say, trying to change the mood, 'let me make you one of my special coffees – for your birthday.'

She smiles and sniffs, and Leo says, with no emotion, 'Mommy did die.'

# NOW

## Maria

*Hout Bay*

Joy will be here at any moment. The painkillers have not yet kicked in. The present is a rope of running water I cannot hold on to. Diego has taken the bottle; I stroke his cheek, milky blue in the darkening room. I don't see my children as I saw them before. Now, I see only their murky futures and hope I will feature in them.

When last did I go on a night out? Was it Nick and Franky's anniversary? That night, I felt like a child dressed in my mother's clothing – my clothes not fitting, my clutch awkward in my grip. But tonight, I will wear my boots, jeans, a casual sweater. It's cold and I haven't the energy to put on an act.

When I tell people I was a model, they tilt their head to one side: 'Oh yes, I could *maybe* see that.' These days, it is only Adam who would brag about such things. I keep quiet and resign myself to domesticity, sometimes pretending to be a sculptor, so I seem interesting, if only to myself.

I think now of Franky, the woman who has been in my life for six years, and yet has not become my friend. How brittle and pale and sophisticated she seems. She is ten years older than me but her skin is untouched with the lines children bring. Her frame with so few curves – like mine used to be, before the pregnancies. I like the way she runs her fingers through her hair, tousling it, rubbing the top of her skull. I think this makes her look youthful and creative. She and Nick are luminous together, in control of their lives, so assured. Adam always said Nick never wanted children. Nick didn't have a happy childhood. He thought he could control the tendencies of history. My mother had been mad when I'd fallen pregnant at eighteen. But how could she complain when she herself had been pregnant with me at the same age? Children will let you down, if only by repeating your mistakes.

I wonder what I will talk to Franky about tonight. There is the obvious topic, which I want to avoid, and then there is her pregnancy. How I would love for my own mother to be here permanently to help take care of my children, like Franky's mother would. Maybe after tonight Franky and I can finally connect. Maybe then I will find the courage to discuss that night with someone other than Wendy.

'Joy's here!' shouts Adam from downstairs, as if I didn't hear the doorbell or their brief hello. Adam is impatient to go – impatient for his first drink.

# NOW

## Maria

*Constantia*

'Would you like to hear our specials?'

I force my eyes back towards the blackboard. There's an elaborate description of pork and glaze, kingklip and asparagus spears lightly tossed in goat's cheese from the Franschhoek Valley.

'So many choices!' says Franky.

My cheeks feel hot. 'I'll have the tuna,' I say, not looking up.

'We're out of tuna,' he says. I feel the smile in his voice even though I don't look at him. He is enjoying this. I sip my red wine and stare at my knife and fork. They lie like lovers inside a carefully folded napkin.

'I'll have the asparagus thing,' says Adam, not waiting for the women to order first. 'And the steak … Just bring them together.' I settle for the pork. Nick opts for steak and Franky orders the kingklip. Our waiter retreats to the fluorescent cave of the kitchen. I steal a look in his direction. He flicks a napkin over his shoulder, smooths out his waistcoat, pinches the bridge of his nose as if soothing a headache, and punches our order into a touchscreen computer. He knows I'm watching him.

There's no way I could have known he worked here. Did he tell me? My mind is always elsewhere when he's talking to me. This is the first time I've been to this restaurant. It has an Afrikaans name that doesn't sit well on my Spanish tongue. Nick made the reservation. I think of ways I can get out of here. I could excuse myself, pretend Joy has called, that there's something wrong with one of the kids. My brain is calculating solutions, possible outcomes, the future rushing towards me. I take another sip of my wine and attempt to make myself appear smaller than I am.

'I haven't even heard of this place! God, I feel so old lately,' says Franky. Nick and Adam are deep in a conversation about golf. 'How are you feeling about … everything?' she says, leaning in. She's always been the type to ask questions and not listen to the answers. Perhaps I shall try this technique myself.

'I'm okay. How are *you* feeling? You must be … seven months now?' I find people would always rather talk about themselves. Politeness is a transparent film over everything, like single-use plastic: pointless and necessary.

'Yes! Seven months this Tuesday.' She lowers her voice, looks into my eyes searching for answers. 'It's weird. Did you ever feel … disconnected when you were pregnant?'

I know what she is referring to, but I'm not as sure of the English words to express myself.

'Yes,' I say. 'But you will be fine when the baby comes. It all just happens naturally.'

I don't remind her I was just a child when Sara was born. I wasn't like the mothers I come across at playgroup, who agonise over birth plans and nursery designs. I was eighteen. Adam and I had no money. We lived with his mother; she paid for everything. No one asked me how *I* was feeling back then. All everyone's energy was focused on was how we were going to afford to look after the child and what religion it would be.

'Did you ever …' Francine starts, but before she can continue, our food arrives. I hold my breath as he places the plate of pork front in of me. Franky is oblivious.

'Did you ever … feel, like, depressed after the kids?'

'Probably,' I say. *My life is fucking depressing*, I think, but this might be too much for our first proper heart-to-heart. 'Kids, they become the centre, you know, the sun. You become the moon.'

'That's so beautiful. God, I wish I could speak another language. You're incredible. Can the children speak Spanish?'

'I try,' I say. 'But it's not easy when they don't hear it all the time. By the time they go to school they forget everything. But I will take them to Barcelona one day soon and then they will pick it up.'

'Just for a holiday?' she says.

Despite everything, I have to admit my pork is delicious. I chew with purpose, spear a slice and chase the jus around the plate before bringing the last morsel to my lips. She's anticipating my response, waiting for me to open the door to my secret life.

'Maybe,' I offer. I wipe my mouth with my napkin, registering the stain I have left behind.

'You must excuse me. I'm just going to the toilet.'

'I'll come with you!' says Franky. Her knife and fork stand to attention on her half-finished plate – a passive-aggressive message for the chef. My plans are scuppered. We walk to the bathroom together and I relieve myself in the closest stall. Franky is still talking in that rambling way of hers.

'Does breastfeeding hurt?' she asks.

'Sometimes,' I say. She clearly didn't need the toilet after all. There is only one thing she could possibly have called me away to discuss.

'How's Adam dealing with the whole thing?'

'He's fine,' I say. The flush of the toilet muffles her next question so she has to speak up.

'Isn't he worried that once Seb gets hold of that list and joins the dots, there might be … questions? Do you think we're … all …' She starts to cry. *Jesus*, I'm not equipped for this, on top of everything.

'He was not responsible,' I say in as neutral a voice as I can, washing my hands in the ridiculously small copper basin.

'He might have been,' she says. Her mascara has made patterns on her cheeks – she does have lines around her eyes, after all. I pull paper out of the dispenser, dry my hands, then offer her some.

'Franky, baby, listen – you're pregnant and you're emotional and you cannot see clearly because of this. Adam did not do anything. No one is going to get into trouble for this, okay? Nick did the right thing. You did the right thing.' I must hug her now; there is no way around this and so I do. As we hug, I feel myself soften. She will be all right, this not-quite-sister of mine. Nick has money, her mother has money – she has nothing to worry about, unlike the rest of us. She is *looking* for something to worry about.

She wipes her face with the tissue and regards herself in the mirror. I reapply my lip gloss. 'There are things about that night, that … none of us know,' I say carefully. 'Trust me, Adam was not responsible. Now, you head back to the table. I just need to call the babysitter to check on the kids. Everything will be okay; you'll see.'

'Okay,' she says. She sniffs and laughs at herself. 'Thank you, for … you know … being the voice of reason. God, you're so … wise!'

Once she's left the bathroom, I allow myself a sigh. Checking to make sure no one can see me, I make my way towards an open door that leads to an outside courtyard and the glowing orange end of a cigarette, bobbing in the darkness.

'Fancy seeing you here,' he says, blowing a cloud of smoke in my direction.

'You think this is funny?' I say, my arms folded.

'It's pretty funny.' He smiles. I clench and unclench my fists, suppressing the need to grab him around the throat. 'Have you told them yet?'

'No,' I say. 'Why would I do that?'

'To protect your estranged husband? Oh wait … he's not estranged, is he? He's just strange.' He laughs at his own joke.

'Please,' I say, 'don't do … whatever it is you're planning on doing.' I turn on my heel.

'I'll bring you the dessert menu!' he shouts after me.

I am angry, angrier than I've been in a while, and I have no one to lash out at. One thing is certain: I will need to tell Franky, before he does. God only knows what he's capable of. And Franky doesn't seem like someone who is good at keeping secrets.

# TEN YEARS AGO

## Maria

*Camps Bay*

'It's the prawns, in the paella.' I prod the glassy, grey-pink spiral with my fork. 'You see here? They're not cooked.'

'Oh, my gosh!' he says, jumping to attention. 'I am *so* sorry! Let me call the manager right away.'

I roll my eyes at Tatianna, who tells me her fish is not good either. She runs her hand through her long hair, drops her fork on her plate with a clatter and sighs. 'I knew we should have gone next door.'

'Mine's okay,' says Ayeong. In my limited experience, South Korean models make the best roommates. Germans, like Tatianna, are very direct. Dutch and French ones are not as easy to box.

The Manager Man striding towards us is taller than the waiter and meaner looking. I'm used to speaking my mind in front of my parents, but I've only been in Cape Town for three months and I worry my English will make me look stupid.

'Adam here tells me there was a problem with the paella,' says the Manager Man. He's going through the motions, shifting his feet like he needs the bathroom. He has a pen but no notepad. He clicks the pen as though preparing to stab one of us with it.

'Yes,' I say. 'The prawns are not cooked. And just so you know, it's *pa-ee-aaa.*'

'Not a problem at all, madam.' His face suggests it *is* a problem. 'Can I get you something else? Our line fish perhaps? Fish curry?'

'No, gracias. My friends and I are not happy with the food. It's not good.'

'Mine's okay,' repeats Ayeong. I widen my eyes at her. She sucks her pout into her mouth and looks away. Her skin is as white as the half-eaten fish on Tatianna's plate, her lashes thick black ticks of positivity. The Manager Man looks at each of us in turn, taking us in. I know that look. We may all look different, the three of us, but we have one thing in common: we are tall and imposing, almost freakishly so. We dress down. Our looks are the language people understand. People have always treated us differently. Usually, we get what we want. I twist my mouth and raise my eyebrows at him, waiting for a better offer. The Manager Man swallows, nods and scuttles away like a frightened animal.

'How about a round of cocktails, on the house?' says the curly-haired waiter, who has reappeared with a tray of colourful drinks. He has a nice smile and he smells like coconut, although that could be the drinks. Once he has left the table, I notice he takes money from his moon bag and pays the barman. *Aa-dumb*, I think, allowing my mind to hold the sound of his name.

Tatianna and Ayeong are anxious to move on to the party we have all been invited to – a designer's house, a pool, canapés and older men. I feel reckless tonight. He hasn't called. Screw him. He's not worth it. I tell them I'm going to stay and have one more drink, then have an early night. They exchange motherly looks. I remind them I have a shoot tomorrow. Their looks are now tainted with something else. I tell them I'll meet them at the house, that they shouldn't worry about me – I'm from El Raval; I know how to defend myself. I may be the baby of our new household, but already, I can tell, I'm the toughest.

So far I have been to Paris, Milan, New York, Sydney, and now … Cape Town. *A gypsy since puberty*, my mother says. Cape Town is an easy city to fall in love with. The alcohol in my drink laps at my senses. I pull off the piece of pineapple that balances on the edge of the glass and suck it. The acid and coconut are a pleasing combination. Across the street, beyond the stream of slow-moving cars, grey waves trim a large, starless sky. Their sound rushes in and out above the beat of the music and conversation. The air is warm and still. I think of the northern hemisphere wrapped in wool, snowflakes settling on jackets, while here in Cape Town we are all stripped down to our summer clothes, drinking, dancing, living outside.

I watch Adam manoeuvre around the room. He has a rumpled quality to him that I like, fresh laundry pulled from the dryer. The desire to smooth and straighten him overwhelms me. He could do with a haircut, maybe better trainers. Did I mention his smile? A kind smile, a cheeky smile. His teeth are white and straight. This is the kind of thing I like.

Adam is not good at cleaning tables. He is clumsy, rushed and obviously distracted by me.

Whenever he goes to the bar or the kitchen nook, I see the staff laugh at whatever he says. He is likeable, carefree, not serious – just like Cape Town. He *is* Cape Town.

I hover at the bar until his shift ends. He offers to drive me home. I say I'd rather walk on the beach. His face lights up. He says I should be careful in Cape Town; it can be dangerous at night, not like in Europe. I tell him I'm sure he can protect me.

The white sand holds the heat of the day, but the water of the ocean is crazy cold – unbearable. I laugh at the pain. He holds my hand to steady me. We kiss. It is he who smells like coconut, not only the drinks.

He tells me he is thirty-one and is visibly rattled when I tell him I have just celebrated my eighteenth birthday. 'You look so much older!' he says, covering his mouth with his hand.

'People say that,' I say, swinging his arm in mine to make myself seem more childlike.

'I have roommates,' I add.

'I live with my mom,' he says with a shrug.

I like him still. I feel safe with him. He will be my adventure.

We make love on the beach behind the umbrellas and pool loungers for hire. He is gentle and less clumsy than I imagined him to be. Nobody sees us. I feel taken care of, almost loved. As I look up at the stars, I imagine the earth spinning on its axis around the sun, so hot on one side, so cold on the other. I'm already thinking which parts of this story I will tell my friends back home.

# SIX MONTHS AGO

## Maria

*Hout Bay*

Carole, Adam's mother, is tying up her affairs. She is getting ready to move permanently to the UK to be with her *other* grandchildren. Carole is not *rich* rich, but she has enough. Her late husband, Adam's dad, was a tooth doctor. Carole writes books, mostly made-up stories set long ago. She's quite famous, I think – Carole Sherman? It's her maiden name. I am the only Mrs Berelowitz now.

Carole loves my children, but she doesn't love me. In fact, I don't even think she likes me. She pretends to, but she still believes I scuppered her son's plans – as if he had grand plans in his curly-haired head before he met me. When she goes in a few weeks, she will leave us her house (which we already live in), her car (which Adam already drives), and all her furniture (which I would never choose for myself). I suppose I should be grateful, but I feel like a bird in someone else's nest.

It's been ten summers since I first fell in love with this city. Whether or not I have been in love with Adam all this time is still unclear. I liked *the idea* of him: his humour, the way he made me feel. And I knew he loved me – more than anyone had ever loved me before. He didn't do dishes, or wash clothes. He was always dishevelled. It was charming. I wanted to be the one to iron his shirts and suggest where he could improve. It made me feel like a grown-up, but now I am a grown-up and he is the child.

And so, perhaps it comes as no surprise that I have decided to take a lover. It seems earned. It seems sensible, even. At least this will be my choice. At this point, I am not sure who the affair will be with.

When we met, Adam was thirty-one – ancient to me at the time, so worldly, even though he'd never lived outside of Cape Town. Three months later, when my roommates were planning their trips back home, I'd fallen in love (with something) and fallen pregnant (with Sara).

Now there are five of us, five Berelowitzes – no more Maria *Marín.* Most days I feel completely forgotten, by my husband, my family, even my children. Their demands are so loud. Mine are never heard, or never expressed, which is the same thing.

As I pull into the school gates, my eyes scan the parking lot. Would I need to select a father who is not married, or would it be more of an adventure if he *is* married? I giggle inwardly that I am even entertaining these thoughts. *What would Carole say?* I think – and the thought makes me blush. Then again, in all seriousness, I can't afford to get a divorce. Where would I go? What would I do? Who would raise my children? My parents are not rich – they are not able to bail me out of my situation. I must accept what I have, and I must also accept what may happen next.

My eldest, Sara, who is nearly nine, and my elder boy, Hugo, who is five, are scrapping with each other in the back of the car, dragging me away from my daydreams. My youngest, Diego, is asleep in the car seat between them, mouth wide, *ready to catch flies,* as my mother would say.

'It's Silly Sock Day!' says Hugo, a look of horror on his face.

'You forgot, Ma!' adds Sara, her tone waking the baby.

*Silly Sock Day?* As if this is something I should have marked on the calendar! I remember now: this is the day where the kids at school must wear different coloured socks with their regular school uniforms instead of the assigned beige ones. For this privilege they are then required to bring money in an envelope, which gets donated to the children of a less-privileged school in the area. (My children only attend private school because Grandma Carole pays for it. Another decision I was left out of.)

Hugo is now crying, quietly – the worst crying there is. Sara is silent, arms folded, nostrils wide. Diego is sniffling, building up to a tantrum. My rage is incandescent. I resisted the urge to slap all three of them. I storm up the school steps with two of them in tow, Diego's cries now echoing around the parking lot through the open window. *Yes, I left my child in the car unattended,* I think. Once I'm near the top step, I sit, pull off my pink mohair socks and hand one to each child.

'There!' I say. 'Wear this.' They look at me as if I am crazy, which I often feel I am. A dark shadow falls across us.

'Did someone forget Silly Sock Day?' he says.

The man offers his left hand and lifts me to my feet. His hair is like mine, in a ponytail, and our skin is the exact same shade. We could be brother and sister. He feels familiar, but also strange and new. In his right hand he holds a selection of colourful socks, like a salesman. Pink socks with yellow bananas, green socks with red cherries, orange socks with yellow-and-green pineapples.

'We forgot last year – that's why I brought extra.'

'Oh, no … it's okay,' I say. 'They'll be fine …' Hugo snatches the pineapple ones from the stranger's hands and wrestles them onto his feet. The man offers Sara the cherry ones and she smiles and says, 'Thank you.'

'Where are you guys from? Your accent.'

'I'm from Spain, but my children are all born here.'

'Cool,' he says, sounding every bit a Capetonian. 'I'm from Durban.'

He is young, younger than me, or maybe the same age. I pull my attention away from his eyes to the boy clinging to his leg. He looks about Hugo's age and is wearing one blue sock, one green one.

'What grade is yours in?'

'This is Caleb. He's my nephew,' he says.

'Caleb's in my class, Mommy!' says Hugo.

'We should do a playdate sometime.' His eyes are green, like the sock.

'I would love that.' I feel an adolescent flush. My fingers tremble as I put my number in his phone. I don't know where I find the courage to say, 'I'll have to make it up to you somehow.'

# FIVE MONTHS AGO

## Maria

*Hout Bay*

Hugo is, thankfully, at an age where I can still choose his friends. He and Caleb are engrossed in their LEGO world. Sara is in her room, eyes glued to the iPad, and Diego is having his afternoon nap.

Adam is at work. I have tidied our house. We make small talk. He tells me he is an actor and I tell him I was a model. He says, 'I can see that.'

He asks after Adam. I am suitably vague, deciding at the last minute to tell him we are separating. I add details like, *It has been difficult*, and *It's for the best. We weren't right for each other.* The lies spill out of me. I feel strangely liberated from myself.

He enquires politely about my background, says how much he likes our house, the furnishings, the make of dishwasher we have. And then, while I talk, I let my hand brush his, and he doesn't move away.

It feels natural. It feels like a dream. It feels scary and daring but also … right. This younger man makes me feel less constrained, less motherly, more like the eighteen-year-old girl who left her mother and father's flat in Barcelona and promised to be back with African beads. He *is* younger than I am. He lives in Constantia with his sister. Three years ago she lost her husband – a boating accident, he says. He lowers his eyes when he speaks, searching for the right words on the floor. Now, he helps out with her kids. He says he stays in a *granny flat* – which, I learn, is a strange name for a cottage on someone else's property.

Most of our encounters happen under the guise of playdates. The first time he kisses me is when he follows me into our laundry room on the third playdate. He reminds me of the boys I had been with in Barcelona, familiar Spanish boys. Groping with clothes on. Safe and not safe at the same time. It's always a thrill, but I can see in his green eyes that he is looking for something more – more real sex and more out in the open – and I haven't decided if I am ready for either.

I am not so much a prude about sex, but Adam has always been … polite. I had not realised I wanted someone to lead me, as in a dance; to take control. I had not realised my husband wanted me to lead him. Wendy says Adam loves me more than he loves himself – which is a problem for us both. *I do love him,* I think, but not enough to make up for the fact he doesn't love himself. This thought is bleach on the stain of my guilt.

'I want to take you to dinner,' he says. 'A proper date.'

'I don't know …' I say.

He grabs my nose between his knuckles, pulling gently. 'What are you afraid of?'

It has been six weeks of this now, and the thrill is starting to feel more like fear. It was an experiment, a pastime, a fantasy to colour my days, and now I feel as trapped in this relationship as I am in my marriage. There is new guilt blooming beneath the old. There is some debt owed to this man. I must finish what I have started.

When Adam tells me about the anniversary dinner, I make my plans. One real-life date, then I will end things. I feel daring and alive, I feel young and free – until I remember I am not.

# FOUR MONTHS AGO

## FRIDAY

## Maria

*Hout Bay*

'You make my skin crawl!' is my final remark. That should do it.

Once I am sure Adam has safely left, I allow myself to imagine the evening ahead. Later, I run a sweet-smelling bath, smarten myself up and wait for Joy. She arrives on schedule at six thirty. The children are already asleep, except for Sara who is watching a movie in her room. Like Cinderella, I need to make sure I am back before midnight. Adam rarely comes home earlier when he goes out, especially when he is with Nick and Francine. I tell Joy that if, by some chance, he does come home earlier, she should tell him I've gone to get milk at the twenty-four-hour place. She seems happy to be part of the lie, especially when I offer her extra money for her compliance. I tell her I'm meeting a girlfriend – in case she double-crosses me.

My lover said he wanted to pick me up on his motorcycle. Usually, when he comes to the house he is driving his sister's car. I am nervous a neighbour might see him with me (we have such nosy neighbours in Hout Bay, you wouldn't believe!) so I have told him I'd rather meet him at his sister's house in Constantia. I explained in my text we could go from there and he could then live out his strange fantasy of having me on the back of his bike. I, in turn, can live out my strange fantasy of a date (and perhaps more) with a man who isn't my husband. And then – all things being equal – I will probably end it. A natural, swift conclusion.

The address is easy to find: on the long winding road from Hout Bay to Constantia, over the Nek. I park my car on the verge outside his sister's imposing Georgian-style home. *Eagle's Nest House* is displayed in large brass letters on the high wall surrounding the property. The gate is painted a soft grey and is flanked by columns that hold large stone eagles, their wings poised for flight. I wonder if his sister pays him to be a nanny for his kids, and the thought is cold water on my attraction.

*What am I doing, here?* I think.

Suddenly, there is real fear. This is not a good idea.

I restart my car and continue my journey around the mountain, arriving in Bree Street just in time to see Nick and Adam climbing out of their respective cars. Adam's face is a picture of happiness when he sees me.

# NOW

## Maria

*Hout Bay*

Diego has been accepted at morning playgroup on Mondays, Wednesdays and Fridays. Adam is not happy about the extra expense, but I have told him I need the time to work out. It's for my health, I argue. What can he say to that? In reality, a desire to exercise is always eclipsed by a need to clean or sleep, or take a painkiller, but what I must do now is honour myself and get back to my art. Wendy says this will be good for me. I need something to take my mind off last night. I need a plan.

After I have cleaned the bath, and the showers, and changed all the sheets, I take a cup of sweet tea in the garden. I feel the winter sun on my face and hope inspiration will bloom. I think of my mamá back home in Barcelona, cleaning the tiny flat I grew up in. Our house in Hout Bay is much bigger – three bedrooms and a garden with a pool – although it's still much smaller than most of the children's friends' houses with their electric gates and winding driveways. This is the problem with sending children to an expensive school: everything else must be expensive or they won't fit in. When she stayed with us, Adam's mother wanted to see my gratitude on full display. I couldn't help but feel insulted. Was my own childhood so awful, Carole? What's wrong with growing up in an apartment and going to a state school?

The door to the wooden hut that serves as my studio sticks as I open it. It's been too long. It's cold in here, so I wheel over the gas fire and press the button several times to make it work; it takes longer than it should and this makes me feel stupid. This hut used to be Adam's father's private space. He liked to fiddle with wood. I think it was the place he went to escape his wife. To me, it has always served the same purpose.

I lay out his gouge and chisels. The wood is heavier than it looks and wobbles on the table. It's still covered in lichen and earth; I hold it securely with both hands and try to imagine what I will do with it. I think of her. I think of him. She forgives me. I will make this for her. I wipe away what lichen I can with a cloth, then unfurl a roll of sandpaper and rub. The oak is hard, impossible to tame. This project will take me forever but the rubbing is soothing; the earthy scent lift my spirits. My body hums. I never had the chance to meet Adam's dad, but something tells me he would have liked me.

Why do we say *dead before your time*? Your time is not your time; your time is God's time and only God decides when it's time for you to go home. Sometimes, when I am working on my art, I try to let God decide in what direction I should go. I close my eyes and feel the shape of the wood, try to understand what he is telling me to make. I am revealing what is already there – his creation, not my own.

The gate bell rings. A faint, almost imagined sound through the wooden walls.

I open my eyes, annoyed that my creative process has been disturbed. I check my phone. It's on silent and there are no messages from school or from Adam. I push the door open and head back into the house, wiping my hands on my apron before opening the front door. There, behind the small gate that separates our house from the street, is a man in a bullet-proof vest.

'Can I help you?' I say.

'Morning, ma'am,' he says, thumbs inside the arm holes of his vest, like he's pretending to be a chicken. 'I'm Detective Jan Pretorius. Do you have a moment to talk?'

'Oh, did I accidentally set the alarm off? I'm sorry,' I say. 'The password—'

'No, ma'am, I'm not here with the armed response; I'm a private detective. I'm working on a case and this address came up.'

'My address?' I'm holding onto the door, repeating his question to buy myself time. I had been told what to say if something like this happened, but I always imagined Adam would be with me. Now I am stunned into silence. I grasp for the only thing I can think of: 'I'm sorry, my English …. not good.'

'Praat jy Afrikaans?' he says.

'Español,' I say. This should do the trick. 'Maybe you come back … later?' I make gestures with my hands to make myself look more linguistically challenged than I am.

*'Are you Mrs C Sherman?'* he shouts. My mother-in-law. I hadn't remembered Adam's car was registered in her name.

'I'm Mrs Berelowitz. You … must have … wrong address.' I make to close the door but his voice cuts in, making it impossible for me to act as though I didn't hear him.

'A vehicle registered to this address was involved in an accident in December. Was this not you?'

'I'm sorry!' I match his shouty tone. 'I don't know what is "vehicle" …'

'Car!' he says. 'A silver Audi registered to this address!'

I close the door and lean against it, retrieve my phone from my pocket and hastily type a message to Adam: *Detective is here. Call lawyer. Come home soon.*

# FOUR MONTHS AGO

## Maria

*Constantia and Hout Bay*

I text him from inside my car: *I'm here xxx*

The gate opens silently and slowly. I see him on his bike, a spare helmet under his arm and a smile on his face.

The drive is colder than I expected it would be. I'm wearing a jacket but the wind finds the gaps, the spaces above the neckline of my dress.

'Took you long enough!' he shouts back over the roar of the wind.

'I had an anniversary thing. Old friends,' I say. 'Where are we going?'

Wherever he has chosen to take me, it's back in the direction of my house in Hout Bay. It feels silly to be leaving my car outside his sister's house. I worry someone will see me: a neighbour, or a friend from school. What excuses will I make? But when we draw up to the parking lot I see he has chosen the most private place possible. The restaurant is in a single-storey mall that houses a laundrette, an ATM and a shop that sells beads and incense. It's not somewhere I would normally go. It's tiny, only four tables. At the centre of each, a green glass wine bottle holds a flickering candle. The wax from old candles decorates each neck like icing on a cake.

'I'm celebrating,' he says. I watch carefully as he pours himself a glass of wine. *How many has he already had?* I wonder. I have kept him waiting for almost three hours. It's already after ten.

'Oh,' I say, shifting in my seat. My wine tastes bitter and is not having its usual effect. This place feels dirty, and on some level, so do I.

'I landed a gig today.'

'That's great!' I say with as much enthusiasm as I can muster.

'Big bucks!' he adds with a growing smile.

I find I can't settle. I can't relax. I think of my children, of Adam, of Wendy. My mind won't stay in this tiny, dimly lit restaurant. My mind wants to escape. *Why did I come here? Why didn't I go home as I planned?*

He talks about work, about his plans for the future, his mother, his father. I nod and smile, occasionally suppress a yawn. He ignores my hints and presses on.

'I think we've made another candlestick,' I say with a small laugh, noting the empty bottle between us. I had only permitted myself half a glass, to add to the one I already had with dinner.

I wonder if I might be able to insist he get us an Uber back to his sister's place.

I check the time on my phone. Christ! It's after eleven. 'I need to get back,' I say.

'I think you should come back to my place,' he says, a lopsided smile on his face.

I feel my body tense and sober up as he says it.

'The babysitter …' I mumble.

'She can stay over …'

'But my husband …'

'*Estranged* husband …' he slurs. He suppresses a burp and the gesture further repels me.

'Yes, well, you see the thing is …'

And this is how the argument starts. He's had too much to drink. The similarities between him and Adam are suddenly striking. Why didn't I see this before? I ask for the bill and pay it myself. He protests but only half-heartedly.

In the parking lot I feel the wind on my face and my annoyance surfaces afresh, as it always does when it's windy in Cape Town. I retrieve my phone from my clutch. It's dangerously low on battery. I need to be back before midnight. My fingers fumble for the app that will deliver me safely back to my car, which will in turn deliver me home to my sleeping children. *Adam will see the charge on our credit card statement. Fuck it. I'll say it was for the babysitter … I'll find a way.* My deception has caught up with me. I now see this affair for the moment of madness that it is.

'Don't play games …' he says now, holding my wrists. This is a cliché that makes my stomach turn. I want out of here, out of this. My eyes sting from the wind.

And then … I see her. I see Charley, standing at the ATM in the parking lot, drawing money. The fluorescent lights make her face look purplish green. She has no make-up on and she's wearing a grey tracksuit. It's her hairstyle I recognised first. I hear the faint whirr of the machine as it spits out her cash.

'Charley!' I call, my voice carrying on the wind. She turns, smiling as she recognises me, and then she recognises him.

'Hey! Keith!' she says, zipping up her purse, walking towards us. He looks confused, drops my wrists as Charley raises her hand in greeting.

'What a surprise! I'm Charley,' she says shaking his hand in an overly friendly way. 'I'm the executive producer on the commercial you're shooting next week. How do you two know each other?'

'Oh,' says Keith. 'Thank you … I'm, yeah. My agent called me. I'm amped!' I can feel he is trying to look less drunk than he actually is. He's also trying to work out how we know each other and what possible consequence this will have for him.

'Are you … on the bike?' she says, eyeing the helmet at my feet.

'Actually,' I say widening my eyes at her. 'I'm not feeling so good, I'm going to call an Uber, but my battery …'

'I'll give you a lift!' She beams at me. Her big, expensive smile. I am still stunned to see her without make-up. Her face looks older than I've ever seen it, although her choice of outfit makes her body look like a teenager's. The contrast from earlier is startling.

Her smile widens and I say as little as possible, so as not to further incriminate myself. I ignore Keith and nod my appreciation to Charley as we walk towards her car. As she disarms the alarm, I hear the sound of the bike starting behind us. Keith shouts a slurred goodbye and disappears. I can't be sure, but it almost sounds like he says, 'You'll regret this!' as he roars off into the night.

# NOW

## Maria

*Llandudno*

'Wendy? Hi! It's Maria. Yes, I'm fine. I wonder if you can do me a huge favour …'

Once Wendy has been entrusted to pick up the kids from school, I phone the crèche and ask them to keep Diego for one more hour. They agree, as long as I pay extra. I tell them I will.

I change, pull the elastic out of my hair, spritz myself with vanilla perfume out of habit, and make for the garage. My left knee jars with every stride. With the button on my keys, I open the electric door and the gate simultaneously and pray to God in Heaven that the detective is not waiting outside in his car. The road is empty, except for the neighbour walking his dog. He waves at me and I force a smile.

'Don't forget tomorrow is recycling day!' he shouts. 'It's easier than you think!'

*Fucking neighbours.*

It's a quick drive to Llandudno, up Suikerbossie, the steep hill that rises out of the valley and onto the coast road. The view of the ocean as you reach the top always makes me smile, makes me grateful to be in Cape Town. But today, even the view can't take my mind off what I must now do. I practise my speech out loud, trying different voices.

I'm terrified – but I must do this now, or I will have two problems instead of one. I will not let my children's father go to jail over this. I cannot go to jail over this. I keep myself calm by reminding myself that the detective was *not* a policeman. He works for the security company. He is *pluriempleo* – the English word is something to do with moonlight. I need to get to Sebastian first. I am sure I can get him to call the investigator off. I can appeal to him. I can make him see.

I have reached the intersection that will take me down to Llandudno beach and Sebastian's big glass house. The last time I was at this house was for his fortieth; I was pregnant with Diego. I believe we were only invited to fill the crowd. As I park I draw a mental map of our relationships. *I am Adam's wife. Adam is friends with Nick. Nick is Francine's partner. Charley was Francine's best friend and Charley was married to Sebastian.* It's a long line. Sebastian and I on either end, far from each other. I like Sebastian. I've always liked Sebastian. Sebastian likes me, I can tell. He thinks I'm exotic. He is drawn to my accent. When we have a social engagement he always asks me the Spanish words for things. I entertain him just by saying, *mesa*, *silla*, *cuchillo*, *tenedora* (table, chair, knife, fork).

I press the button on the black wall that lines the property, straightening myself for the camera. There's a chance he might not be home.

'Maria?' he says. 'What a surprise! Come on up.'

The gate buzzes and I make my way up the stone steps to the huge front door which opens to reveal a barefoot, bearded Sebastian, smiling like Jesus from above.

'To what do I owe the pleasure?' he says as I reach the top.

We kiss each other on both cheeks and he stands back to inspect me before letting me inside.

'You look gorgeous as ever!'

'I was at the beach … I thought I'd see if you were home.'

'No kids? You should have brought them. My kids love your kids …'

'Yes, no … I wanted to …'

'Can I get you a drink – a coffee? You look cold. You're shivering.'

'Sure, yes, coffee, that would be nice.' I rub my hands together to keep up the pretence that I am cold.

He has one of those fancy coffee machines that makes a lot of noise. While he fiddles with it he says, 'I've been meaning to call you, actually. I'm working on a film script at the moment … and I was wondering if you've ever done any acting.'

'Me?' This is the conversation I once dreamed of. The timing couldn't be worse. 'You know I did a few commercials in my twenties – pretending to eat stuff and … not acting, pretending.'

'I think you'd be great. Actors – trained actors – are usually too hammy anyway.'

I'm unsure of the meaning of 'hammy' but I sense it is not good. I nod and try to smile. Sebastian seems excited to have another person to talk to. I remember now that he has no wife and I feel sad for him again, and then I remember: it is myself I should feel sad for. After four months my neck and knee have almost healed, but now, for some reason, the pain is as sharp and real as it was that night. My body is communicating. My mind resists.

'Anyway, I'll send you the script when I'm done. I'd love your take on it.'

More noises with the coffee preparation. Cups clatter on the counter.

'Yes! I'd love that.'

'Anyway. How are you? Kids okay?'

'The kids are fine, Adam's fine …' I take a slow breath through my nose. 'Sebastian, I … wanted to talk to you and see …. how you are doing.'

He slides a coffee in front of me. The froth on top is shaped like a heart.

'Well, I have good days and not-so-good days … Sugar?'

I seal my lips and nod, wondering if today is a good day or a bad day. He seems good but also a little crazy, now that I think of it. The kitchen clock says eleven forty-five. I will not be able to stall for much longer – and Adam might call when he gets my message.

'Adam says you have a private investigator?' I say this to confirm what I already know. I want him to tell me exactly how much he knows, and then hopefully I can work my confession around that. Maybe this way it will not come as too much of a shock.

'Yeah, shit … It's all so slow,' he says, his expression falling. 'I want action, you know? But this guy, Jan, he's working with the cops and they're useless and there are so many different divisions and people to call and no one gets back to you, and there's not, like, an actual database. It's a mess. But I think Jan's narrowed it down to two accidents from the same night. One looks like it was just a burst tyre – which technically could have caused the accident if it happened while the guy was driving. The other one looks like a drunk driver and …'

He is speaking so fast I can hardly keep up with his English. I wonder how many cups of coffee he has had today. Mine remains untouched, so I sip some, to appear polite.

'There's also this news that … God, this is a bit hectic … Not sure if you heard from Nick? Well, apparently there was someone else who could have been in the car with her that night. They found footprints that suggest someone ran from the scene, and that's confusing. I mean, she could have been hijacked – that's possible, but I'm not sure where she was going … So there are lots of unanswered questions there and it's hard to piece everything together, but I'm hoping,' he breathes out a long stream of air, 'I'm hoping I get something before it's too late.'

'Too late?'

'Yeah, if I end up having to go civil instead of criminal, there's a statute of limitations so … I need to get this thing in court as soon as possible, and it's going to be expensive and … I need to make sure …'

'It was me.'

'Sorry?'

'It was me, in the car with your wife that night.'

He laughs. He thinks I'm joking. My expression tells him otherwise and he stops. No words leave his mouth, although I can see his mind searching for the right response.

'Your wife,' I start, 'was at the ATM. I saw her at the ATM that night – drawing money.' Every organ in my body feels trapped, suspended. My hands on the coffee cup burn.

'You … What?' He has gone completely still. 'Maria, why are you only telling me this now … Are you …' There is an animal-like quality to his face now. He has shed his skin and the man I see before me is afraid and exposed.

'Sebastian, please – I want to tell this to you as it is. Not half of the truth, only the *everything* truth.' I pause for breath, knowing I will need a lot to get through this, in English no less.

'I was meeting my lover that night, in Hout Bay, and I didn't have my car with me. We had a fight and he was too drunk to drive. My phone was almost dead and then Charley, she saw me and she offered me a lift back to his house, to pick up my car.'

He is holding his bottom lip in his fingers, concentrating on me with such intensity I feel I might crack down the middle. I cannot go back. This is it.

'We came around a bend, and there was a bright light coming towards us. I screamed and Charley swerved and we hit the tree.' I feel tears running down my cheeks in two straight tracks. My voice is steady, my body still. He does not interrupt me although I can see he wants to.

'Charley's car was making all these noises, *Ping! Ping! Ping!* like when the seat belt isn't on, and I panicked, and I couldn't think because of the *Ping!* I was so close to my car … his house … and I thought I would go and get help because my phone was dead; I couldn't see hers anywhere and Charley was … not moving and the pillow thing, the, the … *bolsa* …' I search for the word in the air with my fingers.

'Airbag?' he offers.

'Yes, the *airbag* was blocking her face and I couldn't see … but she was so still, so still, so I opened the car door and there were no other cars, and my knee and my neck were paining, and I walked fast through the pain as fast as I could to my car parked outside Eagle's Nest—'

'Eagle's Nest Villa? Those are the people who called the police,' he says. 'That's what they told me.'

'Yes! I think they heard the sound, and I told them to call the police, and they tried to get me to stay and I told them I had to go get my children, and so I left.'

This last part is the only lie so far. Of course I didn't walk into my lover's sister's house – Eagle's Nest *House* – or their neighbours', Eagle's Nest *Villa*. I climbed into my car as fast as my shocked body would allow, biting my lip from the pain in my knee. I drove away shaking. The neighbours must have heard the sound and called the police. I knew someone would take care of the mess. This was not my mess to clean up. This was God's mess, God's decision.

'Lo siento, Sebastian … I was afraid – afraid Adam would find out about my lover. I was selfish. I see now. I only thought of myself, but I was scared.' My nose is running and the tears are warm and salty in my mouth. I cannot pause too long. I need to keep talking to prevent him from talking.

'It was bad, and I could not help her … I could not help her … but my conscience is haunting me. I cannot sleep. All I see when I close my eyes is the light … from nowhere,' I say, hoping I am not pushing things too far. 'One light, Sebastian … there was only one light.'

'Are you saying it was a motorbike? Did it seem like a bike?'

'It could have been … I can't be sure; it happened so fast.'

He bangs his fist on the marble counter. 'You need to be sure!'

'Yes! Yes, it could have been a bike … It was a bike.' Let him draw his own conclusions. Sebastian is breathing shallow and fast. I am afraid of him, of his silence. What will he say? He closes his eyes.

'Why was she at the ATM?'

'I don't know,' I say. 'She never told me. We talked about me and Adam, about my lover. She said my secret was safe with her, and then …'

My words trail off to nowhere. He opens the drawer beneath the coffee machine and slowly takes out a knife.

# NOW

## Adam

*Llandudno*

I check my phone regularly to see if she's left any breadcrumbs. She never has – until now. The dot on the screen pulses blue. She is unmistakably here, at *his* house. I thank the Uber driver. A disembodied voice greets me before the door in the black wall clicks open. I take the stone stairs three at a time. Why, after calling me, would she go to *his* house? I knew she was having some sort of … dalliance. I don't know how I knew. I figured it was the next logical step in her general dissatisfaction with everything, but Sebastian? That I could not have imagined. He may have lost his wife but I'll be damned if he tries to take mine. Joy lets me in the front door, their son Leo on her hip. Normally I would say hello, pinch his little cheeks, but my anger is a propeller I do not have the controls for. I push past them into the glass-fronted kitchen. I've forgotten how enormous this place is.

'Adam!' shouts Maria.

Sebastian is holding a knife, pointing it at the space between my wife's eyebrows. This is not what I had expected to find. It takes a while for me to process the scene.

'Sebastian and I, were just …' She hesitates.

'… running through a scene …' finishes Sebastian, '… for my film.'

Maria's face is wet. Sebastian's hair has come loose from its ponytail and hangs across his bearded face. He pushes it back as he lowers the knife. '

'Your wife is a remarkable actress!' he laughs.

I am aware of my own breathing; my heart rate is unnaturally fast. Now or never, I think. *Now or never*. Maria has moved towards me. She reaches for my arm and I shake her off as I deliver my line.

'What the hell is going on here?'

'Adam, let's go. I think Sebastian needs some time on his own. I'll explain everything in the car.'

'No,' I say. My voice rings in my head. 'This ends – now.' I point at the floor, marking the place where *now* might be. I draw myself up to my full height. A selection of overpriced gadgets are lined up behind Sebastian like demo models in a store. I could slap him, this spoilt, long-haired, rich bastard. A guy like Sebastian needs a proper punch, but I've never tried anything like that before. And he is technically holding a knife. But it's a prop. A prop I know he isn't capable of using. I could crush him. I could, you know. 'I'm sorry you lost your wife, buddy, but this is *my* wife. You stay away from her!'

'Take a chill pill, Adam,' he says, dropping the knife on the counter. 'Your wife was sharing some interesting news about where she was the night my wife died. I'm sure when you're done here she'll fill you in. But for now, I think it's about time you both fucked off out of my house.'

Maria is already making for the door. Joy retreats up the stairs with Leo. Sebastian turns towards the sink, presses his fingers to his eye sockets. His shoulders move up and down in staccato movements; he looks like he's laughing. A strange squealing sound emerges from his throat. My tough-guy act wanes and I take a step towards him. The flat of my palm hovers above his shaking back.

'Sebastian, I … I'm so sorry, man. I'm so sorry … What you're going through, it must be …'

'Do you love your wife?' he says, a tear balancing on the end of his reddened nose. He sniffs it back while he waits for my answer, wet lips trembling.

'Yes, I do … and that's why …'

'Then *love* her … Just. Fucking. Love. Her.' Airborne spit punctuates each word. 'Don't let her out of your sight. Do everything and anything you can to make her happy. Money means nothing. Work means nothing. Fuck, even your kids mean nothing! All that matters is you and her – do you understand me? You and her!' He jabs in the general direction of Maria as he says this. I know he's an actor and all, but this is pretty melodramatic. I'm not used to seeing men this emotional, especially when it's broad daylight and no one appears to be drunk. Maria is now at my side, her voice both pleading and firm.

'Adam, it's time to go.'

*

Outside, she hands me her keys and I take the driver's side. The doors shut and there is unnatural silence. Maria is … (could it be?) scared. Even though I am desperate to get away from this place, I find I can't yet summon the energy to move. I look out at the ocean and the miniature shapes of surfers.

When I finally speak, I'm almost proud there is no trace of emotion in my voice.

'You said we needed to see the lawyer.'

'Your car, Adam. Your mom's car – they have it on a … database. They know about your accident. This private detective came to see me today. He was asking lots of questions and I was scared and so I—'

'Ran to your boyfriend for help?'

Her eyes search mine. She's doing a good job of looking confused. 'No, Adam, I came here to Sebastian's house to try to persuade him to call off the investigator, to try to get him to stop, to try to end this. The accident was *her* fault – not yours.'

'We landed the MediVac account,' I say, looking back out the window towards the waves.

'You did!' My eyes find her reflection in the car window. Her face assumes the expression she would use if one of our kids brought home a sticker for good behaviour. 'Oh, Adam! That's so great! I'm so proud of you!' She reaches for my arm and I feel my muscles stiffen at her touch.

'Do you love me?' I say, looking directly at her now. This is not neediness; this a fact-finding mission.

'Of course I do, baby,' she says. 'I love you more now than I did when we were so young and stupid.' She bites her lip and more tears escape from her eyes as she says, 'I love your silly face and your terrible haircut and your white teeth and the way you tell a joke with your eyes. I love you. I want *you* to love you.'

There is more silence. She has never been this emotional in an argument before. I'm usually the weak one. She's the one holding back, thinking secret thoughts while I spill my insides for her. I take a deep breath but the oxygen doesn't seem to reach me. I feel numb.'I'll call the lawyer, make an appointment. I think you should meet with her too.'

'Okay,' she says. 'That's good. This is good. It's going to be good.'

I look at her for a long time – this woman, this mother of my children, convincing herself that the lawyer has some magical way to fix this situation. Maria is a person who trusts doctors and lawyers and financial advisors more than she trusts me. She speaks her mind when she needs to, but she also likes authority to tell her what to do. I am not that. Not any more. I turn the key in the engine and her car sputters to life.

'I think we should see Wendy,' I say, reversing out of the parking space. 'Together, I mean. I think we need to see Wendy, together.' She nods just once, sucks her lips into her mouth. I'm not sure if this is affirmation or confirmation. We'll talk about this later.

# NOW

## Sebastian

*Llandudno*

As soon as they're gone I call Jan. My hands are shaking, from the coffee, from Maria's revelation, from my proximity to the dazzling truth.

'I know who was with my wife in the car,' I say as soon as he answers the phone. I am almost euphoric. He tells me he's on another call, that he'll be with me within the hour. I am unsure what to do with myself while I wait. I'm so energised, so confused. I twist the cheese knife in my hand. I want to call someone. I want to tell Charley, *Guess what?*

I call Franky, but the call goes to voicemail. I think about calling Nick, but although I have his number, he's not someone I would ordinarily call. Deirdre enters my mind and disappears just as quickly.

I suppose I should be relieved that the person in the car was not another man, a hijacker or otherwise, but it still doesn't explain the money. Why was she drawing money? What possible reason could she have for not waiting until morning? Was she going to meet someone, pay some debt I wasn't aware of? A dealer, a shady character she'd never mentioned before?

I've always thought of Maria as an innocent, beautiful with not much upstairs; now I see her as a villain, a serpent, an adulterer, a thief in the night. *Fleeing the scene of an accident is a crime* I remember Jan telling me. She will go down for this; I will make sure of it. I don't care if Adam finds out about her affair – it's about time he found out what a liar she is. She was at my wife's funeral. I remember her face in the crowd, looking down. Now I know why she couldn't look me in the eye. How can she live with herself? And what if … what if Charley wasn't dead? What if she could have saved her? How could she have left her? How could anyone have left her? A wave of sadness rises like bile in my throat.

The gate bell startles me. It's Katie, the top of her golden head just visible on the monitor. One of her friend's mothers agreed to lift her home after Art Club. I splash water on my face while Joy opens the door, Leo still on her hip. Katie rushes past her to me.

'Look, Daddy, look!' She's clutching a découpage pineapple.

I clap my hands together then hug her fiercely.

'I can't breathe, Daddy,' she says, pulling away. I apologise, tell her she can watch TV in my bedroom upstairs. I remind her not to go into our dressing room. 'Leave Mommy's stuff, okay?' and she nods and says, 'I love you, Daddy.'

Jan arrives. He's sweating despite the chill outside, and has a bandage over his left eyebrow. He tells me he was pursuing a bag-snatcher in Hout Bay. He arrested the suspect and had to wait for the police to arrive. The suspect fought back, apparently, clipped him across the eye with a knife. The police arrived just in time and took the man away. When I called him, Jan was at the clinic having stitches and was on a call to his wife. All of this, while fascinating, is hard for me to concentrate on, or give a shit about.

'A friend of mine came around this afternoon and admitted to being the one in the car with my wife. Maria – Maria Berelowitz.'

'A friend?' he says, putting his rucksack down, retrieving his notepad. I have barely let him get through the door. 'Berelowitz?'

'Yes, well, she's the wife of the best friend of Franky's husband.'

Jan squints like he's trying to work out a complicated equation.

'It doesn't matter,' I say, waving my arm. 'The important thing is, she's been withholding evidence. We have her. She can be charged for this. She can give a statement. She's sure it was a bike they swerved to avoid. I'm sure we can match the description, find the fucker who did this.'

'Did she get a number plate?'

'No … she … It was dark, but she said there was only one light. It was a bike.'

'That's not much to go on in a criminal case.'

'It's something!' I slap my hand on the marble countertop; a sharp pain travels up my arm to my shoulder.

Jan is visibly shaken by my performance, or perhaps he's still shaken from his near-death experience with the bag-snatcher. He bends down towards his rucksack and fumbles for his laptop.

'Well,' he says, 'as I told you before, there's only one camera on that road, on Constantia Nek circle. I managed to get the footage released last night, but I'm afraid you're not going to like what you see.' He places the laptop on the kitchen counter and begins typing, punching the space bar hard with his thumb. Is he annoyed with me?

'Can I get you a coffee?' I say. 'You look like you need a coffee.'

'Dankie, that would be nice.' He doesn't look up from his laptop.

I feel like I'm back working behind the bar in Newlands. While I fiddle with the cups and saucers, select the blend, I wonder if the camera will reveal the final piece of the puzzle. I know Charley died before midnight that night; there could only have been a few bikes on the road at that time, crossing the circle, the nek between Hout Bay and Constantia.

The sound of the plastic keys on Jan's keyboard gives nothing away.

'Any news on the other two accidents?' I say, fetching milk from the fridge. 'Did any of them involve a bike?'

'I tracked down a car registered to a Mrs Carole Sherman,' he says, still typing furiously, eyes fixed on the screen.

*Carole Sherman*. The name is familiar … but I can't quite place it. I pour the frothed milk into his cup and note my hands are still shaking.

'Here we go,' he says, accepting the coffee and turning the screen to face me. He shifts his seat, so we sit side by side at the counter. As he leans towards the laptop I register the gun strapped to his side. He runs his hand down his face, as if he's not looking forward to showing me what he's about to show me.

'This is the footage from the night of the accident.' He gestures to the paused screen. 'We're looking at between eleven fifteen and midnight.

The footage is desaturated, grainy. He presses play. We silently watch car after car pass through the circle. There are three exits, four if you count the parking lot at the foot of the mountain where the camera is mounted. Number plates are barely visible as they follow the curve down to Hout Bay, or down to Constantia. The gaps between the cars get larger. At times there is a full minute of no activity on the road at all. I swallow. Each car holds a person, a reason for travelling, a secret mission. I count ten cars passing through the circle in the space of fifteen minutes, and then, there's a motorbike.

'That's our guy!' I say, almost shouting.

'No … it's not.'

He pauses the screen and points to what I now know is Charley's car. I feel a sudden rush, as if I might be able to catch her, to stop what happens next.

'The bike was ahead of Charley and going the same direction. Unless at some point he turned around.'

'Go back,' I say. 'Go slower this time.' I inhale through my nose and will myself into a calm state. This feels like I'm back in the edit suite, back making commercials, not looking for my wife's killer. We watch at slower than real speed. Charley could have taken between two to five minutes to get from the circle to the place where she crashed, depending on how fast she was going. The bike we're looking for will probably be coming up from Constantia towards Hout Bay. I feel a rush of something like joy. We're so close.

The camera shudders and static fills the screen.

'Why is it doing that?' I say.

'At first I thought it was the wind – high winds that night, a South Easter.'

The screen is restored and then, like something out of a horror film, the lens is obscured by the shape of a hand. 'What the fuck?' I say. 'Is that …? Someone's blocking the camera!' The static increases as black fingers close around the lens.

'It's not a person,' says Jan. 'They climb the cameras. It usually happens during the day but they must have—'

'Baboons?' I say. 'But … but they're diurnal.' Jan looks confused. 'They're active during the day,' I finish.

'Full moon,' says Jan. 'It's the first thing I checked, when you mentioned that the cops thought she could have swerved to avoid a baboon. They're active in the day, but during a full moon they act different. They're cheeky anyway but … ja, they're a problem.'

The screen has gone black, timecode ticking by in the corner.

'Fuck!' I say, smashing my coffee cup against the counter. The red ceramic breaks into three neat pieces. Jan flinches, cradling his laptop like it's a baby. There's a long silence.

'How about I go over this again at the office?' he says. 'It's been a long day, for both of us. I'll call my friend at Hout Bay police station and find out if there were any bike accidents we missed. What did you say your friend's name was again? Marie?'

My heart is pounding, caffeine and fear and anger and shame and pain and grief. I think of Franky, I think of Nick, of Adam, of Maria, of that dinner, that night. I think of the baboon's fingers, like a child's.

'It doesn't matter,' I say. 'Nothing fucking matters.'

# NOW

## Franky

*Ocean View Drive, Green Point*

The bag is called a *weekender.* It's an appellation that brings to mind a grand villa, the promise of wine during the day, a starch-shirted porter who will remark, 'How light this woman packs!' Packing the bag has the cinnamon-scented suspense of decorating the Christmas tree. Its slouchy cotton shape, leather straps and cream-and-caramel-coloured pinstripes have the exact flavour of assuredness I am trying to achieve. *I am capable,* it says. *I'm just in and out. Don't mind me.*

Last week Nick and I had his accountants draw up matching wills. His & Hers. Charley had a will. This hadn't really surprised me – she was so organised with everything – but I had never really wanted to get one. I liked to prepare, but this felt a little too much like tempting fate. But now I'm going to the hospital, soon. People die in hospitals.

I'd not known that people named in your will appear in bold capital letters, like the characters in a play. ADAM BERELOWITZ and SILVIA ALLEN didn't look like they belonged in the same sentence, and yet Nick's Best Friend and My Mother were forever united in print as our appointed trustees, to a testamentary trust that would be set up in our children's names, should anything happen to the both of us – *simultaneously,* as the contract states. Of course, at times like this you inevitably start to wonder: what awful tragedy would wipe us both out at the same time? Drowning? A car accident, plane crash, hijacking? Yes, I think, it's never too soon for a will, and therefore it's also never too soon to pack a bag.

This particular bag has been packed for six months, but while I wait for Nick to come home from work, I find myself once again riffling through its contents, rearranging things. This calms me, makes me feel there is some measure of control in what's to come. It's soothing in a way I can't quite articulate when Nick walks through the nursery doorway.

'Hello, my love,' he says. 'Still packing?' He kisses my forehead and smiles without judgement. His expression changes when I lift my anxious face to his.

'Frank … what's wrong?'

I tell him what Seb has just told me. I tell him about Maria, her confession, her revelation that she was with Charley that night. Her secret affair, the lift she accepted, the ATM, the baboons. It all comes out in the wrong order, upside down. I am breathless, light-headed and exhausted by the time I finish. Nick holds my hands and watches me carefully. He knows not to interrupt my train of thought, knows not to saying anything until everything has been thrown on the floor between us – out in the air where we can both make sense of it.

'Are you going to tell Adam?' is my final punctuation mark, and I realise that for the first time, I have no idea what Nick's answer will be. He doesn't answer me immediately.

'No,' he says with a sigh. 'No, I don't think so.'

'But …' I start.

'Could she have been lying?' he says. 'About the bike? Do you think she was trying to protect Adam?'

Maria doesn't seem the type to take a bullet to protect Adam; maybe to protect her kids? I'm not surprised to hear of her affair. I am intrigued that she was the passenger in Charley's car, and in awe of her ability to keep such a secret from all of us. Nick has a resigned look on his face.

'You didn't know, did you?' I say in a low voice, trying to keep all accusation out of my tone. 'I mean … you and Adam and … Maria didn't talk about this and not tell me?' I can feel my voice wobble, my childish fear of being left out of the triangle of trust.

'Of course not!' Nick squeezes my hands tightly. Our knees are touching, side by side on the daybed. I can feel the strength of him, the heat, like a boulder that has spent the day absorbing the sun. I fiddle with the straps on the bag.

'So … you're sure you shouldn't tell Adam?'

'Frank.' He's being gentle with me. There's a paternal energy to him now. I am the child who doesn't understand the ways of the world. He is wiser, calmer; I am the crazy one. This realisation sparks an unwelcome anger, like the first rush of PMT.

'I'd want to know!' I say too loudly, pulling my hands free from his grip. 'If Charley had information about you being with someone else, I'd be mad. I'd want to know! Adam has a right to know.'

He looks at me for a long time. My raised voice echoes in the newly painted room. His eyes read mine. He's thinking of saying something, but he's so much better at monitoring the gate that releases his thoughts into the world. Mine spill out of me. His are checked and rechecked before they go anywhere.

'It's not our place to tell him, Frank.'

I look at the ceiling to prevent the tears from spilling. Once I cry, this argument will be lost. I keep looking up while I say, 'So you can hang out with Adam, knowing what you know and not say anything … ever? He's your best friend. He knows you; you know him. How do you keep something like that from him? Isn't that … cruel?'

'You have to look at the bigger picture,' he says, stroking my hair, tilting my chin back down to face his. 'The bigger picture is more important than throwing the truth out. That doesn't always make things right. You need to get this, Frank …'

All at once it strikes me as strange. Why he would say this – this man who is known for his honesty, revered for it even? He tells people when he thinks the building won't hold the weight, when the balustrade isn't the right height, when the beams need to be larger or stronger or wider or made of steel rather than wood. His job is the truth. When he tells me I look beautiful, I know he isn't saying it to please me or flatter me; I know he means it. I've always believed he means everything he says – and now, this new revelation that he doesn't value the truth as much as I thought he did has thrown me off my axis again. I'm back in the place I was that night. *This man is a stranger*, I think. We may be having a baby together, but what else has he been lying to me about? There's something. I see it. Now I'm afraid of what I might find if I pull back the curtain behind his eyes.

'So, is this bag packed or is there still something missing?' he says, smiling, drawing me out of my thoughts.

'I'm just checking …' I say, not wanting it to seem as if the bag is my life raft, the only thing keeping me afloat. He leans into me and gives me a long, meaningful hug. 'It's nearly time,' he says, kissing my forehead. 'Not long now. Let's focus on this, Frank. This is what matters now.'

'Are you nervous?' I say into his shoulder.

'Excited.'

'Which is different how?'

'I'm quietly confident then,' he says with a smile. He gets up, taps the wooden doorframe as he makes to leave the room. 'Frank, you'll see: this will pass. Adam will be fine. It's their situation, not ours.'

*

I've emptied the room of all its former contents. It's painted white and is sparsely decorated: a dove-grey modernist chair; a chaise longue; an unassembled crib hidden in the confines of the panelled cupboards; a high English dresser that could be a compactum, or just a dresser. On the mantelpiece above the disused fireplace are two framed pictures: one is of my mom and me when I was a baby. She's holding me close, our heads two blonde baubles reflecting the sunlight. You can't see our faces but you know it's us. The other is a picture taken almost six years ago: our wedding day; seven smiling faces trapped in the past – me, Nick, Charley, Seb, Adam, Maria and my mom. It seemed like a good number at the time. The people who mattered most to us, if not the people who mattered most to each other. My father always said, 'If it matters to me, and you love me, then it should matter to you.' My green dress. Charley made me a posy of purple flowers. The only other jewellery I wore was the bracelet she gave me. We took only three photographs: one of me and Nick, one of me and my mom, and one of all seven of us – a motley crew of hairstyles and colourful fabric, the purple posy at the centre of the vortex – just before the panic set in. I remember now, it was Charley who took me to the hospital that day, Charley who took me home. I stare at the picture until the tears blur my vision.

# EIGHT YEARS AGO

## Franky

*Green Point*

'It's lame,' I say, dragging the last word out for as long as my tongue will allow.

'Oh, I had no idea you felt that way,' he says, looking over my shoulder. He waves at someone behind me. It's his birthday; I should feel privileged he's chosen me to talk to when there are clearly so many who want his attention. His question caught me off guard.

'It's, you know ... What's the point?' I have reached a place of no return. I'm on my third glass of red wine.

Charley is on the dance floor, shrieking with laughter. I have a sudden craving to be in on her joke, not here, cornered by her boyfriend, discussing their recent engagement and my thoughts on marriage.

'Well, the point is, two people love each other and they want to spend the rest of their lives together.' His eyes watch mine, challenging.

'Don't get me wrong,' I say, protesting the innocence I know is already lost. 'I love weddings. Love them! I just ... don't see the point for myself. But good for you. Charley's not the same as I am ... so, you're lucky.'

The unspoken truth hangs between us. I can't keep a boyfriend for longer than six months. I've been single more than I have been in a relationship. He thinks I'm sad. He'd like to fix me. He'd like to help. His pity stings. I thought he, of all people, knew me; now he feels like another stranger at a party. I shouldn't have to explain myself to Seb, yet my need for him to understand me pulls like a magnet. *Why would I tell the man who's just proposed to my best friend that I think marriage is lame?* The warning labels on wine bottles aren't nearly as accurate as they should be.

'I think you should wait until you meet the right guy,' he says, jerking his head towards the film-industry types gyrating on the living-room dance floor.

'Maybe it's my dad,' I say, digging myself out of a hole with a spoon. 'It's like, he's not there for the whole walk-me-down-the-aisle thing …'

'Neither is Charley's,' he counters. He's enjoying this, enjoying putting me on the spot. He loves an argument, is energised by it. He's always looking for the rub.

'So,' I say, drawing breath. 'Why *are* you getting married? Why can't you … stay as you are?'

'Well, I guess it's … it's security.'

The laugh escapes through my nose. 'How does being married make you more secure?'

'It just does. We officially belong to each other, forever.'

'So, you've never heard of divorce then?'

He thinks I'm jealous. He thinks I want what they have. He thinks I'm lonely. He thinks I'm a fool. I feel myself becoming otherwise. The smugness is barely concealed beneath his crooked smile. He pats me on the shoulder.

'I just want you to be happy, Frank – like we are.'

'I am happy, Seb.'

'You could have fooled me.' He raises his empty glass and I glare at him while we clink our glasses together, red wine splashing onto the wooden floor between us.

'Love is a decision,' I say, desperate for the last word.

'Eh?' he says, cupping his hand around his ear.

'Erich Fromm,' I shout over the music. 'Look it up!'

# NOW

## Sebastian

*Llandudno*

Her navy-blue blazer is an empty cocoon. It's draped over the back of the chair in our bedroom. I haven't been able to move the jacket, although I've touched it a few times. I like looking at it, the way the light falls across its elbow creases. Dust motes float in the afternoon light. Sometimes I don't like looking at it. I've given Clara strict instructions not to move it.

'Yes, yes, I completely understand,' I say into the phone. Jan says he's unable to pursue the investigation further unless I give him the name of the suspect who fled the scene. I'm not compelled to do this, but he strongly suggests I do. Last night I lay awake, imagining Maria in prison. It was Franky who had put these ideas in my head, clouding my sharp determination for justice at all costs.

'She fucking lied!' I said, the moment she called me back. 'She lied to all of us! She's a fucking criminal.' Franky was silent, but her judgement was loud and clear. Maria was not a criminal; she was a woman afraid of losing everything, because of a lapse in judgement. Maybe she deserved to lose everything – God knows I didn't. But once these truths settled in my mind and the red fog of my anger burnt off, I tried to imagine what Charley would say. She'd say decisively, 'It wasn't her fault.' *But it was … It was her fault!* I argue with her ghost. If Charley hadn't given her a lift, she wouldn't have had the accident. But I'm still not sure where she was going with the cash from the ATM. Was there another destination on her journey? Was the ATM only part of it? Franky has convinced me of a new plan: call a lawyer and see if they can grant Maria some level of immunity from prosecution if she agrees to give her statement to the police. It may help us find the person who was truly responsible for the accident. We may never be able to prove who killed my wife, but there's hope that one day someone will confess and all the pieces will fit together.

Jan wishes me well with this. He'll keep me posted if anything comes up. He will forward me his final invoice. He hopes I'll find closure. He praises me for my patience, tells me not to give up. I say, 'Thank you,' although I'm not thankful for any of it. My mind remains on the blazer and the person who used to fit inside it.

I was the one who had insisted on a walk-in wardrobe. I'd seen it online. Slate shelves, illuminated with invisible LEDs. 'It looks like a pretentious shop,' Charley said, as if to dissuade me. But, true to form, she oversaw all of the details: the crystal handles, the bespoke hangers, the silent but powerful sliders for the drawers. Everything was as I had imagined it. My side of the wardrobe was taken up mostly with shoes, sneakers in every colour – a collection I'd started not long after that first commercial. Her side was dresses, shirts and jackets – colour-coded, from jewel tones to pure black.

On the bottom two shelves her patent heels now gather dust. Every morning she would disappear into that room, emerge as her powerful self. I loved it when she went in there, when I could see how much she enjoyed what I had dreamt up for us.

The other benefit of this walk-in wardrobe is that it has a door, and that door has been shut since the funeral. I couldn't bring myself to move her clothes, and so, instead, I moved mine. The built-in cupboard we used previously usually houses towels and linen, but I found it was just big enough for a selection of tracksuits, T-shirts, jeans, socks, underwear. This cupboard, with its dark recesses, is the one I deserve. The walk-in is a museum of costumes from a previous life. The door isn't locked, but the children know better than to play hide-and-seek in there.

Of course, I thought about clearing the space, moving her things, but every time my mind so much as landed on the idea, I felt overwhelmed. The thought of wading out into that wardrobe, liberating each piece of clothing, was too much. My wife's tomb. Francine offered to help, but her help felt insincere. She wanted some of it, I knew. I wouldn't want Franky wearing any of her clothes, her jewellery, her shoes – and I knew she would ask for some and I would be too embarrassed to say no. What reason could I possibly give her?

As I end the call with Jan, a crazed feeling moves through me. I recognise it as the one that overtook me that day of the lawnmower. It's a sharp and sudden desire for action.

I turn the brass handle and the grey panelled door swings slowly open. Inside, everything is as it should be: shirts, dresses, accessories hung from custom-made hooks, a table in the centre with drawers neatly displaying her jewellery on bespoke black velvet cushions. *Where to start?* A familiar surge of emotion rises. Wendy said this would happen. She told me to put on music, to clear my schedule, to have the kids sleep over at someone else's house. She told me I needed to do this alone. I should embrace, rather than run from, the process.

I have already bought a selection of plastic containers for this purpose. I retrieve them from the garage, clutch one to my chest. *I'll start with the sweaters*, I think. I fold and pile them up. Each one holds a moment, a memory, a photograph in my mind of an occasion when she wore that particular shorn skin. Once the jerseys are finished, I move on to the jackets, then the skirts and dresses. I'm trying to be measured and calm, like Wendy asked me to be, but everything feels leaden, weighed down by invisible liquid. The wooden hangers swing on the emptying racks as if in a breeze. I slide a wooden ladder across the room and make my way up to the higher cupboards. I open the doors and take down the hats she never wore, the shoeboxes of old photographs already digitised, a box of kids' clothes she'd meant to give to charity but never did. It's all so inexplicably heavy. I put everything on the central table. I go up the ladder again. At the back, behind everything I've moved, is a cardboard box. It's light. I slide it out and peer inside. A stuffed panda and an unwrapped Barbie stare back at me. I find I need to hold the doors for support. I want to laugh, I want to cry, I want to scream, I want to run, I want to tell someone, but I do none of these things. I slide down the wall and sit on the floor, my back against the cupboards. *I need a drink,* I think. But I can't get up. I'm so tired. This process is not infusing me with the energy I hoped it would.

What other secrets did she keep from all of us? Did she write a diary? Could that be here? Could there be other clues as to where she was going that night? Do I want to know? Would I feel better if I knew?

I pull myself to my feet, will oxygen into my nostrils and lean on the central table. I open drawer after drawer: rings, earrings, scarves, bracelets; my mind can barely take it all in. And then I find I'm back up the ladder, my arms sweeping the dim cavernous spaces, stirring clouds of dust. Right at the back of one, I find a small Prada box a pair of her sunglasses must have come in. I pick up the box and shake it. It rattles as if full of diamonds. Carefully, I slide off the cardboard lid. What I find inside makes me shudder. All at once, I know.

Of course. This explains her wallet full of cash.

# NOW

## Adam

*Hout Bay*

'Pru?'

The lawyer's face changes. 'Maria?'

'You're … It's you!'

My wife and my lawyer embrace as though they are long-lost family members. It's more than an embrace – they clutch each other; hands grip forearms as they separate, bouncing on the balls of their feet. In our cramped hallway decorated with kids' rucksacks, a pram, golf clubs and Wellington boots we never use, Nick, Francine and I look on in awkward silence.

'You finished law school?'

'I did, obviously!' Prudence's voice is light and girlish, her lawyerly facade dismantled.

'We used to model together,' says Maria, waving away the idea like a bad smell. Franky introduces herself, followed by Nick. Prudence's attention quickly returns to Maria as we make our way into the lounge.

'I haven't seen you in what – ten years? The last time was … that underwear commercial, remember? With the pillow fight!'

Their laugh becomes a squeal. The rest of us remain mute. I look at Nick. He widens his eyes, the corners of his mouth twitching.

Toys have been packed away and we've entrusted Sara to watch the younger kids while we have The Conversation. Prudence is incongruous in our home. Her sharp features and grey suit only serve to show up the stains on our cream-coloured couch.

'Please, sit down,' says Maria. Everyone huddles around a tray of tea and muffins on the coffee table. Maria is flushed and nervous. She's not normally much of a hostess; the muffins are nothing more than a distraction. I'm not hungry, which is never a good sign. As Maria pours tea into cups, Prudence pulls a sheaf of paper from her leather briefcase.

'Right! Everyone!' she says, returning to her professional persona. 'I have some good news.'

No one says anything. We all look at her expectantly. I wonder if I am the only one trying not to imagine her and Maria in their underwear.

'These documents show the timeline of the night of December the seventh.' She points to a highlighted row with a black lacquered fingernail. 'These are the calls to Nick which you made between eleven sixteen and eleven twenty, yes?' I look at Nick's number duplicated on the page – the same number he's had for twenty years, in black ink, highlighted yellow.

'Yes' I say.

'And this' – she shuffles through the papers, places the relevant one on top – 'is the coroner's report showing Charlotte Hastings' time of death to be estimated around eleven forty-one.'

A beat of silence before Nick says. 'That doesn't prove anything. She might have died after the point of impact.'

I look from Nick to Prudence – a tennis match. Franky is quiet and still. Maria's hands are clasped unnaturally on her lap, a schoolgirl waiting to be given permission to go to the toilet.

'Exactly,' says Prudence. She seems to realise Nick is the best person to direct her entire presentation to. He's the one who will understand everything and explain it to all of us again later. 'In law,' she continues, 'we work with the *physiological* time of death, which is when a person's organs actual stop functioning; the *legal* time of death, which is what is recorded on the death certificate; and the *estimated* time of death, which is decided by a medical examiner. And now, thanks to the wonders of technology, we also have the exact time of impact.'

'The car?' says Nick.

'Exactly. The electronic control unit in the Porsche Cayenne logs the exact time the airbags deployed. Only the dealer who sold the car can extract this data.' She takes out another piece of paper, holds it up for us to inspect. We all stare at the words *ECU Report*, typed in bold letters. 'I am now in possession of information that confirms the time of impact to be eleven-forty and thirty seconds.'

'Wow, that's ...' This from Franky, who is squinting to make out the wording on the page. 'Is that conclusive?'

'It would appear so, but obviously we don't want it to have to get to the stage where we have to defend ourselves. The next step is for me to contact the private detective on your behalf and lay out where we are, before he makes any formal application through the courts. He's not allowed to question any of you directly – only a police officer can do that, and the court would have to have enough evidence to action this.'

I clear my throat. 'Do you have to say you're acting on my behalf? Can't I be anonymous?'

'That won't hold up legally, I'm afraid, but, yes, that is the first port of call: considering your car was registered to your mother, I may be in a position to name you as a "family member" and not disclose your full name at this stage – until we know what further evidence he may have. Any statements you may have given can only be obtained with a court order.'

Nick audibly releases his breath. 'Okay, well … any bad news, then?'

She smiles and directs her attention back to Maria. 'Most people consider my final invoice to be a bit of not-so-good news, but we can discuss that later.' A weak laugh ripples through the room.

'So, I didn't … do it?' I say, wanting someone to say the words.

'Yes. Well, I mean, no,' says Prudence. 'No. You did not, *could not* have caused this accident, unless you somehow caused the car crash after you called Nick. But' – she riffles through the papers again – 'the location of the call shows the spot where your car crashed, so the answer is …' She finds the map showing what she has alluded to, places it in front of me. 'No, Adam. You can now rest assured: Charlotte Hastings' accident was absolutely no fault of yours. It is, as suspected, pure coincidence that you and she had an accident on the same evening, on the same stretch of road. There is no connection – absolutely none, other than the fact you knew her.' She shows me her teeth, an approximation of a reassuring smile. 'If this goes to civil court, we will win, but it won't. The PI will have to present our evidence to the complainant. His investigation will need to look elsewhere.'

I catch Maria looking at Franky. Franky is the first to look away. My wife's brown eyes find mine. *I am alive,* I think. *We are all alive*, and it wasn't me who killed Charley. An invisible weight rises from my shoulders, and another one presses itself down on my chest.

# NOW

## Franky

*Bree Street, Cape Town* CBD

I trace the gold lettering with my fingers: *Sunrise Sunset.*

'Looks good, no?' says Gabby, holding the pink-and-orange bottle up to the light.

'It does!' I say, as if realising this for the first time.

I'm feeling euphoric today. Adam is not guilty. I have no more secrets to keep, other than Maria's infidelity, which isn't life or death or jail. It's also my last day at the office before I leave for the seemingly endless ocean of maternity leave and the horizon beyond.

It wasn't exactly love at first sight when we presented our new branding idea to the client, but, in the end, Gabby won them over with her stylish bottle design and her new hairstyle: golden blonde, cropped short. She looks youthful and confident – more so than the sallow, heavily pregnant copywriter at her side. I tried to be trendy that day, but my bulge softened every angle. My roots have grown out. I refuse to colour my hair in case the dye and bleach reach the foetus. At least I can take credit for the name.

'Genius,' declares Gavin, arms folded. 'We're going to miss you.'

'I'm sure you'll manage,' I say, slipping two sample bottles into my bag.

'Here.' He throws a brown paper packet on my now empty desk. It's tied with string and a sprig of lavender.

'They wrapped it for me,' he says.

I tear open the paper. Inside is a tiny babygrow. In silver glitter letters it reads, *I'm no longer a twinkle in my father's eye.*

'Thanks,' I say, leaning forward for an unfamiliar embrace. My eyes water. I'm determined not to let him see he's hit a nerve.

'Any time,' he says, with a smile. 'Good luck.'

Gabby gives my hand a squeeze. 'It's going to be great. All that free time! I'm jealous!' Her smile is contrived, but the hand squeeze is genuine.

I make my way around the office saying my goodbyes, accepting the hugs, the congratulations and the unsolicited advice. Finally, I am in the lobby, pressing the button for the lift. I can't escape the feeling: you don't always know when you might be doing something for the very last time.

# NOW

## Sebastian

*Llandudno*

I'm drunk – drunker than I've been in a while. Katie's birthday party is over. It's her first birthday without her mom. People keep asking, 'Is this the first birthday since …' before they trail off. After the disaster that was Christmas, I was determined not to mess up.

I hired a magician. I ordered a cake. I even spent the whole of last night filling party packs with plastic toys and sweets Charley would normally forbid. The Barbie was wrapped and unwrapped – Katie was happy, for at least twenty minutes, and then she tripped down the stairs and cried and the Barbie stayed on the third step, its legs splayed like a contortionist.

The panda has been re-hidden. I'll wait for the right time to give it to Leo – maybe when he talks about her again. It can be something to comfort him when he needs comforting, although I'm still the one who needs comforting. What I need now is a reprieve from all the pointless conversations with people who pretend to care, people who secretly think, 'So, are you seeing anyone yet? Isn't it time you looked for a replacement?' Deirdre, my parents, everyone was here adding their voices to the milieu. Even Franky was here. I didn't invite her. She invited herself.

I never did finish clearing the wardrobe. Not after that box. The next day I asked Joy and Clara to go in there and pack everything up. I said they could each choose something they liked of hers to keep. Clara chose a grey sweater, Joy a red coat. Neither dared wear them in front of me. I watched as they left, my wife's clothes draped over their arms like dead animals after a hunt.

The rest of her things – jewellery, photographs and shoes – are in clearly marked plastic containers in the garage, where they will sit for all eternity, until someone in my employ suggests I do something with them. I'm not in the mood for that sort of commitment – or any commitment for that matter.

As for the Prada box, I emptied its contents into a paper napkin and threw them in the bin. If only everything was that easy to let go of. Now I am once again alone, surrounded by balls of shiny paper and drooping helium balloons, the scent of vanilla icing and beer an unpalatable combination. And then I see it.

I sit up in my chair, turn up the volume on the TV. It's my commercial, only it's not mine, of course; it's an approximation of the treatment I'd given the client: the lonely road, the tattooed guy, the shiny black car, the changing scenery around the mountain. It's over so quickly, a tune, a logo, the end. I rewind and watch it again. It's Keith, with a fake tattoo snaking up his arm. You literally see him for a split second. He is barely recognisable – and neither, I note, is the tattoo.

# NOW

## Adam

*Hout Bay*

'Daddy, how do you spell *tortoise*?' The productive sound of the just-turned-on dishwasher fills the silence.

'T-O-R-T … O-I-S-E.' I take a sip of coffee and exhale, pleased with myself. I look at my five-year-old son over my mug. Hugo's tongue runs the length of his lips as he writes.

'How do you spell *actually*?'

I recite the letters for him, over-enunciating the two Ls. More scrawling.

'*Necessary*?'

Ah, yes – I know this one! One collar, two socks: 'N-E-C-E-S-S-A-R-Y.'

Maria is gone. This was necessary. She needed to go. She took Diego with her. We said our goodbyes at the airport and she hugged me for a long time. 'Thank you,' she said, as if she'd been waiting for my permission all along. I'm working from home, which is harder than I thought it would be. Six weeks and she will be back. I hope.

We went to Barcelona together after Hugo was born, but the trip could not be described as a success. Maria's mother tried and failed to hide her disappointment in her daughter, and she saw no value in pretending on my account. I was not the man she thought her daughter deserved. That day, six years ago, as I stood in the tiny flat my wife had grown up in, I resolved never go back to that place. It was a mirror I didn't care to see my reflection in. Maria's father spoke no English. He did not shake my hand and did not engage with his grandchildren. He grunted at me over dinner while Maria babbled. I had no idea what they were saying to one another. Every conversation felt like an argument. It was one of the longest weeks of my life.

Hugo looks out the window, scratches the inside of his elbow, searching for inspiration.

I watch transfixed as spots of blood appear on the pale skin inside his elbow.

'Don't scratch!'

'Sorry, Daddy, but it's itchy.'

'I know, my son,' I say, moving to the medicine cabinet above the kettle to retrieve the wildly overpriced ointment that promises to tame his genetic predisposition to eczema. I can never remember its name. I know it sounds vaguely like the spell a magician would issue at children's birthday party: *'Alacazam!'* I apply the ointment gently, saving some for my own baby finger, which is red and flaky.

'Oh, Huey, I'm sorry, I'm afraid you've inherited your eczema from Daddy.'

He watches me rub the cream in, and he says, 'And my cleverness!' I feel a sting behind my eyes – something like pride, and something else.

'Possibly,' I say, resisting the urge to berate his mother.

'Definitely,' says Hugo. 'Mommy doesn't know how to spell words.'

'Mommy's first language isn't English, Hugo – you know that. She was clever at school.' I have a sudden desperate need for my son to see his mother as a sharp, intelligent woman, the girl who finished school at sixteen with straight As so her parents would allow her to embark on a career as a model. I, on the other hand, spent my final school year in a cloud of marijuana. Who knows what my actual results would have been? They weren't good enough for medical school, or dentistry, I can tell you that much.

'How do you spell *eczema*?' says Hugo, returning to his homework.

I hesitate before glancing at the tube still in my hand.

Wendy said Maria and I need to *work* on our relationship. We need to put time and effort into each other, *to reap what we sow*. She wants us to write a diary of our feelings while we are apart to see what comes up. All I can think of is my father. *Bide your time,* I think. *Bide your time.*

'Daddy, can you spell *miserable*?'

'Huey, what's this story about?'

'It's a surprise!'

'For what?'

'Father's Day.'

It strikes me off guard. *I* am a father. *I* am that person for my son. I am the one he looks to for all the answers. I don't have them. I can spell *miserable* and *necessary* and *tortoise* but I can't spell *eczema*, despite having the condition for most of my life! I don't actually know everything. My father didn't know everything. All this time, I've been feeling the lack of his compass-like presence, and only now does it dawn on me: he was probably no different. He didn't have all the answers. He said, *Bide your time*, not because he thought that was the answer, but because he didn't *know* the answer. All he knew was that I would find my own way, if only I gave myself time and space.

*Is that what you meant, Dad?* I think.

The phone rings. It's Maria.

'We need to talk,' she says.

# NOW

## Sebastian

*Llandudno*

We open on a Spanish villa, no, a French château … a whitewashed Grecian village … an Italian farmhouse. All of these places seem desirable. Writing about it isn't quite the same as being there. It's not that I need a holiday; it's that I need my mind to be transported somewhere, anywhere else.

The cursor mocks me. *Go on*, it says, *I dare you. Say something that hasn't been said before.*

After several more failed attempts, my fingers find an old file of writing material. I open each document in turn, cringing as I read my musings – the thoughts of a man who still had a wife.

My laptop goes dead. My wife is dead. I am dead inside.

I open the drawer of my desk to retrieve a charger. The purple notebook Charley gave me looks back at me, gold-lettered 'NOTES' winking. *There you are.* I inhale and open the book. My own handwriting is illegible. I've written in the margins, up the side, made small sketches, underlined words. I wonder at this person who once had so much energy, so much to say, so many opinions and ideas. I was so arrogant, so self-assured: confident someone would find meaning and delight or even comfort in what I had to say – *my vision.* I smile to myself as I read, 'The narrative is easy to change. The hard part is defining what you actually want to say.' And there, underlined in red, the words 'Disappointment vs awe – explore.' Yes, I think. I am … *disappointed.* That is the purest and truest description for how I feel right now. I am immeasurably disappointed. Such a weak and functional-sounding word that doesn't nearly have the strength to carry everything I feel, and yet, I am disa*fucking*pointed. How and why did I write this? I flip over the pages and there in the middle is her unmistakable cursive, so much clearer than my own. 'I love you forever. Keep writing. xxx'

I take out a pencil and write all the ways I feel disappointed. My wife died, I'm not as good a father as I thought I'd be, I haven't made the film I want to make, I'm lonely, I'm tired, I'm afraid; and then, when my fingers hurt and my hand starts to cramp, I turn the page and write AWE. What am I in awe of? The fact that the world is constantly spinning. My children grow up with or without me. People still phone me and want to be around me, even though I am miserable. Nutella toast tastes so good in the morning. I don't need a gardener even though I've always thought I did. My mother and father are alive, and they love me. My sisters love me. I am loved. I live in a massive fucking house in the most beautiful place in the world.

I close the book as my laptop restarts with the single note of a symphony.

# NOW

## Sebastian

*Hout Bay*

I know her from somewhere. I can't place her. Her eyes are on me.

'Hi,' she says. We're outside the coffee shop, the place I like to come to write. I'm seated at a small wooden table in the shade. She clutches a bunch of white roses in one hand, a takeaway coffee in the other.

'I feel like I know you,' I say. 'Could we … have worked together before?'

'I'm in advertising. You?'

'I'm a commercials director.'

'That must be it, then. Have you worked with Smith & Sergeant?'

'No, but my wife … my late wife's best friend worked there.'

'Oh, Frank?'

'Yes, how did you know?'

'You're the husband … Charley's husband.'

'Yeah, that's me … guilty.' I try out a laugh. She smiles.

'Who are you buying flowers for?' I say.

'Oh it's … I just like to buy flowers for myself on this day every year. I don't know why. It's not my birthday or anything … It's just this ritual. It's silly.'

'I'm not judging,' I say, experimenting with a smile. She looks at me as if reading my thoughts.

'Could I … could I join you?' she says. I think of all the excuses. She takes in my silence. 'I'm sorry, you have your laptop – you must be busy.'

'No, I'm just … No, I mean yes, I would love to have a coffee with you.'

'No industry chat!' she says with a nervous laugh.

'I wouldn't dream of it.'

She pulls out the chair and as she sits down and stretches out her legs, I make the connection. Her hair is different. She's the woman from Wendy's bench – a fellow nutcase.

'I'm Gabby, by the way.'

# SIX MONTHS AGO
## FRIDAY
23:56
## Nick
*Constantia Nek Road*

The moon is as bright as I've ever seen it. There is something not quite right about the car. It's not just that it's upside down; the front windows are open and Adam is nowhere in sight. The engine ticks. *Fuck*, why am I thinking about my shoes at a time like this?

'Adam,' I call, not wanting to raise my voice for reasons I am not entirely cognisant of.

There's movement in a nearby bush. I use my phone as a torch. He shields his eyes as the light finds his face between the leaves.

'What the fuck, man?' I say. 'Are you okay?' I crouch down to his level.

'Shit, bru, Franky's mom is *lank* pissed at me,' he says, blinking away the after-vision from my phone light. 'She was banging on the window just now: *'Wake up! Wake up! Get out the car, you fucking idiot! You need to hide!'* I was just resting my eyes, bru, and she was like … upside down and it was like this weird dream, man …'

I look behind me before reaching for his arm to lift him up. 'Are you hurt?'

'Nah, I'm totally fine. Just, like, need to pee …'

'There's no time, Adam, seriously. Let's go. We can talk about it in the car.'

Adam has an almost Pavlovian response to the word 'go'. Whenever I say we need to go – anywhere – he says he needs to pee. He's always been an old man, even when we were teenagers. He follows me in a ragged line towards the hard shoulder of the road, looking back mournfully at his car.

'Maria is going to go apeshit …'

'Come on,' I say, willing him to move faster.

'Where's Franky Frank?' he slurs once we're in the stillness of the car. I lean over him and buckle his seatbelt before buckling mine.

'She's with her mom.' I check my rear-view mirror before pulling onto the road – the acceleration makes Adam lurch in his seat. I hope he doesn't get sick in my car. It's bad enough that we both have mud on our shoes. I open both of our windows for air.

'Where we going?' He's completely unconcerned, like he'd just asked me to pick him up from the side of the road and hadn't almost killed himself in the process.

'How much did you have to drink?' I say.

'I have noooooo idea … Shall we go get something now?'

'Adam! We're going to have to get as far away from your car as possible. The cops will be looking for you and you're, you're … not in the best way, bud. It's not gonna look good.'

'You're not taking me home!' Real fear reaches his eyes. 'You can't take me home. Maria can't know yet … I need to think first.'

'Relax,' I say, my eyes on the road. 'Let's go to Franky's mom's place. She's closer. We'll get you something caffeinated to drink and figure it out.'

'Shot, bru,' he says, stifling a yawn.

We are our own double act. I know him, sometimes better than I think he knows himself. I wonder if he knows me as well as I know him. Twenty-four years is a long time to know someone, but does the knowing make you closer? Or do some of us pay less attention than others?

I've always loved detail. It's one of the things Franky says she admires in me. I see more than other people do; I notice. Franky hears more than other people do. She can pick up songs on the radio, news headlines from the other side of the room, but when I'm jogging she'll pull out of her parking space and I'll wave at her and she won't even see me, her eyes fixed on the road. Franky and Adam have a lot in common. They're both good with conversation. They make friends easily. It's probably why they are the two people I'm closest to. Of course, I know both of their insecurities – but I wonder, do they know mine?

I pull up to Silvia's familiar front gates. I knew Franky's mom would follow me. She has a nose for things like this. I remember Franky telling me about the time Silvia chased after that bag-snatcher – no fear. My mother would not have reacted in the same way.

The gate opens, as if by magic. I see Silvia's car behind me. Despite everything, I trust this woman, almost as much as I trust myself.

# SIX MONTHS AGO
## SATURDAY
### 00:05
## Nick

*Sillery Avenue, Constantia*

Franky is outside, deciding how best to formulate an argument about something that needs no argument. Adam is at the kitchen table and Silvia has pulled me into the relative privacy of her lounge.

'Nick, I need you to protect her, no matter what. Do you promise me you'll look after her?'

'Of course I will, Silvia. What's the matter? You're shaking.'

'I don't know … I don't know … There are no cameras on that road, are there?'

'Not that I know of. I think there's one on the circle.'

'Will you be able to check, on your phone?'

'On my phone?'

'You know you young people can do so much on your phone these days. Don't say anything to Francine. Promise me? She'll only worry.'

'Of course, Silvia. It's fine. You're fine. Adam's fine. We're all fine.'

'I know, but you know how she worries and analyses everything … I just don't want her calling the police. You won't call the police, will you?'

'Why would I do that? I don't want Adam to go to jail.'

'Good. Good. Yes. I told him he needed to hide – not sure what I was bloody saying! Seemed like the only thing for it at the time. It seems rather silly, now that I think of it. It was all so confusing. I think I just needed to get out of the car, get some air. I thought about taking him away myself, but then I wanted to be there for Francine and I was very … We're on the same page, aren't we, Nick? No police?'

'Silvia, I think you need a cup of tea.'

'I think I need more than that!'

'You go and get Franky. I'll handle Adam. Don't worry, Silvia. Let me handle this.'

'Oh, Nick, you are so … Thank you, my boy. Thank you.'

I hold her in my arms and she feels like a smaller and frailer version of my wife.

# TWENTY-FOUR YEARS AGO

## Nick

*Newlands*

'She's your girlfriend?'

'Pretty much,' he says. 'Labels. You know?'

'Right.'

It's one of those days where the sky is so blue it's almost purple. We're trapped on the grounds of my new school, trapped under the oak trees. Well, they're trapped. I can leave at any time. I usually do. I can see my bike glinting invitingly in the afternoon light. Molly and her orange ponytail shrink to nothingness as she gets closer to the school building beyond.

'Smoke?' I say.

'Why the heck not.'

He has good teeth. His hair is curly, falling over his eyes. Pieces of it stick to the grooves in the bark like Velcro. He looks up at the leaves as if looking for a lost ball. I know he's a funny guy but he doesn't seem happy right now. He's popular. I'm a loner. Nobody finds anything I say or do funny.

'Dude, have you been … crying?' I say.

He laughs. Maybe he's been crying with laughter, or he's been smoking weed. Maybe that redhead has just broken his heart.

'My dad died.'

'That sucks large.'

'It does indeed.'

'So, you and Molly … I wasn't interrupting anything was I?'

'She's been my rock.' A laugh travels through his nose. 'I'm kidding. She's not a rock, she's … just there.'

I want to ask how his dad died, but I remind myself that I don't like being asked heavy questions like, 'Where are your parents?', 'Do you not have a dad?' and 'How come your mom's in the hospital' Questions need answers, and I'm not good at that, unless we're talking square roots and compound fractions. I let the question hang in my head like the stream of smoke that has left my mouth.

'Cancer,' he says. 'He had cancer, in his brain. One year: that's what they gave him, and that's how long he lasted.' He reaches for my cigarette. 'You smoke a lot?'

'I'm not as think as you stoned I am,' I say. He smiles. I have made him smile – this funny guy with his sad eyes and his white teeth. It feels like a triumph. I'm wise today. It's a feeling that comes over me when I know the only person I can trust is myself.

'Lots of things don't make sense. No point overthinking,' I say.

'Shit happens?'

'Continuously.' I exhale another small cloud. 'Adam, right? I'm Nick.'

# TEN YEARS AGO

## Nick

*Constantia Nek Restaurant*

It's her. It's fucking her. Jesus. Fuck. This is not happening.

'Maria, this is Nick ... Nick, Maria.' He's beaming. Widening his eyes at me as if to say, *I know, pretty amazing, right?* She stretches out her hand and there's a pause before she says, 'Nice to meet you ... Nick. I've heard almost nothing about you!' She squeezes my hand, a silent communication. I feel like I've lost the ability to blink or swallow.

Adam is bursting with pride. 'You guys get to know each other ... I'm going to get us drinks at the bar,' he says, striding away.

'Well, this is awkward,' I say, attempting a laugh.

'You never called.'

'I was going to ... or no, I ... that isn't true – I wasn't ... You said ... you said you were going back to Barcelona.'

'I booked a job. The agency wanted me to stay longer. Relax, Mr Freak-out; I won't say anything, if that's what you're getting at.'

'But you'll go back to Barcelona? Adam said you were here for ... a while?'

'Maybe, maybe not.' She twirls her hair in her fingers, examines the ends, brushes the tips against her chin like a paintbrush.

Our conversation ends at the re-emergence of Adam.

'You can stop talking about me now,' he says, all smiles. He launches into the story of how they met, even though he's already told me this – albeit without the important facts like her actual name, occupation and the fact she's from Barcelona. She squeezes his arm at intervals, smiling and stroking the back of his head. I watch them interact and my mind can't quite connect with the scene in front of me. A month ago, this woman was leaving my house at 5 a.m. –

make-up smudged from the night before, same black dress. She said she had a shoot; she was leaving for Barcelona the next day. I hope I can fake responses Adam won't see through.

'Nick, you all right, bud? You seem kind of off. You've gone like, totally red in the face.'

'Yeah, I was on site today; you know, too much sun. Could be sunstroke. Listen, guys, I have an early start tomorrow, so I'm not sure I can join you for dinner, maybe just …' Adam looks hurt and confused, trying to read my eyes. I squint into the middle distance, like I've just seen something I need to decode.

Maria breaks the tension. 'My roommate Tatianna was going to join us, but she's running late. She comes here every season. She's been showing me around Cape Town. If it wasn't for Tatianna we wouldn't have gone to that restaurant where Adam works.' They look at each other. Adam runs a finger down her cheek.

'Worked,' he corrects.

'You quit?' I say, slamming my glass on the table harder than I intended.

'Yesterday. I have so much to tell you! Ten years is too long, man. I'm out. Time for a change.'

'What are you going to do?'

'Well, this regular customer has a software start-up he wants me to join him in.'

'Software?'

'I'll figure it out as I go. He says I have the right personality for customer-facing, says he'll send me on a few courses, you know, get me started. It feels right. It feels like this is … you know … it.'

'Wow, that's … wow. A big change. Congrats.' I lift my glass with shaking fingers and we say cheers. Maria lifts her glass, clinks it against Adam's and then mine, looking in my eyes for longer than necessary. Shit, I think I might actually hate her. Please let her just go back to Barcelona where she belongs.

# NOW

## Nick

*Claremont*

Terror is not an emotion I am familiar with. The palms of my hands are slick and each elbow joint pulses with some strange new sensation. I am known for my calm energy, lauded for it even – my steadiness, my ability to handle a circular saw – but when she looked at me and said, 'It's time,' I felt our roles reverse, like one of those family-friendly films where the characters inexplicably swop souls.

To say I have done nothing for the last nine months would not be fair to me, but I have felt helpless in the face of all of Franky's physical changes. While she's mostly the same person, her belly has stretched and pulled with each week, tiny elbows and knees pushing to the surface like coat-hangers in a laundry bag. Her breasts are enormous, which makes me feel like I'm having an affair. I'm a moderate cook, I clean when I need to, but generally these things don't come naturally to me. Most of the time I feel useless. The only thing I know I can do is keep her calm and upbeat. Franky has a tendency to veer towards the negative. She firmly believes worry is a form of mental dress rehearsal.

Franky has had the bag packed since she started showing. I am only now coming to understand the significance of this preoccupation: the scented sachets, the new underwear that will provide easy access to the breasts I will now share. She likes to be physically, if not mentally, prepared. I am the opposite. I throw things in at the last minute, but I always know the route I'm going to take before I take it. If only there were an app for the fastest way to get this baby out of her with minimal pain and limited problems. Adam could design one. She has given me but one instruction: *Make sure the anaesthetist gets here before it's too late.*

Franky is not one of those women who have a birth plan. She's a fatalist. She believes this is our child's birth and not her own. (Maybe she read this in one of the books that now form a toppling tower on her bedside table.) She will not pretend to know more than the doctors. She doesn't want to know the sex, doesn't want to settle on a name or assemble the crib. All this, she says, is a way of curating her worries, one thing at a time, lest she imagine too far into the future and then be forced to grieve the loss of the figment. When we have these conversations, I tend to glaze over. She's the one carrying the baby. I guess my function will become clear to me when the baby bursts into existence. I'll admit – my imagination is limited in that respect. She wants children and I'm fine with that. I want her to be happy; it's the only thing I want. The only thing I've ever wanted from the first moment I saw her.

Some might say it was timing. Isn't that always the way? I was ready for a relationship, ready for something solid. When I was younger, girls were never an issue. I set myself a challenge: find the most beautiful girl in the room and make her mine. It worked, almost every time. But the more beautiful the girl I dated was, the more I saw a pattern: insecurity, neediness, weakness – my mother. I was earmarked as the person to fix it for them. I always pushed back on being cast in that role and it always ended quickly. Sometimes a phone call. Sometimes a lack of a phone call.

Heather was the real deal. She was my first experience of love, but she changed her priorities, I changed mine, and then her father involved himself and it was too late. I've always wanted to live my life as Dale Carnegie says, in day-tight compartments. Every woman I've ever been with wanted to project me into her future, but not Franky.

Franky's voice was what attracted me to her: the words she used and the way she said them. I knew, from the moment I met her, she was a woman I could grow old with. It took me a while to convince her, and even longer to convince her mother, but we made it there in the end.

The anaesthetist is on his way. The small-handed nurse told me this after she unceremoniously thrust two of her digits inside my wife. Franky looks at the miniature television, hung high in the corner of the room. A cooking show. A woman silently cuts lemon in half before inserting it into the cavity of a raw chicken.

Franky might not have a birth plan, but she does have a playlist and this is what's keeping her calm. I stroke her hand and in the spaces between songs I tell her things I know she wants to hear. I feel as though we are about to be strapped side by side into a roller coaster – the metal bar in place, no escape as the car shudders to life on the track.

Franky is overjoyed to see the anaesthetist, who is comically thin and bent forward, not unlike the needle itself, which is much larger than I expected it to be. As he plunges it into the space between two of her vertebrae, I tense every muscle in my body. What if my wife is paralysed for life? What if they get it wrong? What if they hurt the baby? Shit, I should have read some of those books; at least that way I'd be more prepared – I would know What To Expect. God, why would anyone want to be an anaesthetist? 'All done,' he says without triumph.

Franky relaxes back onto the pillows. She is serene. I have never, ever seen her this calm. It's charming, if not a little disconcerting. If she is calm, then what am I? What part is there for me to play? I have fulfilled my purpose. Maybe I should do what the small nurse is asking of me and sit in the easy chair expressly provided for my pleasure. I might change the channel on the ridiculously small TV to the golf. Or would that be even less appropriate than the cooking show?

The gynaecologist wakes me. I gasp for air. Is it a workday or a weekend? Franky's eyes are closed and she's smiling like she's deranged, a cable in her wrist and wires hanging out of her ears. The nurse takes over Franky's mantra: 'It's time.'

What happens now defies description. *Don't look* is what some of my colleagues at work told me, but I can't help myself. My wife's body folds in on itself. The hump of her belly becomes the shape of a Toblerone. Her legs are splayed and her exposed flesh seems to bloom outwards like a time-lapse flower; at the centre a round shape, slightly purple and grey. Is that the right colour? I'm holding her hand tight now – for me, and for her. To my left the doctor tells her, bizarrely, 'Make a poo!'

Franky looks at me with a mixture of embarrassment and confusion. 'Did he say that?' she laughs. 'Isn't he supposed to say *push*?'

She's laughing and the doctor tells her to keep laughing. 'Say something funny,' she says, and I say, 'I just saw you poo!' and she laughs and the laugh ripples her belly and the baby is out, and I can tell Franky doesn't know this, probably because she can't feel anything from the waist down, or maybe because her eyes are full of tears of mirth or exhaustion and the doctor is handing *me* the baby, and it smells like blood and metal and sex and I look in Franky's eyes and I feel myself choke as I say, 'It's … a little girl.' As if I'd expected it to be anything else.

# SIX MONTHS AGO
## SATURDAY
### 07:55
## Silvia

*Sillery Avenue, Constantia*

It rained last night and for this I am grateful – one less task for me to complete. Running a home with a garden this size isn't easy at any age, but at sixty-nine I feel I am almost at a point where I could give it all up. The sprezzatura of my European garden in Africa is not easily achieved. I have *some* help, of course, but not every day, and a garden like this needs attention *every* day.

The first thing I notice is the new roses, quietly unfurling just for me. I marvel at the depth of their colour before my eyes run the length of a star jasmine. During the night, the jasmine appears to have stretched and curled one long tendril around the trunk of my Norfolk pine. I smile to myself at the jasmine's cheek: a stubby suitor, yawning its arm around the waist of the tall object of its affection. How did the jasmine know, I think, without eyes or ears or senses of any kind, its partner was so near? I inhale the clean morning air and feel grateful I am here to see it all.

The creeper needs the tree. It is not a certainty that the tree needs the creeper, but the roses need me and I need the roses; of this, I am sure. Birds call to one another across the garden. I fetch a slice of orange, drizzled with honey. I place it just so in the centre of the ornamental fountain in the driveway and watch as the birds descend. Some seem to look at me with their beady eyes, an acknowledgement of sorts. *Yes*, I think, *I see you too.*

Back inside the house I make myself a cup of black coffee, with a sugar-free rusk, as recommended by my doctor after my latest round of blood tests.

I've grown used to the cardboard taste, almost look forward to it in some way, despite my initial displeasure. I spread out the newspaper on my lap. My daughter keeps trying to get me to read the news on the iPad she insisted on buying me for Christmas. I prefer the feel and smell of the real thing. Young people and their screens!

After the headlines and the rusk, I head back into the garden, secateurs in hand, ready for pruning. I have my eye on the old red grapevine that snakes around the decorative wire arch. The leaves are starting to turn brown and the tendrils of the vine have thickened to the size of a child's arm. It needs to be tamed or it risks squeezing the life out of every other plant around it. A vine is not as charming as jasmine. A vine is a pushy suitor, demanding a *feel.* I will be the one to rescue these other plants from the vine's aggression. I will put the vine in its place.

I think now of my daughter and the tiny seed germinating inside of her. Will it be a girl or a boy? How much of my own genetic code will make it through? Will it have her father's blue eyes? I hope so.

Graham and I were married for four decades. We witnessed apartheid, and its death, the new government and its challenges. We had only one child, Francine, a real South African with Irish skin. She is mostly like her father, although lately I have seen more obvious similarities with myself: the furrowed brow, the folded arms, the wild imagination.

After attacking the vines, I absent-mindedly pull the heads off the rose blossoms that have died in the night. I pull away the bald rose hips, so the plant can focus its energy on what is alive instead of what will never flower again. I hope my daughter will stop worrying and worrying and worrying as she does. Now that she has something to concentrate on, to keep alive, perhaps it will take her mind off all the 'what ifs' that seem to loop continuously in her mind. She's obsessed with illness, always running to the doctor, accumulating lotions and potions for every minor ailment. Perhaps all young people are like that nowadays – searching and searching and googling and googling: fruitless.

I don't see myself as a curmudgeon as such, but I have had it out with life. When Graham died, I was jealous of people whose coupledom remained intact. *It'll happen to you,* I said in my mind, wagging my finger like a witch in a fairy story. *You'll see, you'll lose the one you love too, eventually, so best you wipe that smug smile off your face!*

It sickens me that I harbour such negative thoughts. I usually wash them away with white wine and a good round of house-cleaning. First the cleaning, then the white wine, of course – I'm not *completely* deranged.

I look back and admire my work: leaves swept, trees pruned, roses restored. I bend to pull at a few stray weeds, enjoying the stretch in my legs, before I make my way back towards the French doors. I hear the faint chirp of my phone, which sits in my favourite chair, next to my now cold coffee.

'Hello, my darling,' I say. 'How was Charley?'

'Mom.'

'Franky?' I instantly sense the negative tone, feel the skin prickle on the back of my neck. 'What's wrong?'

'It's Charley, Mom.'

'Yes.' Instant relief. A picture of my daughter's best friend clear as day in my mind. The baby is okay. Francine is okay. Everyone is okay.

'She's dead.'

'Oh.' My mind scrambles from relief to disbelief.

'She's … how?'

'An accident, in her car.'

'Oh …'

'Mom? Are you there?'

'Yes, dear. Yes. I …'

'I'm coming over.'

'Okay … I'll just …'

I am barefoot and the wet grass is a welcome relief after stepping through the gravel. Gravel always looks grand, but unless you remember to wear shoes, it's torture. I look down at my toes, chipped nail polish no one is likely to see, except my daughter when she arrives. I pick up the phone with trembling hands and call the only person I know who will know what to do.

# SIX YEARS AGO

## Silvia

*Alphen Hotel, Constantia*

S*marmy*. That is the word that comes to mind. *So bloody sure of himself.*

I've met her boyfriends before, of course, but this one takes the cake. He has a vaguely threatening quality. He's ridiculously handsome. I am instantly distrustful and braced for a fight.

'I'm so sorry I am not able to meet Franky's father.' He holds my gaze, a challenge dancing in his eyes. 'He sounds like he was an amazing man.'

I know just the thing to put this little fucker in his place. 'Do you have parents?' I ask, feeling my throat burn. Francine squirms in her chair, admonishes me for – as she likes to say – *stating the obvious*. Well, from where I'm sitting, the most obvious thing about this situation is that this bloke (and he is *just a bloke*) is not someone I want staking a claim on my daughter and her time. And one thing she doesn't have right now is time.

I fell pregnant with Francine when I was twenty-nine – quite the story back in those days. I remember the looks my mother gave me, my father's assertion I must be a lesbian just because I cut my hair like Twiggy. Graham had swooped in and saved the day. His stethoscope pressed into my father's barrel chest as he counted the beats of his failing heart. My father was young, too young for a heart attack, they said, but *these things did happen*, even while on holiday in South Africa. He was lucky he went on to live as long as he did. Graham was the one who saved him, kept him alive so he could eventually witness our wedding and his only granddaughter's arrival.

I named her Francine because it sounded distinguished, strong and fearless. I was fascinated by her. She looked remarkably like Graham's sister – the one who had schizophrenia. This kept me awake. Graham assumed I had some sort of motherly devotion preventing me from sleep, but it was my shock that I had been handed someone else's baby. While she breastfed, I regarded the contours of her face, even drawing it in charcoal again and again to forge some sort of *knowing*. She was a stranger. All I related to was her anger. Her fists were constantly curled in indignation. She didn't recognise me and I didn't recognise her.

She was a nervous child, afraid of everything. She had a seriousness to her even as a toddler that quite unnerved me. I had dreamt of a tangled-haired artist, someone I could paint with and explore, someone I would discuss art and music and flowers with – but she didn't like the paint on her hands, and had a disproportionate fear of snails, which made her scream in terror if she encountered them in the garden.

She was an early reader, devouring books on every subject and reading the labels on the back of everything. *Why rinse and repeat, Mommy? What's E220?* My answers were made up and always seemed unsatisfactory. She became precocious, and then moody, difficult to live with in her teenage years. When she spoke to me I focused on how she said things rather than what she said. I watched her mouth move, the lines form on her forehead, the tears of frustration slide down her cheeks.

Graham always deferred to me. 'Silvia!' he'd call, if Francine came to him with any kind of question. He felt I was best placed to soothe our daughter's womanly concerns. I wanted to solve things for her, but the world she inhabited was so different to mine. I struggled to find the commonality that could offer her any kind of relief from her frustrations. I loved her fiercely. I wanted her to be healthy and happy and alive, but I didn't understand her in the way I thought I would understand my only child.

I was fired when Francine was nine. One of the children in my class had complained to their parents that I had *caned* her with the end of paintbrush. It was hardly a caning (which, by the way, was still legal back then); just a clip on the back of her thick skull. She had dipped her classmate's ponytail into a pot of red paint, for God's sake! Either way, it didn't go down well. After a bit of convincing, they agreed to let me teach at the high school. I was less likely to hit people my own size – or at least that's what I think they thought. I took a forced year of absence before I began teaching teenagers, hoping for some insights that would help me when my daughter became one of them.

Never once did I hit Francine. I was proud of that. I hugged her as often and as hard as I could in an effort to stem the flow of tears. She was so *fragile* and I wanted to infuse her with my strength. Then, one day, I had it in my head: perhaps I was a less-than-capable mother. Had I caused my daughter's fragility? Did I not listen enough? Was I too hard? Too expectant, too demanding, too self-absorbed? 'You are who you are, my darling,' Graham had said, not quite filling me with confidence. 'Don't worry,' he would say. 'I'll tell you when it's time to worry.'

I never once worried that Graham would die. I never considered we wouldn't have the retirement we'd planned. Silly of me. I was delusional, I see now. When he died, the shock nearly killed me. In fact, I would go as far as to say it did kill me, but the ghost of myself remained, fooling people into believing I was still there. It was my daughter who brought me back to life.

In those awful months that followed, I saw Graham in the shape of her eyes, the contour of her jaw. He was there in her laugh, in the way she sighed, even the way she changed the channel without asking. The way she cut cubes of cheese and threw them into her mouth instead of going to the trouble of making a sandwich. I felt horribly guilty, of course. I had been so impatient in those early years – so desperate to see myself reflected back to me – I couldn't properly appreciate this other woman who had been given to me, the rare creature who was mine but never mine. We've become so close, my daughter and I. I've let myself fantasise: one day I will have a grandchild, a child who will be even further removed from my gene pool, but one I will cherish. This time I won't agonise over who looks like who. I will get another chance.

But time is running out for all of us. She's had so many false starts! Why can't she just find a nice man like Sebastian? Someone rugged and creative and charming – a successful artist, that's who she should be with: someone who can complement her serious nature. Charley always had it easy with boys, Francine was always so goddam worried about making a mistake.

'I hear you and Francine are thinking of moving in together?'

'We're not sure yet,' he says.

Bingo.

'Yes, it's important to be sure,' I say, fixing him with my gaze. 'You learn a lot about someone when you move in with them. Towels on the floor!'

I've made him laugh. That's a start.

# NOW

## Nick

*Bishopscourt*

I need to move away from the drilling so I can hear myself think. The throbbing in my head is a testament to the fact that I've been on site for too long, or that I haven't slept since the baby's been born. Either way, I'm not myself today.

The house is set inside a curve of excavated rock. Teams have been drilling for months, and now the Swedish owner wants to see progress. There have been so many stops and starts, neighbours complaining, council pushing back (as only they know how), not to mention the crumbling rock face. Geologists have been hired and fired. The architect is relying on me to push this through, to get it done. The plan runner is on his way with the council's latest feedback on my drawings. A flick of my wrist, a rubber stamp, and it will all be over. I hope. I decide to wait in my car for him. My car, my safe haven, the last place I can truly say is my own.

I have never cheated on Franky. I have lied. I have omitted the truth. This comes easily to me now after years of practice. Is it *lying* if you do it to protect the people you love? Adam and Franky are the only two people I would do anything for, but does that mean I would do anything for the people *they* would do anything for? I've always been comfortable with my decisions – but something changed the morning my daughter was born. A hairline crack that may split me in two.

My history with Maria is long and complicated, but we have an understanding. Over time, I've come to realise: where there's a will, there's Maria. She makes things true by believing in them enough. We've come to trust each other but trust has never spilt over into any kind of affection. Adam loves Maria; I tolerate her. This has never been more clear to me than right now.

When I met Silvia, I knew she was going to give me a hard time. It was as though she saw the worst possible version of me under my skin. What I hoped was that her lack of confidence in me wouldn't rub off on Franky. Franky was the one I wanted to keep, the one I wanted by my side in sickness and in health. She was practical; she talked through things, listened and made me feel that I had more to offer than my traditional 'knight in shining armour' role. She needed me but she wasn't needy.

The night of the accident, Silvia was the one who needed me. At first I couldn't understand why, but the next day she called and the truth hit me like an anvil to the head of a cartoon hero. I was alone in my car driving away from Adam's house, Silvia's voice booming through the car speakers like a radio deejay's.

'I've known her since she was a little girl, Nick!' she wailed, coughing and sobbing and gasping at the same time.

'I know … It's – it's so hard for us all, especially Franky. Do you want me to get her to call you?'

'No, Nick … it's you I need to speak to.' She sniffed, gathering herself. A phone call from Silvia was rare; it only happened when she couldn't get hold of Franky.

'Hypothetically,' she began, 'if someone were driving and then someone else came in the opposite direction on the wrong side of the of the road and they swerved to avoid you … that wouldn't be their fault, right?'

'Silvia, where are you going with this?' I heard her swallow, then sigh, the dryness of her mouth audible through the speakers.

'Nick, I don't trust people. I need someone I can trust and I can't tell any of my friends. I can't tell anyone. You're the only one who would … understand.'

Adam was not responsible – of this I was now sure – but once Franky told me a private investigator had been hired, I knew that wouldn't stop the connection being made. Silvia's red Mercedes may have caused Charley to swerve, but, as far as I knew, her movements weren't recorded. Adam's were. When Adam found the lawyer, I made a mental note to see if Prudence was someone I could trust. I tested her out with Adam before I met with her alone the next day.

'This is quite the situation you have here, Nick,' she said, drumming her nails on the glass top of her desk.

'You're telling me,' I said. 'So, are you up for this?'

'You know my rates. Why wouldn't I be?'

*

The next day I collected Silvia while Franky was at work and took her to meet with Prudence. Silvia was mostly silent during the meeting, looking out the window, briefly commenting on the cloud formations. When she did speak, she spoke slowly, enunciating her words as though she was unsure Prudence's first language was English. She seemed confident of her innocence but wary. She knew there was a universe in which she would be sent to prison. Prudence charmed her, played to her assertion that it was Charley and not her who was on the wrong side of the road. We agreed the matter should remain private and Franky and Adam should be kept out of the loop for as long as possible.

'We don't need to prove you weren't responsible, until someone suggests you might have been. Silvia, you need to trust me on this. There are no cameras on that road; no one will be able to prove you and your car were in any way involved. You did not *flee* the scene of an accident, because you were not *involved* in an accident – do you understand me?'

Of course, never in a million years could I have anticipated that Maria would have been a passenger in Charley's car – that she witnessed the whole thing and lived to tell the tale. That was a curveball of note. Barely a scratch on her, except for a sore neck, which was hardly unusual given she was a mother to small children. Ten years of omitting the truth meant I knew I could trust Maria. Our truth was so deeply and safely buried in the past, she had to be on my side.

'Ai, ai, ai!' she said when I called her on the day I found out about her involvement. I decided I had to trust her with Silvia's secret.

'You're fucking kidding me! I'm sorry, Nick, but I'm not letting Adam go down for something she did. This is my family we're talking about.'

'Of course, that's not what I'm suggesting, Maria – I just need you to not say anything to any investigators that could incriminate Silvia. Nothing. I need you to promise me. You're the only one who can do that. I promise you Prudence will get Adam off, but you cannot say or do anything that would hurt Silvia. I need you to swear.' Her sigh was the only reply. 'Maria, when have I ever asked you for anything? I kept your secrets; now I'm asking you, no, I'm telling you to keep mine. Adam doesn't know you were the passenger, he doesn't know about your affair, and we can keep it that way. We will keep it that way.'

'What about Sebastian? I told Sebastian. What's stopping him from telling Adam? He seems pretty fucked up right now; he's capable of anything.'

'Franky will handle Sebastian. She knows what to do. I trust her, you can trust her too. We're all on the same side here.'

'Are we? Are we all on the same side, Nick – or are you always on the side that makes *you* look good?'

'Maria, please. You want an old woman to go to jail over this? It was an accident, a fucking accident.'

'Like Sara was an accident.'

Silence hangs on the line. I inhale what feels like the last scrap of air in the room. I wait for Maria to speak. She sighs again.

'Yes, Nick. Of course, you know you can trust me. You take care of your friend, and your mother-in-law. I'll take care of the rest.'

A rap on my car window startles me.

'Jesus! Fuck!' I say.

'Sorry, big boss,' says Mo as I wind down the window. 'A few tweaks and we're home free.' He smiles, handing me the hollow roll of drawings. Once I'm out of the car I spread the sheets of paper on the bonnet, squinting at the sun's reflection. Mo puts his hands in his pockets and waits for my response.

'They signed off on this?' I say. 'Where are the changes?'

Mo gives me a knowing smile before handing me a folded square of paper. I know that when I open it, there will be a number written on it. I also know I will pay. One way or another, someone's going to have to pay.

# NOW

## Franky

*Alphen Hotel, Constantia*

The branches of the oak trees bend with the warm northerly breeze. Luminous buds hold steady. A berg wind, they call it. (*Berg* is Afrikaans for mountain.) It's akin to a rainbow, or a bolt of lightning – something that should be commented on, appreciated, like the first anniversary of a death. The trees lean in as if to better hear our conversation.

'Mom, how do you know Prudence?'

'Oh, we're old friends …' My mother flaps her napkin on her lap.

'Didn't you say you taught her … at the school?' says Nick, cocking an eyebrow. Prudence stands statuesque, smiling benignly above us, one manicured hand on the back of Nick's chair.

The outside area of the restaurant is full. We were lucky to get a table for six. Opposite me, Gabby is self-conscious, touching the ends of her cropped hair (back to its original shade of brunette). Her hand rests on Sebastian's forearm. When she sees me looking she drops her hand into her lap, fiddles with the earring in the cartilage of her left ear. I feel the weight of the child in my arms.

My mother seems to sit up straighter, perhaps overly aware of Deirdre next to her, exuding sophistication through her porcelain skin: two women thrust together by the closeness of their children, one of whom is no longer here.

'Yes, yes, of course, that was it! Prudence, how *is* your art coming along?'

My mother's voice is unnaturally loud. As well as I know her, sometimes her motives are incredibly hard to decipher.

'Not much time for all that these days, I'm afraid, Mrs Allen,' she says, shaking her head and giving Nick a pointed look. 'Lovely to see you all again. Forgive me, a client and I are celebrating. I must get back to her.'

I instinctively turn my neck in the direction of her outstretched hand. A vaguely familiar woman with a blunt fringe is sitting at another outdoor table, her face obscured by dappled light.

A waiter places a silver champagne bucket in front of her, which reflects a sunbeam. As Prudence takes her seat there's a muted pop and a girlish cry of pleasure.

'Lovely girl, isn't she? So clever.' My mother gives Deirdre a knowing look, 'And such a good artist. Brains, creativity and beauty all in one!'

Nick clenches his jaw. There's a strange current between us all today. Lack of sleep might make me imagine things. I want everyone at this table to be happy, but I remind myself that I am not responsible for this. How curious that my mother taught Prudence at school, and Nick knew and never thought to mention this to me. I chew on this information and the side of my cheek. My daughter's eyes roll in the direction of her grandmother, then follow a squirrel up the trunk of a tree.

'Squirrel!' I say, sounding demented. 'That's a squirrel!' Her blue eyes find mine. A tiny fist clamps around my index finger, confirming her presence, sweeping away all other thoughts, worries and doubts.

Seb's arms are folded as he nods to whatever Deirdre is saying at the other side of the table. I try desperately to tune in but my mother is still holding court.

'I'm proud of you … both,' she says. I'm not sure who she is talking to: Seb and Gabby, Gabby and me, Nick and me?

'Thanks, Silvia,' says Nick, raising his beer to her wine glass. They say cheers. I watch them carefully.

'It's been a long time coming, hasn't it?' she says.

'Mom!'

'Well, it has. I mean, renting is such an awful business. You have to get on the property ladder while you're still young.'

'Mom, I'm forty; Nick's pushing fifty.'

'Steady on!' says Nick.

'And I'm sixty-nine!' says my mother with a laugh. 'Can you bloody believe it? But we're all still here; that's what counts.'

Seb catches my eye, gives me a wink. I smile back, understanding everything. Deirdre will be gone tomorrow then he can exhale. I'm grateful Adam isn't here to further complicate this moment. My mother puts a hand over Nick's and gives it a meaningful squeeze.

'Do you know, I've just realised I'm your daughter's only grandparent.' Her voice wobbles.

'And I've just realised I have no family *other* than my grandchildren!' Deirdre's laugh is tight and high. My mother nods in acknowledgement, swallows hard and uses her free hand to pat Diedre's be-ringed fingers.

'You guys still going away?' says Seb, moving his arm around the back of Gabby's chair.

'June,' says Nick. 'Our belated anniversary gift to ourselves – a visit to Barcelona to see Adam and Maria in their new life.'

'It's a beautiful city. We went there for a job once,' says Seb. I see him turn the memory over in his mind, Charley's face. He reaches for Gabby's hand. She smiles nervously before she says, 'Did you see the Gaudís when you were there? I've always wanted to see them.'

Gabby has become a teenage version of herself. Less sarcastic, more energised, a sparkle in her eye I've never seen before. I couldn't have imagined she would quit before I did – and I could never, ever have pictured her with Seb.

I wonder what Prudence made of our strange tableau. Did she clock who Seb was? That the woman next to him was not his life partner but someone he'd been with for three intense months? Did she understand that Deirdre was the mother of my late friend, her relationship with my own mother complicated and competitive? Did she sense I am officially unemployed, not sure what the future holds or what part I will play in it? Did she note the absence of Adam? I'm sure she'll find a way to make contact with Maria and get the full story.

Lottie wriggles in my arms, places her palm on my cheek. I search her blue eyes as the strange berg wind swirls around us all.

# ONE YEAR AGO

## FRIDAY

23:12

## Charley

*Llandudno*

Our home is a glass box perched on the side of the mountain. Warm-white outside lights illuminate the tropical garden as if ready for a performance. The rest of the house remains in blue-black darkness. The road leading from our driveway to the nearest ATM is a black snake ready to strike. I know its contours well, but as my car slides up its back my stomach contracts. Twelve minutes past eleven is admittedly an unusual time to be leaving the house. On some level, I relish the crazed freedom of it – the cool night air on my skin as I contemplate the faces of the three sleeping souls I've left behind: my husband, my daughter and my son.

Before leaving the house I searched frantically in pockets and wallets, bags and boxes. I upended jars, opened drawers, but it was no use. No one uses cash any more, except for the goddamn tooth fairy.

A collective total of around forty teeth are expected to fall from my daughter and son's mouths during their brief childhood. The first was momentous, the second thrilling. By the third, family enthusiasm had started to wane.

The morning after Valentine's Day, Katie shook me awake at 5 a.m., tears ripening in her eyes. 'Mommy! She didn't come!' She held up her tiny shell-like incisor in her palm: proof of this cruel injustice. Seb came to my rescue then, his eyes still half closed, his voice hoarse: 'No, sweetie; you see … your tooth came out *after* 5 p.m., right? So … the tooth fairy has you on her roster for the next night. That's how tooth fairies work. Don't worry, baby girl … She will come. She always comes.' Katie's watery eyes searched his for signs of subterfuge. She is six; only one more year until we reach seven, the milestone of Innocence Lost. Seb and I laughed about our parental ineptitude at the time, but the shame of the mistake stayed with me for days, like a bruise.

This morning Katie lost her fourth tooth. Despite it now becoming a non-event, she squealed with delight. The tooth looked naked and exposed in the flesh of the apple, yet in surprisingly good condition, given it had spent so many months crunching Oreos and Milo-flavoured cereal. I promised myself I would not forget.

But earlier, as I climbed between our clean sheets, tired and drained from a long day of decision-making followed by talking, drinking and dancing, the pleasure of well-deserved sleep stole me away. I woke with a start just after eleven, heart pounding, mouth dry. There was still time.

# Acknowledgements

Thank you to my first readers: Anna Vayanos, Ruth Barnes, Sara Hilliard-Garrett, and Tinet Anelli – your forty-eight-hour turn-around times gave me hope. Catriona Ross, I'm so honoured you agreed to edit this book and I can't thank you enough for championing this story from the moment it hit your inbox. Thank you, Matthew Blackman and Michelle Matthews, for demystifying the world of publishing, and Robin Goode for implying that the world *does* need more stories when I insisted we probably had enough. John Hayward, thank you for getting the ball rolling, so to speak. May we always be on the same side. Abby Price, there is no story without you. Your trust, faith and sisterly support have propped me up for nearly forty years (I know, I'm rounding up!)

I am forever grateful for the support of the entire team at Curtis Brown Creative including Anna Davis, Christopher Wakling, Simon Ings, Danni Georgiou, Jennifer Kerslake, Abby Parsons and Jack Hadley. Dewan Bronkhorst, thank you for providing information on police procedure in the Constantia Valley, and Jan Booysen for helping me create an accurate map of the place I call home. Thank you, Karabo Mosia, Marida Fitzpatrick and the rest of the Penguin Random House team for holding my hand while I flipped my first pancake.

Evon Greenwall, Mom: you were the first person to read this story. You read all seventeen drafts along the way – and even though you offered many alternative endings, I hope this one holds the truth. You are my best critic, my biggest cheerleader and the most well-read person I know! Georgie and Riley, the tooth fairy is real. Don't believe everything you read in this book. Robin Fryer, my love – thank you for believing in me, with zero evidence to go on. You *are* my rose, my gardener and my best friend. I love you always.